WAR AND PRESERVATION

WAR AND PRESERVATION

BOOK 2 OF THE TEXIAN TRILOGY

KAREN LYNNE KLINK

SHE WRITES PRESS

Published 2025
Printed in the United States of America
Print ISBN: 978-1-64742-866-2
E-ISBN: 978-1-64742-867-9
Library of Congress Control Number: 2024922327

For information, address:
She Writes Press
1569 Solano Ave #546
Berkeley, CA 94707

Interior Design by Kiran Spees

She Writes Press is a division of SparkPoint Studio, LLC.

I dedicate this book to
All those men and women who fight for their country,
regardless of "sexual" orientation.

The only thing that makes life possible is
permanent, intolerable uncertainty:
not knowing what comes next.

Ursula K. Le Guin, *The Left Hand of Darkness*

Characters

Blue Hills

Paien Villere, Creole papa from New Orleans

Lucien Beau Villere born June 1831, eldest son from first marriage—m. Joanna Camden from abolitionist family

Adrien Denys Villere born August 1841, first surviving son of Madeleine and Paien Villere

Bernadette Louise Villere born July 1842, daughter of Madeleine and Paien Villere

Marcus Holland, overseer, Paien's good friend and Isaac's papa

Betta Holland, his wife and Isaac's mama

Isaac Holland, their son and Adrien's supposed "brother" and close friend

Esther Davis, cook

Simon Thatcher, butler

Gideon and Amos Tainter, young man and grandfather that Jacob assigns to help out at Blue Hills

Hartwood

Randolph Hart, owner of Hartwood Plantation

Jacob Hart, born September 1832, and eldest son—m. **Porscha**

William (Will) Hart born January 1841, youngest son and friend of Adrien

Lily Hart born September 1843—m. **Andrew T. Garrison**

Colt Alvaro, half Tonkawa and Jacob Hart's companion

Terry's Texas Rangers (8th cavalry) and citizens
Ethan Childs, Adrien's new friend and companion
Katherine Wheatley, Ethan's betrothed

Chapter One
1861, Houston

Ethan

If a fellow asked Ethan Childs how a man from Louisiana ended up in Terry's Texas Rangers, he said it was because he lost his Houston enterprise in a card game. Truth: his partner caught him in an indiscretion that meant he must sell his partnership in the saloon and leave town. *"Indiscretion" my great-aunt's fanny*—he mentally kicked himself in the behind. He had let desire overcome caution.

He would put a decent piece between himself and Houston, and his mouth watered for the taste of a fresh beignet.

In Galveston, he discovered there weren't any ships bound for New Orleans, as Galveston ports were under Union blockade. The long-faced man at the ticket counter winked and spit three feet into a brass pot. "Come back next week and maybe I can get you on a ship to Nassau. You can prob'ly get a ship to New Orleans from there. No guarantees, though." The fellow laughed like a pig squealed, coughed, slapped his knee, and turned red in the face. Ethan walked away to the sound of fading coughing. What the hell. He wasn't the sort to let a little war ruin his life, not with his pockets full of silver.

Back in Houston, he treated himself to a good meal of expensive blockade-run shrimp, oyster stew, and a couple drinks. Got in a game, got out of it, had a few more drinks. Maybe more than a few.

When he crawled out of bed the next evening, an entire day was gone. He barely recalled signing up with Benjamin Terry's cavalry. The girl with him (he was being circumspect this time)—Ginny, or

1

Jenny—thought he was a hero. He recalled drinking with a hell of a bunch of jolly fellows.

He later discovered some of the rowdy Texas recruits couldn't read, but there were plenty of educated clerks, lawyers, and other such, who proved they could sit a horse better than average, and shoot. Many fellows from surrounding counties were turned away before the remaining thousand or so were split into companies of a little over one hundred men each. They were to be sent in two groups, one after the other, to join the army in Virginia by way of New Orleans, which must have been why he joined. He could not recall. That was the trouble with mixing bourbon and beer. Even what happened *before* he started drinking faded into oblivion.

He became part of the first half of recruits to be sent overland from Houston. The rest would follow a few days later.

Ethan's group, along with their horses and gear, rode in boxcars to Beaumont, Texas, where they boarded a steamboat up the Sabine River to Niblett's Bluff. In Beaumont, there was no room for horses on the boat, and they were told every animal must be left behind.

"But we're cavalry," a fellow said.

An older bearded recruit to Ethan's right squinted from under his dusty flop hat. "You're in the army. Get used to such goings-on."

Upon arrival in Niblett's Bluff, they were crammed into two-wheeled ox carts, standing room only. Ethan leaned his elbows on the side of the cart and ruminated on Texas cavalry being treated in such a manner.

"I'd rather be on my own two feet than jounced along by a pair of dumb cows," the grizzled individual next to him said, and held out his hand. "Name's Crane Forbes."

"Ethan Childs." Forbes, who was older than most of them, conversed some on the surrounding territory, but not too much, so turned out easy to be alongside. His knowledge of birds and plants they passed was nothing short of astounding. "Been through Louisiana a couple times afore," he said. Ethan was too embarrassed to admit he'd passed his childhood in Louisiana and didn't know half what Forbes did of the flora and fauna. Ethan was born in New Iberia, wandered her streets and levies, then finished his growing in New Orleans, never exploring much beyond the houses. He turned fifteen before mounting a horse, and that occasion caused him to learn to ride right fast.

Forty miles later Forbes got his wish about walking on his own two feet when the ox carts and their Cajun drivers abandoned the recruits. If the men weren't so miserable, they might have laughed at the idea of cavalry trudging one hundred miles across Louisiana on foot in the rain.

This was what a person ought to get used to in the army—things not being logical. When his father went off to fight Mexico, he said that's how it was, and having someone you trusted at your back was essential. A professional gambler, Ethan must be careful who he called friend. A man rarely remained a friend after you took his money. Ethan would watch the goings-on, test the waters before he decided who he would trust at his back in this coming fight. *Test the waters*, he smirked as he splashed his way through another muddy creek, or hole, or damn whatever. Fast and accurate judgment remained a prerequisite of his calling.

As they trudged past miles of cane sugar through Louisiana mud, he noticed a well-dressed young fellow. His smooth-combed canvas trousers were double-seamed. The fawn-colored deer hide jacket, though worn at the edges, covered a finely tailored cotton shirt. Silent beneath his wide-brimmed hat, the boy rebuffed no one's friendly advances, but was stingy as a banker with his responses. He was soon limping along like the rest. Hand-tooled leather riding boots were not made for walking mile after mile; neither were riders.

Perhaps this mark, how quickly they became marks, might be interested in some sort of diversion from this daily murk and toil.

That evening after supper, Ethan joined seven others huddled around a campfire. A few of the recruits had brought a slave along to help tend their horses and persons, but no colored accompanied the men at this fire, including the young gent he had noticed earlier. The soaking rain slowed to a drizzle, then stopped. The young man's hat projected low over his face as he sat on a stump cleaning a .36-caliber Colt revolver.

"That's a fine piece," Ethan said.

"My papa presented it to me."

"Appears you've taken good care of it. Used it much?"

"Enough to hit that at which I aim." The oil rag stilled. Poking from beneath the hat was a straight, refined nose above a sparsely whiskered chin. "Tin cans, mostly." The rag was off again, no less busy for the interruption.

Ethan was too tired for a game, anyway. Everyone soon collapsed on their bedrolls, complaining of the usual—they joined the cavalry for this? He tossed a coin and won a somewhat dry spot beneath one wagon.

As tired as he was, he had never been one of those gents who could nod off soon as he closed his eyes. Had he heard right? He had lived in New Orleans with his mother until sixteen, and knew French Creole, even if mangled by Texas drawl. Did a kindred soul present itself this way? Old Mamsy Dee would tell him so. He recalled her dark, wrinkled face, her bright red tignon with the crow feather stuck in its folds. The other boys had feared her piercing black eyes and gravelly voice. He'd spent his favorite Sunday afternoons visiting her and her raucous parrot in their cottage near the wharf, though he quit believing in her spells and pronouncements when he left other childhood fancies behind.

Two days later, he saw the same youth again, much changed.

They had arrived late the night before at Spanish Lake on Bayou Teche, a glorious encampment of cropped grass, spreading oaks, gum, and cypress trees. Palmettos rattled in the soft breeze. Their company being near last in line for washup, Ethan slept well until after the sun rose. They washed by finding a partner, soaping up, and pouring buckets of cold water over one another. Not everyone took such care, which soon determined who slept near whom. This was followed by a breakfast of ham, spicy Cajun sausage, cornbread with butter, scrambled eggs and coffee—rich, black coffee, coffee he remembered.

He spied a big log near the water in warm, morning sun, unoccupied, no less. The perfect place to eat what looked like the best breakfast in weeks. How happy he felt among all the familiar smells and sounds—the nattering of so many birds, the soft breeze redolent with the smell of flowers. He'd left home to get away from anything that reminded him of his childhood. Yet here he was, looking forward to being home and seeing it all again, even his mother.

A young fellow was heading the same direction. Ethan would know those boots anywhere. It was the same fellow who'd been cleaning his pistol that night. Cleaned up and without the hat and scruffy semblance of a beard to hide behind, he appeared younger than Ethan first believed.

He ambled forward with his biggest grin.

The boy turned, a look of hesitant anticipation in his eyes—deep-set black eyes that met his, slightly slanted and set above prominent cheekbones. Ethan was reminded of Louie, a boy he'd known years ago in the Quarter—the son of a French cotton broker and his beautiful quadroon mistress.

Ethan offered his hand. "Never introduced myself. Ethan Childs, Houston. Before that, New Orleans."

"Adrien Villere, Washington, Texas." Something melancholic hovered about his face, then he smiled with a hopeful look and a curious twist to the corner of his mouth. A fine mouth it was, too, made sensual by a full lower lip. And that delightful inflection again. It had become a habit, the way Ethan's speech adjusted to that of the other person. A good habit to acquire when you wanted someone to relax, to trust you more than he ought before a game.

Ethan nodded toward what appeared to be their same destination. "Will you join me at this fine log?"

They dug into their cooling eggs and spoke between mouthfuls.

"Are you glad to be going home to New Orleans?" the youth said.

"I'll surprise my mother, a few old friends."

"I have never been, but I hope to find family there."

"I thought I recognized your accent."

"*Maman* was French, though she grew up in Savannah. She loved the way Papa spoke, which was familiar and different from Texas cow hands. He came to Texas through Virginia, but was originally French Creole from Louisiana. She insisted all of us converse with what she declared proper diction." His spoon hung suspended above his plate for a moment of silence, as though his mind hovered somewhere beyond where they sat at present. He continued eating.

"I don't recognize the name Villere," Ethan said. "But I have heard the name Villeré, with the accent at the end. You might ask for that name if the other doesn't work."

"I have an address where Papa wrote her."

"It's a woman you're looking for, then."

"Yes, my papa's sister."

They talked off and on into the afternoon. He learned the youth had an older brother and a younger sister and somewhat of a life on a Brazos tobacco plantation. Adrien made nothing of it, but Ethan was familiar with those Texas families who colonized the Brazos River. They came from Louisiana, Tennessee, other southern states, and nearly all from wealthy plantation families. What the devil brought one of their sons to join up as a lowly roughneck horse handler instead of using family influence to gain a commission? *I better discover the fellow's inclinations up front.*

"You may as well know my father was a gambler and my mother runs a fancy brothel on Rampart Street. I grew up in the place. It's where I learned to read and play a little piano. If my breeding doesn't suit you, say so now."

"You suit me fine, Ethan. Maman played piano. She taught me, yet I could never play as well as my sister."

He lost years from his face when he smiled like that. He also looked . . . innocent. So many of these country boys were. *How many will be alive six months from now? Is this a mistake, getting so friendly? But I can't go into this thing without pals.* His father had been damn frank about his own experiences fighting under Commander Scott in the war with Mexico. Never volunteer, son, he said. So why had he? Hell if he knew. Being full as a tick at the time didn't seem a good enough answer. But if you're in, find someone to watch your back. He'd said that too.

Maybe he'd figure it out before this thing was over, and it being over in a month or two wasn't likely. He knew too much about the North to be so fanciful.

He chanced a glance at Adrien as the boy took a gulp of coffee. Fellow was from a first-class family and was educated, which would keep him from being bored in the weeks ahead. Kept himself clean and didn't smell like dog roll. *Maybe I won't displace him of everything he's got, after all.*

Chapter Two
One of Them

Adrien

Since joining up in Houston I had met a number of congenial fellows, most as educated as myself and all friendly, but none too friendly. No one looked askance at me as though I were unfit for the task ahead, or as though he might devour me. It appeared that once you were accepted by Terry's 8th Texas Cavalry, there were no further questions concerning your manhood. Perhaps later I would think about home and why I was here, but meantime I wanted to relax in the camaraderie of men who accepted me for what I appeared to be—one of them.

After all, I had been born on a tobacco plantation in Washington County, East Texas, like them, and learned to ride at an early age, like them, and shoot, like them. I sounded pretty much like them too, but for that bit of accent and precise diction from my French mother, which I would abandon—the diction I was sick of being teased about. The rest, well, the rest was a sign of decent education and in her memory; something I'd keep, or attempt to. She deserved that much. She had been good to me, for the most part, if a little *too* good. My sister thought so, and Berni was generally correct about most everything.

And there was Ethan. Something about how he radiated understated confidence made me want to be his companion. Ethan was easy to talk with and appeared to be a gentleman of the first water, as Papa would have said. I liked listening to the timbre of his voice and what he had to say. His smile turned his eyes the warmest brown.

It would be quite fine to have him as a friend for whatever was to come, as long as he never got too curious.

As long as no one learned of the one way I was not like them at all.

Chapter Three
New Orleans

The first group of 8th Texas Cavalry arrived at temporary quarters in a cotton press building on the west side of New Orleans. The nearly forty-foot-tall steam compressor rose at the far end of the enormous room like some iron giant out of a new age. Small, square windows near the rafters bathed the men in beams of late afternoon sunlight.

No evidence of horses or uniforms presented itself.

Ethan doubted most of these fellows had ever slept so far from home. Everyone provided their own gear and weapons which they dropped onto the plank floor, throwing clouds of cotton dust into the hot air. The vast space muted sneezes that joined thuds, scraping of boots, and men's voices.

Chattering of what sort of food they could expect, of when they would get mounts and if the mounts would be any good, one eager young man said, "Sure hope we have time in the city before we move on." As did Ethan. He expected plenty others would like to experience the delights of New Orleans.

They had no sooner settled than Benjamin Franklin Terry strode in and heaved his six-foot frame up onto an elevated section of the cotton press with the alacrity of a much younger and smaller man. A neat goatee matched dark brown hair combed back from a wide brow, and his steady eyes, calm face, and attitude bespoke confidence and authority. The recruits already thought of him as their commander.

Terry, along with John Wharton and Tom Lubbock, was responsible for the Confederate States War Department's authorization of their cavalry regiment.

Terry congratulated every man for volunteering to fight for their home state, which prompted cheering and flinging of slouch hats, coonskin caps, and sombreros. "We'll be headquartered in this building until the next group arrives and we get orders to depart. Y'all will have plenty of time to visit the city. You are now members of the cavalry of the Confederate States of America and representatives of the great state of Texas. I expect you to act accordingly." Another tremendous cheer rose to the rafters. "Regarding passes, anyone not back to quarters by midnight will be considered absent without leave. Anyone found drunk and disorderly will lose subsequent passes to town. No exceptions." He left them to ponder the last, which quieted them down a mite.

Eventually nearly every man wandered over to the compressor to take a closer look, but only a minority were comfortable around the contraption. Ethan watched Adrien prowl about, his head moving up and down as he surveyed its ins and outs as though he might figure how it was put together and did its job. *I suppose it's useful in that it mashes cotton into bales half its original size. But it's ugly.* He'd read about the industrial age that began in England and was considerable in the northern states. Everything about the industrial age was ugly— made ugly cities, made rich people richer and poor people slaves, white and Negro. He didn't want that here in the South, thank you very much.

After a much-appreciated supper of fried chicken, wheat biscuits, chicken gravy, greens, potatoes, and berry pie, the companies drew lots for passes the following day.

Next morning Ethan and Adrien stood in line for a hearty breakfast of ham, beef, scrambled eggs, cornbread, biscuits, and ham gravy, which most ate sitting on their bedrolls or perched wherever they could find a moderately comfortable spot. The biscuits disappeared first as most fellows had been brought up on cornbread, and wheat flour was a luxury. Square windows near the rafters let in light, and now and then little bits of cotton fluff escaped from high overhead, drifted down in the early sunbeams, and landed in someone's coffee.

"I have always liked Louisiana," Adrien said, while digging into a juicy piece of well-smoked ham. "The folks here appreciate the importance of a good breakfast."

Ethan barely heard him over the clash of tin plates, metal utensils, and voices of so many hungry men. "You've been to Louisiana before?" Adrien had given him the impression he'd never been in the state. The boy didn't appear the sort who would appreciate good food, or lots of it—not an ounce of fat on him.

"I went to Centenary College in Jackson for a couple years, but Papa made me promise to never set foot in New Orleans. I surely wanted to and nearly did come down the river with a friend from school. I could not break a promise to Papa, though. He thought New Orleans was an evil place, but now I wonder if he was concerned I would discover relatives he didn't want me to meet."

"I take it they didn't get along."

"He would not discuss them, even led us to believe they had all passed on. But I overheard him and Maman discussing his sister once, and I found letters from her hidden in his desk."

"You never asked him about it?"

"You would have to know my papa." He placed the fork carefully alongside his plate. "I was afraid of what he would say. Now I am here, and I must learn why he would not speak of her."

Adrien picked up the fork and pushed at the last piece of ham. "I feel torn. Is it really my place to go digging around in Papa's past? Except she is my family, and there are few of us left." He looked down at his plate, opened his mouth as if to say more, closed it. Began a tentative smile as if at himself and took a deep breath.

"What's the address? Maybe I know the area," Ethan said.

"857 Rue Toulouse."

Ethan remained silent—farther down the table he heard laughing and someone dropped a metal plate. The address was a curious one for a plantation owner's family, unless—no—that would be a few blocks east. "Are you sure?"

"I have had it memorized for years."

The address didn't seem right considering the location, but how would he know? He had been gone for over ten years. Situations changed. Unless, being New Orleans, not so impossible. Some things never changed.

He and Adrien had become at ease with one another in only a few days. Maybe their camaraderie had something to do with sitting together at night listening to frogs sing, neither finding it necessary to speak. People who filled every moment with meaningless talk were tedious.

"Listen," Ethan said, and leaned forward, forearms on knees. "I can show you where the place is if you want."

"I'd like that, Ethan." Adrien gave him a curiously vulnerable smile.

Ethan flashed a return smile, then looked down at his plate and saw he'd eaten everything. "I'll get these," he said, grabbed Adrien's empty plate and headed for the wash tubs. His chest had clutched back there and, damn, he wasn't going to take care of some puppy. What mad notion'd got into him, anyway? He was after one thing and one thing only—distraction from what might be a bit of a slog. He rolled up his sleeves and dunked dishes and utensils in the soapy water, scrubbing with vengeance.

Neither Ethan nor Adrien received a pass the first few days, and they spent hours cleaning gear and themselves of travel dirt. After a couple enterprising fellows returned to camp with fine shirts of deep red, red shirts became part of their unofficial uniform.

The third morning, Ethan, Adrien, and a couple other fellow rangers strolled into the French Quarter as far as Conti Street, where the other two went off to Gallatin Street.

"I figured you'd want a decent meal, see the museum and other sites rather than head straight off for trouble like those other two," Ethan said.

"You are right. First, I want coffee and beignets, and I will leave the rest up to you, though I wouldn't mind some good music later. I have never heard opera."

"I hope you brought dress clothes. I'll get us tickets before we leave." The day after they'd arrived, Ethan had sent a note to inform his mother he was in New Orleans. "We can clean up and change at my mother's place," he said, steering Adrien clear of a filthy gutter as they hurried along the banquette that kept pedestrians above water and muck. Built over a swamp, the city had a problem with rising water. "She'll be offended if I don't call on her by tomorrow afternoon. I'll show you where your aunt's house is afterward." How would Adrien react to the reality of his mother's bordello? Likely the youth did not frequent such establishments.

Fortunately, they had three-day passes, and the next sweltering afternoon presented themselves outside his mother's two-story Spanish-style house.

The door and outside trim were freshly painted white, otherwise the same red brick facade Ethan remembered glowed in the early afternoon sun. Tall, etched glass windows on either side of the door sent beams of sunlight streaming across the cypress-floored foyer. Between the beams stood Jackson, seemingly not a day older but for curly gray hair. The huge mulatto bowed, a big grin on his face. At sight of that welcoming grin, Ethan's anxiety at arriving home settled.

"She been on pins and needles waiting for you suh. I spect you know the way."

"It's good to see you again, Jackson. Is she alone?"

"Only Nancy be with her at present."

"Thank you." He headed up the carpeted stairs, running his hand along the familiar polished walnut banister, glancing at Adrien, who followed. The first door on the left was ajar, and after rapping once he entered.

Nancy stood in front of a small table to his right, but she hardly mattered. No other woman mattered in any room which contained Annette Porcher-Childs. Memories flooded Ethan along with her lilac scent.

She smiled from the silk damask chair at the opposite end of the Oriental carpet. "Ethan," she said and raised her lace-draped arms. She was prepared for the evening in embroidered satin and heavier powder and paint than he recalled.

He went to her and dropped to one knee. Their embrace was brief, a surface touch only. Her touch had never been more than superficial. Maybe she saved emotion for her clients. Her eyes and mouth bore new lines, and her moderately round face displayed hints of puffiness, though her hair appeared deep brown as ever, her eyes lively emerald. He stood back. She yet radiated beauty and accomplishment.

"It has taken you overly long to visit," she said. "I should have borne a girl who would remain with me."

"You have ever preferred men, Mother."

"Yes, I have. Handsome and entertaining ones, at any rate." Her pupils enlarged as she peered past him.

"This is Adrien Villere, from Texas."

She beamed like a schoolgirl at her first ball, and languidly raised a hand to be kissed. "I adore Texians. Texas men are so magnificently masculine, yet gentlemen to the core."

Adrien bent, took her hand and brushed its surface with his lips. "I do not know about that, ma'am, but I always hope to behave as a gentleman should."

So, he did know how to thrill the ladies, a side Ethan hadn't seen.

"He looks like Louie Menard, doesn't he, Ethan. Louie was too beautiful for his own good. He and Ethan were exceedingly devoted as boys. Then Louie's maman discovered he could earn more money than she."

Though she had begun speaking to him and ended speaking to Adrien, she never drew her gaze from Adrien's face.

"I don't believe Adrien is interested in hearing of Louie, Mother." Surely, she knew not to speak of such things to a gentleman, not a real one. What was she up to? Able to find underhanded means to penalize him for the slightest transgression, she had been deft at keeping them secret. Despite the passing years, she yet aroused an angry coil in his gut. He knew what it meant if he let it strike. Sweat dampened his brow.

She was still speaking to his guest and conversing in French, no less. Good Lord, she was flirting—with a man younger than her son. She could never desist from playing the coquette, not even with his friends. He had found more than one slipping from her room at odd hours.

"Adrien is too much the gentleman to say, but he has an early evening appointment and we must clean up beforehand. Is the cottage available?" Ethan managed to keep his tone amiable. After ten years, he had hoped, but Mother would never change.

"You mean the *garconniére?* I made sure it wasn't let when I learned you were coming. See how dear is your maman?"

She still played her French card and reserved a special place in her heart for Creole gentry. Though most of her clientele were "Americain."

"I can't stay," Ethan said. "I have responsibilities to the army. I am forever in your debt." He bowed, one tight fist against the small of his back, placating her as ever.

"I hope your debt is to me only," she said. "Not to half of Louisiana as was that of your dear departed father."

He motioned Adrien toward the door. *More like half Louisiana was in debt to Father.* Ethan pressed his lips together to keep from speaking the words, which would start a screaming argument that would end with her throwing bottles and whatever else she could get her hands on as he ducked out the door. *I am too old for that, and with Adrien present. Mother never cared for Father's gambling, though his successes bought her a fancy house and most of what it contained. She ignores my following the same profession until we argue, then blames my "vile habit" on Father, as well. Yet she accepted my friendship with Louie and runs a brothel. Mother's moral compass is beyond my understanding.*

Nothing remained in the cypress-wood cottage to show he had lived there, save for the locked trunk at the end of the bed. The trunk contained everything important he had left behind, and he would leave more inside before continuing to Virginia. He couldn't help but consider the bed for a moment or two, recalling partners with whom he had shared its cozy boundaries, both male and female. He had a preference, but that preference was perilous.

One of the pretty dark-skinned girls brought them soap and filled two copper tubs placed on the little porch beneath the flaming wisteria. Adrien wouldn't remove his trousers until she left.

"She has seen more unclothed men than you have, I expect," Ethan said as he slid into the steaming water.

"She has not seen me." Adrien sank into the tub quickly enough to make water splash over the side. "Ahhh." He dropped his head against its high back and closed his eyes.

Adrien could be strange. He behaved as a disfigured man might, but there was nothing to be ashamed of. Quite the opposite. "Don't get used to this—"

"I know," Adrien said, "I have had a taste of the military. The very fact this bath will soon be rare is why I am enjoying it to the utmost. Look up there. Here we are in glorious, perfumed hot water surrounded by flowers. And honeybees. Hear them? And there is a butterfly."

Ethan watched it flutter by. He had never paid much attention to such things and glanced at Adrien, eyes tightly closed and lower lip in his teeth.

He's embarrassed for speaking of flowers and butterflies.

"This is glorious," Ethan said. "I always loved this little cottage, but never considered why." As a boy, he had been sometimes lonely here, even with the company of girls and his young friends.

He wanted to ask Adrien what he thought of his mother. Why did he care?

"Your mother is a lovely woman, Ethan. You never said she was French."

"Father married her in France when she was sixteen and brought her here to his home. She pushes the French accent a bit to impress her clients."

"She put my accent to shame."

"I happen to like your accent." He grabbed a bar of soap and sank beneath the water.

Chapter Four
The Yellow House

Blue, humid twilight settled upon the city. Ethan and Adrien found the graceful yellow stucco house nearly hidden behind banana trees, palmettos, and gardenias. The scrollwork house number was partially obscured by morning glory blooms, their livid petals having recently closed, and more lacy scrollwork decorated two second-floor balconies. Lace-covered windows glowed warmly on both sides of an arched and lacquered door that beckoned from the end of a brick walk.

"I'll go now," Ethan said. He didn't want to interfere in a private matter, and suspected a mistake, either with the address, or some secret he wanted no part of.

"Please. I mean . . . no need. If you don't mind." Adrien touched Ethan's sleeve, drew his fingers away to a button on his own coat, then dropped the hand to his side.

"Of course, I don't mind." Gratifying that his new friend wanted him present at such a moment. He shouldn't be gratified, wouldn't be if Adrien were anyone else, if—*Face it, if he didn't remind you of Louie. You are going to make a fool of yourself again if you're not careful.*

They passed through a wrought-iron entrance gate and Adrien lifted a brass fox-head knocker. Ethan remained two feet behind, not entirely comfortable considering this part of town.

A blue-black Negro in white gloves, black frock coat and frilled shirt starched to a fare-thee-well opened the door. "May I help you, sirs?" He spoke slowly and as meticulously as Adrien.

"I am looking for a lady by the name of Madeleine Yvonne Villere. My name is Adrien Villere."

His palm on the doorknob, the man's eyes went from Adrien to Ethan and back again. "Would you wait here a moment please?"

"Of course."

He left the door ajar, but did not invite them in. Strange. Male voices wafted from within. Adrien glanced back at Ethan. The door opened wide.

A different man stood there: gray eyes, clean-shaven face with thick, curly gray hair, wearing a silk cravat and dark blue velvet coat with gold buttons and gold studs in his sleeves. He might be any distinguished gentleman except for his toast-brown skin.

"I am sorry. There is no one by that name here. You have come to the wrong house." His words were clipped, his face compressed with determination.

"My papa wrote to this address. Possibly you moved here recently?"

"We have lived in this house for three generations. You have the wrong address." The man closed the door.

"I didn't think this was the right place," Ethan said, "but I hesitated to say until we checked." But why was the fellow rude? Perhaps he had had a bad experience with some other white man from out of town. Such a thing had been known to happen with whites with little or no contact with free Negroes, particularly with a Negro as prosperous as this man appeared to be. Ethan hoped he hadn't made his relief obvious.

"I do not understand. I was sure I had the right number," Adrien said.

"Can't be, Adrien. This whole area is where the Creole *gens de couleur* live."

"Free people of color?"

"Yeah. They are well-off, as you can see, and many own businesses. Some own their own slaves."

"It seems I have a lot to learn about New Orleans."

"I'm sorry you didn't find your aunt. But I know of a place that will take your mind off your disappointment."

Ethan didn't care for the beaten-pup look on Adrien's face, though he didn't appear shocked by the idea of moneyed free Negroes. To tell the truth, Ethan was keen for a decent game, and the place he was considering would make his new friend happy at the same time. Generally, it took only one thing to lift a young fellow out of despondency. He might enjoy a little canoodling himself before the night was over. With such a tempting companion, it was best to keep his own appetites on the straight and narrow.

A mockingbird sang from a pomegranate tree in the center of the yard as they left.

Maison Coquet was similar to his mother's house with the addition of card tables and a roulette wheel, and the games and girls were clean. Pretty mulatto boys in tight satin trousers and embroidered top coats served champagne and chilled oysters. Ethan added to his finances playing faro while Lysette, a sweet, frisky bundle of auburn curls, led a hesitant Adrien upstairs.

Several hours later, as they headed west on Rue Royale, Adrien had obviously drunk too much champagne. He declared, "She is an angel, Ethan."

Ethan grabbed an arm as Adrien swayed dangerously close to a cast-iron picket fence.

"You don't know what she has done."

"I have a pretty good idea." Ethan grinned. Thank God, Adrien wasn't a morose or violent drunk.

"She made me laugh; we laughed so hard. I could even love her. I do, tonight, love her." His voice drifted into a murmur. He drifted as well, and Ethan grasped the back collar of his top coat to set him in the right direction again. Adrien laughed, a hiccough, "If there was such a thing as love, if I deserved it. . . ."

That's what his mumbling sounded like, but Ethan wasn't certain.

"We'd better catch a cab, or we'll be late." Besides, he didn't wish to carry Adrien so many blocks back to headquarters, and it had begun to appear he might.

"Like champagne . . . how it makes me feel. Pleasant and numb." More mumbling. Then, clearer, "Not all that important, is it?"

"What isn't?"

"Anything."

Ethan caught the boy under a shoulder as his legs folded, then whistled up a cab.

❧

"I thought I would wander around town on my own today and see where it takes me."

Adrien was blocking Ethan's sunlight. Ethan didn't look up, but continued with his needle. He sat cross-legged on the ground against a sunny outside wall, the shirt across his lap. *On his own, huh?*

For once Adrien hadn't been up before Ethan, and it was obvious why, from the way he had crawled out from under his blanket like a whipped dog. So many had come in late last night that the cooks had obligingly produced breakfast until nine o'clock. The local ladies frequently presented them with baskets of hot buttered biscuits and spicy Creole sausage. Late evenings and late breakfasts had become a habit with most of them in New Orleans, and few were anxious to move on to Virginia.

Adrien's announcement sent an unwelcome swell of annoyance through him.

"Watch your pockets, don't go above Canal Street, and stay away from Gallatin—"

"I am grown, in case you did not notice."

Ethan poked his needle into the fabric and squinted up. The sun glared white over Adrien's left shoulder. Ethan had seen him dump a pail of cold water over his head shortly after rising—only marginally improving his bleary-eyed appearance. His hair looked like a bird's nest drenched by a rainstorm, making him even younger and appealing as hell.

"See you later," Ethan said, and returned to his needle. Good. He hadn't been alone since they arrived. He would reacquaint himself with some people he knew. *Damn!* He sucked on his needle-stabbed finger.

✤

Wandering old haunts throughout the afternoon, Ethan found none of his former friends. One had gotten married and migrated to California. Two had joined the New Orleans Regulars. He was told the last got himself killed in a duel.

"A duel!"

"Still happens. Though most don't talk of it."

Well, Gil was Creole. Hot-tempered and proud, as Ethan recalled. But dueling? Common back in the thirties, but to get killed in a duel in these modern times? *Damn foolish. Damn.*

As he'd guessed, Louie Menard was in Paris.

"He will not return," Madam Menard said. "They never return once they go."

She referred to all the young boys like Louie. Those who could escape the stigma of being a Negro in the United States lived a life free of injustice in France. He would not blame Louie, who could pass for white.

Madam was still beautiful. More so than his own mother. She had a lady's maid, a cook, and a lovely little cottage on Rue Chartre.

"I only see old friends now," she said. "I need not see anyone else."

He understood what she meant without her having to elaborate. She was well taken care of by Monsieur Menard. Monsieur cared enough to give their son his name, despite what his legitimate family might think.

"Surely you recall my daughter Marie has a protector and a fine house on Rue Toulouse," she added. "We have been fortunate."

New Orleans was full of beautiful women, most tinted with color.

✤

That evening, musing upon his afternoon experiences broke his concentration as he perched on an overturned pail and considered the hand of cards he had been dealt. The other three men with him hemmed and hawed at their own hands. Crane Forbes, the boney, dark-haired fellow he'd met earlier, threw a card down onto the piece of old, gray board they were using for a table and asked for another from Jim Matthews, who dealt this round. Forbes had lit the kerosene lamp hours ago. Ethan's bottom was numb and his back ached. If his mind had begun to wander from the game, this should be his last round.

Lanky Will Moore ambled over to watch. Having been a cow hand before becoming a ranger, Will was more bowlegged than many.

"I'm out after this hand, if you want in," Ethan said.

"Long as it's not too stout."

"Penny ante," Matthews said.

"Count me in, then."

No one spoke while the round played out to Crane's win. Ethan stretched and found unwinding his stiff self from the pail a mite difficult.

"Say," Will said, as they do-si-doed one another, "I saw your compadre come in 'bout an hour ago all dandied up, I hardly recognized him. I reckon he's got himself a fancy lady friend or two in town already, hey?"

"Beats me," Ethan said.

"I'd hang tight with that one if I were you. Be like a bunch of heifers around the only bull in the county. You'd be bound to rope one sooner or later."

Shush, shush, shush—the cards flew out from Forbes's hands into piles.

Ethan had an urge to smack the back of Will's head and shove him face first into their makeshift table.

About midnight, Ethan crawled in next to Adrien's back and light snore.

Next morning the youth was up and gone. Good. A little space was just the thing. Ethan didn't see him at breakfast, either, when word came along that all passes were canceled.

Benjamin Terry strode into the enormous room—only it didn't seem so huge with him in it—clambered up again onto the compress and tucked his thumbs into his belt. Ethan was close enough to note him scanning the room while everyone quieted down.

"Fellas, I had hoped to announce we were to be favored with tents and gear, but Commander Twiggs has seen fit to deny us such things on grounds that men from Texas are so tough as to not need them."

"Hurrah!" Ethan yelled with the rest, but thought it mighty clever of Terry to put it that way. Twiggs was the bigwig officer in New Orleans and, as far as Ethan could figure, had not done a damn thing for them. Local folks provided all their food.

Terry rotated as he continued, catching the eyes of fellows as he did so. "It also appears that Albert Sidney Johnston desperately needs us to chase the Yankees out of Kentucky. General Johnston is known to me personally as a fine Texas gentleman, which means we would be riding under one of our own. As no one has voted for officers and the other companies have not yet arrived, I did not believe it fair to change our plans without a vote taken among all those present.

"I realize that not joining our Texas brethren in Virginia will be a disappointment, but General Johnston is in need of a strong fighting force of superb cavalry." He raised his voice and pumped the air with his fist, "and I told him that would be riders from Texas!"

With all the cheering and hurrahing after that, it was obvious how the vote would go. They would head up north by rail that night.

As their half of the 8th Texas Cavalry boarded the train, Adrien, with a sheepish smile, took the empty seat next to Ethan. Ethan glanced at him and looked out the window. He was not one to poke into someone else's business without being invited.

Chapter Five
The Note

Adrien

The morning after Ethan and I visited Maison Couquet, I found a note in the pocket of the dress trousers I had worn the evening before.

> *If you wish to locate Madeleine Yvonne Villere, be at Café Mes Amis on Rue St. Anne at noon. I will meet you. Come alone. Tell no one.*

How in God's name? The note might be a hoax. But why? No one knew but Ethan and those people at the lovely yellow house.

I would do as the note suggested. My heart beat faster as I stuffed the note back in my pocket.

Near noon on Rue St. Anne, *Mes Amis* was easily found. The first gentleman I asked gave directions to the southeast corner of Jackson Square. Hundreds of masts bobbed above the Louisiana and Texas Railroad Building that stood on the Mississippi wharf beyond. Four finely dressed gentlemen sat drinking coffee at two small, round tables beneath the eaves of *Mes Amis*. Beyond them the café's two large multipaned glass windows twinkled in brilliant sunlight slanting between the leaves of an old oak trailing ivy. A pretty mulatto girl in a bright yellow tignon, her tray full of sparkling glasses balanced in one hand, smiled and slipped gracefully aside as I approached the open double doorway and stepped down into the dim interior. Cherry wainscoting ran along the walls, and smooth cypress floors glowed with polish. Enticing aromas of meat, fried fish, and spices as well as the pervasive tang of beer permeated the room. Three large oak kegs lined the far end of the bar, and behind and above it hung a three-by-five-foot oil painting of what I took to be the Battle of New Orleans.

I found an empty table against the far wall and ordered a beer—a bite of the dog that yet muddled my brain—from a maid with tempting décolletage. She returned with an inviting smile as well as my beer, which was cold, frothy, and excellent, possibly the finest I had ever tasted. I liked this city more and more and could not imagine why Ethan had left. Or why Papa had left. My hands trembled as I took a couple of swallows of beer. I had had nothing to eat since breakfast, and it would not do to be tipsy for this meeting.

How nice to hear French, to know I still understood the surrounding speech despite not having used the language since college. Papa had ceased speaking French after Maman passed on, and refused to teach me or Berni much Creole French.

An accent I could not place rose above others at the bar—Irish, perhaps? Here was that familiar ache again, of wanting to know, to experience the unknown, the world beyond.

The men were elegantly attired in frock coats of various shades of gray, brown, and black. I considered Marcus and Isaac, how well they would blend in, how fine they would look dressed the same.

Had Isaac succeeded? Was he somewhere in Mexico or at the bottom of the Rio Grande? I had not thought of those last moments with Isaac since arriving in New Orleans. I took a deep breath and another sip of beer.

A deep voice startled me. "*S'il vous plaît*, may I join you?"

The gray-haired gentlemen of the evening before wore cream kid gloves and carried a silk hat and brass-topped cane in one hand.

"*Oui, merci*, do." I had the urge to stand in his presence, but the man was already sitting, placing hat and gloves on the table, the cane against the wall. The maid magically appeared, as though she had been waiting for the gentleman's arrival.

"A small glass of whiskey please, your finest," he said, and turned to me after she left.

"My name is Gilbert Villantry. Will you first tell me how you found our house and, again, who you are? You will understand why I ask later."

Why should I tell this man anything, a stranger? Villantry? Had he taken his master's name, as so many Negroes did? I had been at that house. This was the only lead I had, and the fellow appeared to be a gentleman—*un monsieur de couleur*—according to Ethan. If I would play the fool again, I wanted to know now.

"Then you are Paien Villere's youngest son."

My voice came hesitant at first, but speaking became easier as I continued. "*Oui.*" I grasped my nearly empty glass of beer so tightly I might very well have broken it.

"I will not waste your time nor mine mincing words," he said. "I am a free man and you came to my home last evening." Then Monsieur Villantry carefully lifted the tiny crystal glass. The white ruffle at his cuff hid his lips as he drank. His hand trembled slightly.

I swallowed, a dry lump in my own throat, and took a last gulp of beer.

"My wife sets much store by the truth. That family should know family, that blood is thicker than water, no matter the consequences. She is generally the wiser in such matters, so, in spite of my doubts, I will do as she wishes. If you have finished your beer, come."

A brisk walk took us past Spanish and Creole houses decorated with fanciful iron scrollwork and colorful wood carvings, accompanied by the perfume of hundreds of flowers that vied with the stink of ever-present overflowing gutters.

It is not too late to scuttle back to headquarters. Excuse me, sir, I have made a mistake. I have changed my mind. My shoes kept moving along with the other man's polished shoes, right there on the cobblestones. Left, right, left, right, like a march, like the infantry would, looking for battle—or trouble. *I am looking for trouble, doing this.* If only the man would speak, if only I didn't find myself overcome by longing? Dread? I had done something wrong and was marching to Papa's office for one of the few switchings I had received when I was a boy, all shivery and short of breath.

This time the door opened immediately, as though we were expected, and the same butler took Monsieur Villantry's hat, gloves, and cane the moment we entered the vestibule. I followed Villantry down the carpeted hall through a door to the right, where we entered a small, elegant, yet cozy room with tables and chairs of heirloom quality. Lace curtains decorated the windows on either side of the unlit marble-lined fireplace at the opposite end. A pale, thin woman sat on one of the two facing settees in front of the fireplace. Her black hair was streaked with gray, parted in the center and gathered in a silk lace net at her neck. She smiled—a familiar smile. We approached, and she held out her hand.

"This is my wife," Monsieur Villantry said, "Madeleine Yvonne Villere Villantry."

I took her soft, cool palm, only I could not pull my eyes from her face, from dark eyes that looked so much like Papa's. This free man of color said she was his wife; she was married to him. She was as white as Papa. This could not be allowed, even in New Orleans, could it?

"You are my brother's son. Is that true?" Her voice was deep.

"Yes." Breathing difficult, I had spoken.

"Please sit," she said.

My hand located the chair first, cool damask, thank God, as the floor beneath my feet tilted.

A different servant, not so black as the other, brought in a tray and poured tea.

"Do you take sugar?" Madam Villantry said.

"No, thank you."

"I prefer a little honey in the evening, and my tea not so strong as in the morning." She took a sip, and the white lace at her wrists did not entirely hide her mouth, rather wide for such a petite face.

The cups were so delicate, I could see the tea through them, and my hands were unsteady.

"Did Paien tell you of me and our family?"

"He has told us nothing. I found your address in his letters. Your letters, ma'am. He does not know I am here."

"Ahh. He has not changed then. Nothing has changed." She put her cup carefully onto its saucer, folded her hands and raised her eyes to me with the same quizzical look I got from Papa before he decided whether I might be trusted with a new gun or horse. I held her eyes—I did not want to be found lacking by this woman. Was she about to tell me something that would make Papa less or my own life less? I should never have come, never learned of the letters.

"My brother left New Orleans for Virginia to make a new life for himself," she said. "What was left of our family at the time, Maman and I, understood. We also understood and forgave him for wanting to leave the truth and his past behind, though it was difficult, especially for Maman. I believe you will also find truth difficult and may wish to leave before hearing more."

Another chance to end this right here. *I cannot. I cannot even stand. Or breathe.*

"There is very little you can say that would create a truth more difficult than one from which I am already running. Maybe this one I can face." *That sounds good. Please make it true.* I swallowed, or tried to.

She regarded me calmly. *What if she asks me what I mean? What will I say if she does? Why did I say such a thing in the first place?* Thankfully, she let my comment pass.

"Very well. You are already wondering how it is possible that I married a free man of color. My mother was a woman of color from Santa Domingue, your grandmother."

My grandmother, a woman of color. My blood. Papa's secret. My secret now. My sister Berni, my brother Lucien.

Lily. Had I once thought to marry her? I felt no different. Why would I? I did feel different. I could not get air into my throbbing chest and that beer was coming up. I swallowed it back down, again, and again. I placed the little cup and saucer carefully on the table in front of me before I dropped it.

This woman—my aunt?—lied. To hurt me. To hurt Papa. Why would she? No, she did not lie.

Dear God, I am one . . . one of them.

I nearly asked if she were sure. I was suddenly cold.

"Here." Monsieur Villantry held a small glass. By the smell, it was liquor of some kind. I took the glass and gulped the contents entire—warmth flowed down my throat, brandy or something like—and my eyes watered. My papa, Paien, was passing himself off as a white man. Had been all these years. *God help me. Us. Did Marcus know? Had Maman?*

Monsieur Villantry offered another glass. "No thank you, Monsieur. I am sorry." I spoke, though it came out breathy and soft, a whisper.

"Do not be sorry, and call me Gilbert, please. You are my nephew by marriage if you will allow."

The man's voice, the voice that spoke to me. I hated it, wanted to bash him for such insolence, to break everything in this wretched room. She watched me, her black eyes so like Papa's, hands still folded.

"Do you wish to run now, Adrien Villere?"

"I—" I was blinking away tears—from the brandy. But she sat so still, waiting. Her lower lip trembled, and she bit down on it. This small act was what forced me to stay, forced me to think of Maman. I would be more the fool to run.

"If I may, I would like to hear more, if there is more." I might catch some mistake, a mistake that made this right.

"Oh, my dear," she leaned forward and put her hand on mine, to stop it from trembling, "there is much more. You have cousins and aunts and uncles who will be so happy to know you, and you must remain for supper."

"Don't worry," Gilbert said, "we have learned to be most circumspect, and none of this will get back to your people."

My people. Who are my people now?

I hardly noticed my route through the dark, late-night streets, so engrossed was I in the disjointed ramblings of my mind. My entire history was a lie.

They, *my relatives*, had asked about Ethan and how long we would remain in New Orleans.

"We are with the 8th Texas Cavalry and will leave when we receive orders." A statement no sooner out of my mouth than I wished to swallow it. We must defend our homes from the Yankee intruders. The federals claimed another cause. I had not joined up to keep those people enslaved—now *my* people. My people? I helped Isaac escape. Papa's slave, no less.

That mysterious note had changed everything. Denying, accepting, denying again. The deaths of Maman, Abby, and Jules had affected me the same. Every morning I woke as usual, before remembering that my entire world had collapsed out from under like a riverbank during flood.

Who was I now? How could I face my new friends? How would I face Ethan?

How did Papa do it all these years—pass as a white man?

Wandering the city all evening had not served an answer.

I stopped, closed my eyes, and curled my fingers into my damp palms. The earth turned beneath my feet and I opened my eyes for fear of falling over. This damn burden of one secret, now another. If Jacob had known, would he. . . ? Of course, he would. White men forced Negroes all the time.

I believed I had understood how they, how Isaac, had felt. Papa's adamancy over not fraternizing with our people that way now shone under a different candle. Dear God, what would happen to Berni if my family were discovered to be Negro? I jerked to a stop and flung both hands up to my head, knocking my hat askew. No one must learn of this!

I was among the darkest in our company, although J. J. Petty, whose mother was Mexican, had eyes and hair as black. The warm red-brown of his skin would now give me a fleeting sense of security. Such stupid reasoning. If anyone ever learned of my breeding, it would not matter a whit if I looked as white as a full moon on a clear night; I would be considered colored.

I should have heard it sooner—the soft scrape of a shoe on the banquette behind, too close behind, and the back of my neck prickled like hair on a frightened cat's tail. I was in the warehouse district, only four blocks from headquarters—but devoid of other people and gas lights few and far between—the thought blew through as I moved how Jacob had taught, how Isaac and I had practiced over and over.

Adrenaline firing, I crouched and spun, right elbow powering into my assailant's midsection. A *huh* exploded from the man's mouth as he curled forward and a wicked blade spiraled from his fingers, clattered off the corner of the banquette and plopped into the miasmic gutter. My shove, fueled by a flash of hot-burning anger, sent the fellow face-first after the knife.

Barely time to grab the wrist of the second man and continue its downward thrust—farther than the fellow planned and right on around so I could pump my knee into a kidney and throw him into the wall of the nearest building.

The third, driving in with the second, snagged me. Fire sliced through the lower left side of my new red shirt. What must be the first man, spitting, pumped a vicious fist into my abdomen that turned my legs to water and dropped me to my knees. A brutal kick into the gash left by the knife lifted me up and onto my back. My stomach heaved from the searing pain and what little supper I had gotten down came up as I landed, the back of my skull bouncing on the wood banquette. I would not have to worry about being Negro, after all. My own puke dribbled into my right ear.

"Hey! Stop! You there, you sons-a-bitches!" Sufficient to wake the whole block, but only warehouses and cotton press buildings lined the street. Shouting and someone running down the street sure enough sent my attackers reeling off into the dark.

The two who trotted up wore red shirts of rangers. One was tall and lanky, like Ethan, the other a short fellow. They stood up there against the inky sky, two dark forms topped by floppy wide-brimmed hats, a little blurry and spinning among the hazy stars.

"You all right?" tall and lanky said, as he offered a hand.

I sat up, but was not quite ready to rise any farther for the moment. I removed a linen cloth from the breast pocket of my coat and wiped at the side of my face. "Sorry." What I would do for a glass of clear water.

The tall one held his hand out again, and I accepted it. Once up, I had to lean over, palms on my knees, to keep from sinking back down. Lord, my bones hurt.

"You saved my life," I managed to say as I slowly straightened, leaning a little to the left, my fist hovering over the seeping wound.

"Let's see that," said the shorter fellow, leading me under the nearest streetlamp.

"It is not deep—I think he barely touched me." A hot iron burned a furrow into my skin. My hands shook.

"We saw you well ahead of us a ways back and wondered why a fellow so duded up would be heading this way on his lonesome," said tall and lanky.

"I am with Company K."

"By jings, I told Sol you had to be a ranger, coming this way so late." I could see nearly all the fellow's teeth in his smile. "I'm Ned Brown and this is Solomon Autry, Company G."

Autry might be short, but his shoulders threatened to burst his shirt seams. We shook hands all around, the newcomers more enthusiastically than me.

"You look a mite peaked there," said Solomon. Both possessed matching Texas drawls as long as a hot summer day. "I reckon that's going to take right smart of stitches. I'll hold that fancy coat if you want to wrap your shirt round there good and tight till we get to Doc Hill."

"Don't mind Sol," said Ned. "Back to home blacksmithing warn't enough. He must doctor everything in sight, as well."

I took him up on the offer. No point getting blood on my frock coat, as well. I did feel a mite woozy. And all-around sore. And wanted to beg these fellows to accompany me back to quarters. By jings, as Ned said, they did so without my asking, and once or twice when my legs threatened to fold out from under, Sol supported me with a surreptitious grasp of my arm. Wonderful fellows, none better.

We arrived in quarters with no more incidents, and the two guided me straight to Bob Hill, who sewed me up in no time with eight neat stitches over a rib. "Lower or higher and you'd be worse off," Hill said. I even got in a few good sips of bourbon. Otherwise, I might never have managed to sleep, despite my exhaustion.

The following night, we rangers grabbed gear and boarded the train, boxcars, of all things, for Nashville. I was relieved to find a seat on a plank next to Ethan. I had been avoiding him all day, had considered making a run for it, considering what I was. But I was also Adrien Villere, Paien and Madeleine Villere's son, and I held a duty to my family and to the Brazos River people where I grew up. Without that and without the rangers, I was nothing. My life was theirs.

Fortunately, I had written a letter to Papa earlier to let the family know where to write to me. I added that I met Mrs. Villantry, but no details. Papa would understand without more.

Chapter Six
Texas, the Last Time

Lily

Lily had never been so angry as the afternoon Jacob forced her to leave Adrien behind in the tobacco barn. He had promised not to kill Adrien if she left. Her brother had never lied to her.

She nearly kicked her mare into a furious run that would hurtle them both to a crash on the uneven, rain-slicked ground. Drizzling rain puddled her saddle, which served to fuel her anger. The mare, ever sensitive to her rider, tossed her head and fought the bit the entire way home.

Father was off somewhere, thank God. Lily hastily changed into dry clothes and waited in the parlor on pins and needles for her brother to return. Nearly two hours later, he did.

Her hands in fists, she practically ran at him. "What have you done?"

Jacob remained insufferably calm. "Your lover is on his way to Houston to join a company of cavalry. He'll be as safe as our brother, whom you seem to have forgotten."

"You had no right."

"I had every right. I introduced you to a liberal education believing you had more sense. I hoped you would use that education to your advantage. It appears I was wrong. I do not like being wrong, Lily."

"I would marry him."

"Dear God, hear yourself. Where would you live? Not here at Hartwood. At Blue Hills with Adrien and his family? How long before

they must sell the rest of their land? You really expect you could live in
some sod hut with him, peeling potatoes and slopping hogs?"

"You exaggerate."

"You reckon so, do you?" he said with a crack of laughter, jutting
his chin.

"I hate you."

"Because you know I am right. You will thank me later."

She turned from his smug face, her own face burning, lifted her
skirts and flew up the stairs to her room, where she need not look at
him. She would not cry. She absolutely would not.

This God-awful marriage to that railroad man would be the last
time she obeyed her father and brother.

Six weeks later, Lily, as gloriously trussed as the seven-layer wedding
cake on the sideboard downstairs in the dining room, trembled before
her bedroom mirror. She must rid herself of all these more colorful,
yet similarly dressed clucking hens.

"Please. Give me a few moments alone with Bernadette."

Understandable, since Bernadette was her maid of honor.

She turned to acknowledge the smiles, the expressions of affection, *swish, swish*, of crinolines and silk and, last, with a flick of her
wrist, sent her girl Mae out the door after them. Mae, ever on her toes,
closed it behind her with a soft click.

Lovely Berni, in lavender marquisette over silk, held her matching lace gloves in clasped hands before her. She waited calmly not
four feet away at the window she had previously opened to cool
October morning air heated from so many flushed and anxious
females.

"I've wanted to speak with you alone since he left." She was sure
Adrien's sister knew who she meant, though she had no idea how
much he had told her about their . . . assignations.

Berni stepped close, reached for her hands and, with dangling
gloves, took them in her own. "You must forget him, Lily. You are

about to be a married woman. Adrien surely left to make this right. No good comes from pining for what cannot be."

Pining? I never pine. "I must know if he is alive and healthy."

Berni took a deep, quick breath. "I promise I will tell you if we hear otherwise."

Oh, God. Her emotions were slipping back and forth from vexation to relief to dread and back again. She was sure the same thoughts flickered in Berni's eyes as they clasped one another's hands tighter.

"We're still friends, aren't we?" Lily said. "I could not bear to lose you. You are my only true friend."

"Of course, we are." Berni leaned forward and hugged her. Her eyes filled as she grasped Adrien's sister tight.

※

The Garrisons took their honeymoon in a special railroad car to Shreveport. He promised her Paris someday. Alas, the war.

With its plush maroon velvet furniture and matching swag drapes with gold tassels on every window, the car was rather ostentatious, Lily mused. She pushed up the window above the small table where she sat until the train rounded a corner and coal smoke from the engine blew into her face.

She slammed the window shut and brushed coal ash from the bodice of her dressing gown. The gown, ivory silk bordered in French lace, a wedding gift from her older brother Jacob's wife, fit perfectly. Garrison poured two glasses of red wine and sat across from her.

"When we are alone, you will call me William, and I will call you Lily," he said.

"As you wish."

"My lawyer said that was quite a prenuptial your father had drawn up." He took a cigar and engraved silver scissors from a wooden box on the table.

"Let me," she said, and deftly cut the tip, leaned forward and held a match while he drew and huffed clouds of gray smoke above their faces. "Actually, the addition was Jacob's idea. With my full concurrence, of course." She blew the match out with a soft puff, watching him.

"And I thought I was getting some naive maiden."

"This is Texas, not Virginia. We have learned to survive on our own."

"So it seems. I will get everything out of you I can in the years I have left, including an heir, and I may live longer than you think."

She would not let him know of the fear that clutched her chest. She had never missed her monthly before, but she had missed the last. She and Adrien were always careful. Knowing their time together would soon be over, at Oak Creek they had made love more than once. They were not properly prepared for the last—she thrilled, reflecting on what came to mind. Last, last, last, she could choke on that word. It had been the last, and she hadn't known.

Perhaps missing once meant nothing. She would know soon enough.

Chapter Seven
Forgiveness

Bernadette

This morning I retreated to the quiet solitude of my room where I can write my letters in some semblance of peace, having received two of Adrien's letters since last September, not including the note I found under my doorway begging forgiveness for not personally saying goodbye. If he had not appeared so dogged and desperate when I encountered him in the library, I never would have forgiven him. I am of the opinion the affair with Lily sent him off. Only a kiss, he said all those months ago. But from Lily's behavior at the wedding, it hadn't ended there. I should have realized, but I had been too caught up with Will, with my own wedding. Now, my dear brother has gone off to this dreadful war.

Papa has become strangely reticent since receiving Adrien's first letter. Papa's face went pale, and he abruptly excused himself, taking the letter with him. The family shares our letters, but Papa no longer shares all letters from Adrien, not before reading them. Of course, I do not share everything Will writes to me, but that is different, is it not?

I find myself staring out my bedroom window, seeing nothing. Drat. The ink in my quill dried, and I must begin again.

After two days of October rain, the afternoon has turned sunny and all the windows are open to let in fresh air, which explains why I hear a galloping horse arriving at the front of the house. Who has ridden up so hurriedly? They have not come from town or I would have seen since my window faces east to the main road. I must finish these last few sentences.

Voices downstairs. One male and the other is surely Joanna, in the parlor with her baby. Papa and Lucien are working in the fields and Isaac has taken the boys out back to help Betta in the garden. At a rambunctious five, Renee is best outside as much as possible, and Gabe wants to be with his older brother. What a relief how my oldest brother, Lucien, has softened since marrying Joanna and becoming a father.

The male voice rises louder. I do not like the sharp, frustrated tone of Joanna's response. Drat. Nothing for it but to go down there and see what this folderol is about.

"You mustn't," Joanna said.

"I have to." That voice matched the windblown profile standing on the carpet in the parlor facing Joanna, his hat grasped tightly in one fist—Joanna's youngest brother, Joe.

"You're only—" Joanna caught me in the doorway. "Tell him, Berni. He plans to go to this ghastly war, and he's only sixteen."

Joe turned, his face dark with emotion. "I'll be seventeen in three months, and Adrien is barely two years older. My friends are waiting and I'm going with them. I only came because I had to tell someone." He faced Joanna again. "I couldn't tell Papa or Mama. You know how they are. I assumed you would understand. Of anyone, I thought you would."

"Because I'm married to a slave owner?" This burst from her in one fierce exhalation. I had never heard such anger from Joanna. Though the comment had been made to Joe, I felt I had been slapped.

"That slave stuff is abolitionist propaganda." Joe smacked his hat against his thigh.

"How dare you." Joanna's voice had risen an octave. Arms stiff at her side, fingers clutching her skirts, her entire body trembled.

Despite my fast-beating heart, I stepped farther into the room.

"Please, we are all family here. Don't say anything further that you both will regret."

Both stared at me, mouths slightly open, eyes widening, as though they had forgotten I was there. The baby on the sofa let out a long wail. Joanna's eyes filled with tears. She spun to pick up her child and sat, burying her face in the baby's middle and patting her back.

"Sit down, Joe," I said.

"I can't stay. My friends are waiting."

"You may be years away with your friends. You can sit with me and your sister for a moment or two."

I sat next to Joanna. The baby quieted to hiccoughs. "I take it you are joining the Confederacy?"

Joe, on Papa's armchair, sat forward, hands on his knees, dangling his hat. "Yeah. I don't want the North coming down here and taking our land, telling us how to run our affairs." He studied the low table between us where lay a copy of *Harper's Weekly* and then looked at me. "Matt, my older brother, you remember him? He rode out last week to join up with *them*, the North I mean." His glance took in Joanna, who, from her stiffened form and intake of breath, I realized had not known. "So now there's just my oldest brother, Rob, Jr., and his family, Mama, and Papa at home." His hands became fists, squishing the brim of his hat. "They don't realize, don't know I left, yet. Me and Matt waited till after harvest," he said to Joanna. The tone of his voice, the way he looked at her, he hoped this last would receive her approval. He peered down at his hands, absently turning his hat around. "Course, Matt didn't know I'd be going, too."

"Oh, Joe," Joanna said, holding her baby tight. A tear coursed down her cheek.

He looked up, mashed his lips together, lowered his head again, grasped his hat ever tighter, whitening his knuckles. He popped up off the chair. "I better go."

Joanna carefully lay the now-silent baby among the sofa pillows and rose. "I'll see you to the door." She followed him out of the parlor. Then the murmur of their voices on the porch and soon after the receding gallop of his horse. I hoped he would take care of that horse after galloping all over creation like that or it would not carry him far.

Joanna returned with red eyes and sat next to me. "I'm so sorry," she said. "Will you forgive me?"

"Of course," I said, "there is nothing to forgive." Holding one another for a few moments felt splendid. I suspected we would all need a good deal of holding in the year to come.

Chapter Eight
Tennessee and Kentucky

Ethan

E than would later recall camp at the fairgrounds outside Nashville as a frolic, a last hurrah. The town came to symbolize his life *before Nashville* compared to his life *after Nashville*. Deterioration crept up over a period of weeks. Even after December 17 at Woodsonville, he had no idea how bad war could get.

In early October, the rangers behaved like big children playing games at a picnic, with the biggest game yet to be played. They entertained Nashville citizens with a show of riding ability by tearing back and forth across the fairgrounds doing tricks on horseback, including snatching coins—contributed by locals—from the ground, while galloping at full speed. Nashville ladies brought the Texas heroes pies, biscuits, honey, and marmalade. If Ethan wasn't careful, he would outgrow his trousers before their first battle. Since leaving New Orleans, no one ought to complain about ending up here. If anyone did, Ethan would personally boot them in the behind.

They lay their bedrolls on soft grass, and the prettiest clear creek rambled right along the edge of camp. The weather cooperated—cold, but sunny. If only these boys would take advantage of the sinks they had dug the first day instead of peeing right outside the tents—some wouldn't even use the sinks for squats. Holy Mother of God, the place stunk. Good thing they weren't any closer to town or they might not be so welcome. He hoped they'd soon vote for officers before everything got entirely out of hand.

Word passed around that they were supposed to remain in camp. But men snuck into town, and no few brought liquor back with them. Without officers, who could do anything about it?

Adrien was another concern.

They weren't in camp twenty-four hours before Ethan heard a story about a ranger who'd gotten rolled—knifed and nearly killed—returning to quarters the night before they'd left New Orleans. He'd been "all duded up and alone." And he was from Company K, all Ethan needed.

The two threw down their bedrolls among clover and beneath a brilliant red sassafras tree. After Adrien removed his shirt, Ethan plucked up the edge of his undershirt, exposing neat thread tracks that ran across a blue and purple field on one of his lower ribs.

"Hey." Adrien shoved the hand, flopped onto his bedroll, and pulled off his boots.

Ethan stared down at him, arms dangling.

The youth removed his trousers and tugged the blanket up to his chin before he looked up at Ethan, who hadn't moved.

"You are going to get mighty cold standing out there all night," Adrien said.

Ethan folded his arms to his chest and tightened his stomach muscles. He would not suffer such foolishness.

"Holy cockroach, Ethan. You are not my papa. Stop acting like some, some—" lips mashed together, he sat up and threw off the blanket. "I did not go to Gallatin or any other place I should not have. It happened on Tchoupitoulas Street, mere blocks from quarters."

"You were dressed like some wealthy fool and out late at night alone."

"I was *not* alone, or I would not be speaking to you at present."

Ah, Ethan thought, *at least he's aware of how close he came.* His fists clenched.

"I will allow I was stupid, not paying attention. If I had heard them earlier, I would have run like a rabbit."

"Would you?" Ethan surprised himself with his own sharp tone.

"You must think me an idiot to stand against three men. By choice, that is." He peered up from under tousled, black hair, regarding Ethan with an innocent look of suffering endurance, forearms dangling over pulled-up knees.

The devil. Ethan joined Adrien on the blanket, pulled off his boots, and turned to face him.

"Don't make a habit of wandering down dark streets on your lonesome. Once I get used to a sleeping partner, I don't like to change."

"I feel the same." Adrien gave him a crooked grin.

⚘

The first sickness was blamed on hangovers. It was measles. If that didn't beat all. Having been raised in the city, Ethan had acquired measles as a child. Most of these fellows were country boys, had never left Texas and never encountered the disease. Measles was serious when it latched onto an adult.

In mid-October, a week after their arrival, the regiment received orders to cook rations for three days and move again. Ethan wondered if the move was an attempt to outrun the sickness that snatched men from their ranks every day. If so, the attempt failed, for no sooner had they arrived in Oakland, a little town not far from Bowling Green, than a fellow died from measles that turned to pneumonia. Their first casualty.

In Oakland they finally received tents and equipment, elected staff and field officers, and Terry officially became colonel; Tom Lubbock, lieutenant colonel; Tom Harrison, major. The men elected Bob Hill assistant surgeon along with a Dr. Royston. The original one hundred and fifteen men of Company K still healthy voted Ethan one of their four sergeants. His immediate superior, First Sergeant Gayle P. Alexander, chuckled when Ethan learned of the appointment and threw his metal cup at the dying fire.

"You won their money, Childs. They voted you sergeant out of spite."

"Blast."

Adrien, perched on a nearby log, snickered into his coffee, then coughed. Ethan didn't care for the sound. He had heard enough of that dreaded hacking around camp already. He ambled past the fire and placed his palm on Adrien's forehead.

"Son of a, you could fry bacon on there. Get on over to the surgeon's tent."

"They are full up. He will instruct me to return here and lie down."

"Well then, go lie down."

Rather than make some remark about Ethan giving him orders, he got up like an old man and dragged himself to their tent.

On the other side of the fire, Arch Lovell and Jim McGehee brandished their usual shenanigans. Arch was the youngest at eighteen and Jim was a year older, same as Adrien. Inevitably together, the two had become the cutups of Company K. Always laughing, snickering, and stamping their boots into the ground. Ethan didn't generally pay them much mind.

"Will you two dunderheads take it elsewhere?" Louder than he meant. The two went silent, as did the other six men at the fire.

"You're in a rare pucker," Forbes said, and continued popping peanuts into his mouth. At forty-six, the oldest in Company K, his pockets were always full of nuts.

"Hand me some of them goober peas, eh?" Alexander said with his hand out, nice and calm like.

Ethan stared at the fire. His cup had rolled to the far side where Forbes snatched it up, unwound himself from a decent-sized boulder, and ambled around to stand next to Ethan.

"More coffee?" he said, presenting the battered tin.

Ethan took a deep breath, blew out through his teeth. "Don't mind if I do."

He was up all night heating stones and applying a steaming black pepper and mustard poultice to Adrien's nearly hairless chest. Alternately shivering and sweating with fever, Adrien mumbled to himself or folks absent. Ethan sat, elbows on knees, and watched, warm from the rocks he kept hot in the fire at the tent entrance. Adrien didn't appear soft like some wealthy planter who did nothing but tell slaves how to do their jobs. Lean muscle and a scar or two defined his arms and ribs. Though his hands were fine-boned, his fingers and palms were laden with calluses. Ethan wondered how much the boy hadn't revealed. He still thought of Adrien as a boy. Shit, Forbes, the oldest in their company, had called Ethan a boy before he became a sergeant. Now it was "Sarge," with a glance that made Ethan want to wink at him.

Adrien had been mighty shifty ever since leaving New Orleans. Before then he'd been eager to talk about family, especially his sister Bernadette and that fellow Isaac. Lately, he'd avoided anything about his past and wouldn't meet Ethan's eyes. If he had gone back that day and turned up his aunt, why wouldn't he say so?

Ethan supposed everybody had things they wouldn't reveal, though there was nothing he'd kept from Adrien. Well, almost nothing.

The next afternoon, Assistant Surgeon Hill came round collecting the sick, including Adrien, and put them on the train for the Nashville Hospital. In a cold, October rain, Ethan worried about those in his squad, too many of them coughing and not having the sense to keep warm and dry, trying to prove what tough Texians they were here in this pit of trickling springs, wet caves and wetter sinkholes that dropped out from under your feet before you saw them. Then cold rain turned to wet snow.

Arch and Jim took sick the following Wednesday. Their squad of ten was down to seven, and they'd never yet been in a skirmish.

November approached with virtually half the company sick and a third of the regiment in the Nashville Hospital or recovering in private homes. Everyone was assigned picket duty off and on as, with so many ill, anybody able performed double duty. They molded bullets and oiled their weapons, preparing for the battle it seemed they would never get into.

On a gray day some two weeks after he left, Adrien hobbled into camp with eyes as droopy as an old hound dog.

"You don't look much better," Ethan said, fists on hips.

"Mercy me," Adrien said. "I was recovering in a house under quilts and care of the most handsome lady you can imagine. Her hands smelled of rosewater and were soft as petals, which I knew because she placed them on my brow at least three times a day along with cold packs on my face. She was hard-hearted though—tied my wrists to the bed so I could not scratch and turned a deaf ear to all my pleadings.

"I swore I could not but stumble down the stairs, but the scarecrow who called himself a doctor said if I could take a piss on my own I could return to this God-forsaken place. So here I am." He punctuated this revelation with a hack into a trembling hand.

Ethan told him to go to bed and made him stay there, which was easy the first few days. Thereafter on a rare sunny afternoon Ethan found him perched cross-legged on a boulder sewing the left brim of his hat up against the crown. A small can of what looked like paint and a brush sat next to him.

"Where'd you get the paint?"

"A fellow in Company C got it in town—a bunch of us threw in for it." He lifted the faded, once-dark gray hat to his face and bit through the thread, held the hat at arm's length to inspect his handiwork, then raised one knee and reached into his boot for his Bowie knife. "We don't have tin stars, so everyone is painting them on the brim . . . for Texas." He used the tip of his knife to pry open the can of paint.

"Mighty jaunty, I'd say."

Adrien went still, an arm across his leg, dangling the knife. "That's the idea, I expect."

"Hey, you're starting to sound like the rest of us, throwing words together like that."

Adrien squinted up at him, grinning. "Must be the constant company of you ill-bred types." With that he flushed, turned away, and coughed into his hand so hard he scrambled to get his feet on the ground and bent over.

Ethan put a hand on his shoulder. "You all right? Maybe you shouldn't be up yet."

"I'm fine," he croaked, and coughed again.

Adrien stayed hunched over, swallowing the cough away. Ethan's hand was still on Adrien's shoulder, and he squeezed a bit, dug into the muscle some, digging the tension out until he felt Adrien relax a little. He slid his palm up to the back of the boy's neck, under the soft hair where the skin was warm and damp, and pressed his fingers deep into the tendons there. Adrien dropped his head forward and let out a moan of gratification.

It was the moan that caused Ethan to clench his fist, turn, walk away, and not look back.

He was playing against himself. Had been from the start.

Nearly a week later mounts appeared out of nowhere. Those on their feet drew lots for them. Adrien managed to perform his share of picket duty and would not be left out. The horses looked decent, though a mite wild, like their riders. Ethan liked a black gelding with steady eyes, strong legs, and one white stocking on his off pastern. Adrien picked a compact bay, quiet and deep-chested.

Ethan reminded the fellows in his squad that their horses came first, always. First to be rubbed down, bedded, and fed. He needn't have worried. These boys were from Texas.

Colonel Terry was determined to make some sort of cavalry of them, despite the sick. Those who could get out of their bedrolls drilled. They learned Poinsett's Tactics and rode stirrup-to-stirrup, charged, retreated, swung left and right all in proper order, their horses' hooves flinging snow and clods of mud every which way. They learned bugle calls that told a rider when to walk, trot, gallop, or retreat—temporarily, of course. Considering the racket their own companies made charging about, it became clear that the only sound they would hear above the musket and cannon fire of battle would be a bugle.

Ethan's black did not take to being behind another horse in the second rank of double drill and fought the bit for three days. Before long, they all took to their assigned places, and the horses learned the bugle calls nearly as fast as the men—in some cases, faster.

Ethan hadn't expected to take to military life so easily. He couldn't deny his excitement and pride at being part of this regiment. The bark of orders, the regiment's united response to bugles, and so many horses stomping and shaking their heads infused in him a belonging to something bigger and finer than himself. All were here for the same purpose, taking care of things, doing what was needful. He learned the name of every man in his mess, every face reflected in the firelight, who would ask for the other's leftover greens and who would bum tobacco or make a joke at someone else's expense.

He tried not to treat Adrien differently than the rest, but whenever his eyes wandered to the youth, he pulled them away. He stayed up until sure Adrien was asleep before crawling into their tent after him. Ethan draped an arm over the boy's torso, and pressed himself against the firm, masculine curve of him.

They all slept that way, spooning, to keep warm.

More infantry arrived nearly every day, and a group of flying artillery from somewhere in Kentucky drilled on the other side of the field, firing cannon hourly. The harsh banging took getting used to, for both men and horses. The sharp odor of gunpowder mingled with that of horse dung, sweat, and mud. Soon Ethan hardly noticed; the smell of coffee overrode everything else in the morning, got him up and going. Along with bugle call.

Companies were sent out on scout, and many brought back food, weapons, and prisoners.

"General Johnston wants the Yanks to believe there's more of us here than there are," Captain Walker said. "We should cover up to twelve miles an hour, sixteen at a good gallop, so let's hit them often and hard."

More like twenty miles to Ethan. Unlike most of these boys who rode since they were knee high to a grasshopper, Ethan hadn't ridden horseback much until he found it necessary to leave home when he was fifteen and fell into herding cows on the Opelousas Trail between Texas and New Orleans. He had learned fast. The first week on a horse his entire body had ached, and exhaustion had put him to sleep at night. Many weeks later, the riders got paid, and he joined a card game. He soon learned not to play with men he rode with, yet cards called to him as they had his father.

At twenty-two, he was done with aching bones and swimming rivers with panicky longhorns. He won enough at cards to dress whatever part he wished to play, and thereafter made his living at gambling tables. A dang good living, too, for a while. Still, he learned that keeping a good horse under him from then on was advantageous.

Ethan wondered how the men in his squad would do when they faced an enemy who fired back. He'd been under fire a couple times when herding cattle, and everything had happened so fast there was never time to think. Neither side had been out to kill so much as to see who could scare the other the most. Some trail bosses would even let a steer go if the thieves were a family who looked desperate for something to eat.

Ethan never argued over cards. Money wasn't worth a ball in the gut from beneath a table. A man who cheated or who'd accuse another of cheating wasn't about to face you honorably. Not unless he had something to prove. Consequently, Ethan never carried a pistol where it could be seen.

Now he owned two revolvers: a Colt Navy six-shooter he shoved under the front of his belt, and a LeMat that shot nine balls from the top barrel and a .60-caliber scatterload from the lower. He kept the heavy LeMat in a holster to the right of his saddle. Nearly everyone carried a shotgun.

On an overcast day, Ethan eventually learned how his squad would do facing enemy fire. It was one of the few dry days they were on patrol, and Company K's scout's warning got them off the road and spread behind a bluff before they could be overrun by approaching Yankees. Ethan heard the approaching creak of wagons, jingle of harness, and muffled shuffle of booted feet. They'd been playing at soldier for weeks, and the game part was about to be over. He had killed a man once. That man deserved to die. Even so, Ethan sometimes had nightmares of that killing, and would rather it had not been necessary. Would shooting those unsuspecting fellows on the road or receiving return fire bother him more? He glanced at Adrien on the bay to his right. As though he noticed Ethan's eyes on him, Adrien turned his head and his eyes glittered like onyx beads beneath his turned-up hat brim. The youth's face was blank of expression, nothing like what Ethan felt gripping his own stomach and inner thighs. Adrien's thumb rubbed back and forth on the reins in his left hand.

"At 'em boys!" Captain Walker.

Company K tore over the ridge and came down upon the soldiers. Some fired back, but by the time Ethan fired two shots from his Colt, most had dropped their shiny new rifles and raised their hands. He doubted he hit anyone. Someone shot an officer sideways off his horse, which trotted on down the road about fifty yards before coming to a slow stop and looking back to see what had become of its rider. Two more bluecoats lay in the mud, their arms flung back, staring at the sky. One fellow sat on the edge of a far wheel rut, rocking, his right hand tucked under his left armpit. He was eighteen at most, blinking up at them, tears streaming down his face, blood seeping down from under his folded arm.

His own horse stood quietly but for rippling hide while Ethan reloaded his pistol and shoved it into his trousers. The barrel was barely warm. One of the bluecoats, relieved of his weapon, went over to the boy, crouched down and murmured something. The boy wiped the back of one sleeve across his face while keeping this ball-mangled hand in his armpit. The soldier put an arm around the boy to help him up, and Ethan turned his horse away. Watching them embarrassed him, as though he claimed no right to witness such an intimate scene.

They took forty-eight prisoners and their weapons, four wagons of supplies, sixteen mules and one horse. Later, Ethan learned the boy lost his hand to the surgeons.

When Company K returned to camp, fellows jawed away in excitement, reliving the entire episode. Adrien remained silent while unsaddling and rubbing down his horse. Ethan and he took their time and placed grain bags over their horses' noses. Adrien, leaning his arms across the back of his mount, peered over at Ethan.

"That boy looked like someone I knew at Centenary. He wasn't, of course, but he could have been."

Ethan said nothing. He didn't think Adrien expected him to. Adrien stood a moment more, picked up his gear and headed for their blankets.

A couple days of rest back in camp, then out they'd go again, mostly in freezing rain or wet snow, trying to run down Yankees and make them believe in more able-bodied Confederate soldiers than actually existed. The measles had devastated them—most 8th Texas companies were fortunate to put out fifty men out of a company of one hundred. They'd return to camp from a three-to-eight-day scout, and ask the first man they rode up to, "Who's gone?"

Company K rode the countryside more than they stayed in camp: raiding, scouting, skirmishing. No time or energy for putting up tents. Ethan "requisitioned" himself a Yankee gum blanket from that first raid, which he lay between their other wool blanket and the ground. Their second gum blanket kept the rain off, with a hope and a prayer. They were usually so exhausted that neither moved until morning, and often Ethan woke with his mouth open, drooling in Adrien's hair.

Then came Woodsonville.

Chapter Nine
Woodsonville

Adrien

The morning sun blessed us as we jogged up the Nashville Pike outside Woodsonville under a pale winter sky. Heads lifted, nostrils opened wide to the sharp December air, our horses swiveled their ears in anticipation, as if aware this was not a typical morning. Silence reigned in the ranks. Terry and perhaps 250 men were on the north side of the Green River, along with a Yankee force of 100,000 men and artillery—the left flank of General Hindman's brigade. Terry had ordered half our regiment—the part not ill—off in another direction.

"We're the fat mouse boys." Lt. Morris had told Company K earlier. "We lure Yankees across the river where our own artillery can get at them." He winked at young Ash Lovell. I believe he did so because Lovell's chum, Jim McGeHee, had not yet returned from the Nashville Hospital, and Lovell was no end of lonesome.

I did not care for being a mouse—not in the cat's territory.

Ethan had given me a thin smile when we abandoned our gear back at the bridge—gear we would not require for battle—and I had forced a pinched smile back. I had not felt like smiling at anyone or anything. Ethan assumed I was someone I was not, and I already cared too much.

A lingering cough shook me. I felt light and woozy in the saddle, as though I would float out of it. How long ago that September afternoon when I had wished a Minié ball might end all troubles? Might death be fast and painless, an abrupt end to guilty musings?

My gloved fist was clenched so tight around the reins it shook.

A bird warbled from somewhere in the field on the right. A pretty song, like a bird back home. Lucky if the thing made it until spring when it *should* be singing.

What am I doing here?

I had not killed or injured anyone. During one skirmish, a Yankee dropped his rifle and raised his hands. Would I have pulled the trigger if the bluecoat had hung onto his gun?

Crane Forbes said there was often no time to reload in battle. That night I had imagined firing twelve shots from my Remington—which included changing cylinders—six from the Colt Papa gave me, then both barrels from my shotgun, as fast and accurately as possible. On horseback. Under fire. What would such a battle be like?

I would find out today.

I had seen what a ball did to a man after that first skirmish. Such a neat little hole where it entered his chest. But when we turned him over, the mangled flesh, gangly pieces of sinew, and shards of bone played havoc in my mind. Dear God, fast and painless was to be remotely wished for.

I palmed the shotgun in its scabbard beneath my thigh, touched my Bowie knife then the Colts in my belt—I had lost count of how many times I had done so since dawn.

Riders galloped down the slope at the front of the column—our scouts. Officers' arms raised along the line ahead and everyone came to an abrupt halt, leather creaking, horses snorting and blowing, kicking up half-frozen clods of mud and last year's dead grass. I tasted mud in the back of my otherwise dry throat.

My own gelding, who I had named Bandit, settled right down. Ethan's black, ever contrary, arched his neck and sawed at the reins.

"I pray this cussed animal is as ornery with the Yankees," Ethan said.

I wished to turn my splendid horse out of line and gallop off, jump off and back on from one side then the other like we had at the Nashville Fairgrounds. Everyone would laugh and carry on, including the Yankees. All would note how ridiculous it was parading around out here in the cold, preparing to slaughter one another.

The line began moving again, and Bandit moved along with it. We crossed a different bridge back to our own side of the river, where maybe there would be no fighting.

We were on high ground in the trees when Captain Montrose called a halt and signaled our two companies to spread to his left and right. The officers kept their voices down; the horses shuffled gingerly in the wet sponge of leaf litter and mold. Surely the enemy knew we were lined up over here. Lt. Banks murmured that we'd wait in the woods until the infantry moved up.

"Dang, let's get this over with."

"What?" Ethan said, from his black.

"Nothing." I had muttered that aloud. I leaned low over Bandit's neck to peer through bare overhanging branches. The ridge fell away onto a sun-gilded meadow where hundreds of bluecoats poured out of the woods on the far side of a shimmering water course—the same creek we had crossed earlier? Yankee lines faded off to the right through lifting ground mist. Bayonets pointed up through it like porcupine quills, and morning sun probing the woods beyond flashed warnings of many more. Officers on fine, healthy chargers trotted before those lines as though on parade.

Bandit shifted from one foot to the other, rocking me. Some other horse snorted. Numerous clouds of horse and man-breath wove in and out of ragged meanders of mounted men and bare gray and white trees—the cold air smelled of damp leather, horses, and rotted leaves. Someone among the Yankee soldiers down there yelled an order—sounded like a child from here.

There was a pop, another—a frenzy, firecrackers on the Fourth of July. My blood rushed. Something whizzed by my ear. The air was full of hornets and someone yelled, "Form ranks!" The bugle blew accordingly and Bandit reacted almost before I signaled with my thighs. The popping became one loud, continuous rattle-whizz.

At Terry's "Charge 'em boys, charge!" My heart jumped into my throat. Everyone leaped forward, screaming, and I screamed with them—I had not expected to, but I did. The screaming got my heart back where it belonged and let me breathe—my last clear thought.

The charge became a dream, a nightmare: drop reins, shotgun in one hand, revolver in the other. The air buzzed with speeding hornets and Bandit's ears signaled that fluttering smoke-popping blue gash in the black and holly-green thicket full of flashing bayonets and clouds of blazing smoke. A tremendous rumble and hot blood flared on me from the horse at my left before it disappeared with a thud.

Enemy right there and I blew him into bloody pieces and hung on with my thighs and knees and fired my shotgun and pistols. Bandit quivering beneath me, I attempted reloading with trembling, slipping, sweaty fingers, damn, damn! Heard sharp short whizzes, screams—bangs—thuds. Blurs of color, slashes of blue, gray, brown, pitiless red and open angry mouths—burning air. My body flared and sang with a rush I had never before known. Gasping. World gone mad.

At last, Yankees fled from behind their fence and I rode from the field until Bandit stood, legs wide, heaving. I sucked at rancid, smokey air, salt sweat burning my eyes, that same sweat soaking my hair, my clothes, congealing in my boots. I slid from Bandit's back and spewed breakfast. Limbs threatened to fold beneath me, ears rang with afterthrum. I ran hands over myself: my limbs, my ribs, my arms. Miraculously free of holes. Every part intact.

Ethan found me. "You all right?" Ethan's raspy voice seemed to come from far away down a long tunnel. I coughed, looked up at Ethan's dirty face, and whispered, "yes." Then louder, astonished, "yes." In spite of all I had seen and done, this thing bubbled up from inside—the urge to laugh—or howl. Ethan smiled, and I mounted, glorying in a surging sense of invincibility. Sweat, or tears, burning my eyes.

Our squad gathered as we rode back to camp, every one having survived, every one stained with blood, sweat and horse lather, our faces and hands black with gunpowder.

That night as our squad prepared our fire and supper, Ethan brought me boots and a pipe taken from federal dead.

"They'll no longer have need of such, and I saw your right boot's worn through, the left nearly so. Got a pair that fit me, too. And this—a nice briar. I prefer corncob, but I figured a fine gentleman such as yourself would require a pipe more befitting his stature. Sit here and we'll give er a try. Take that battlefield taste out of your mouth. Mine too, I expect. Being a tobacco grower, you ought to do your daddy proper. Let me light that. Draw in the air, short ones, that'll do it."

What a ramble. Never gave me a chance to get a word in edgewise before the stem was clamped in my teeth. I had to accept the thing or it would have fallen onto the damp ground. I hacked once or twice, never having smoked before, but the taste was all right; I had to focus—not to draw too much—which kept my mind from other thoughts and stopped my hands from shaking.

Ethan gave me a sly grin through the smoke, lit his own pipe, and blew a couple of rings. "Not bad, huh?"

"No. Not at all."

Other boys were laughing and congratulating one another, going from fire to fire, showing off their loot.

"I was scared as hell at first," Ethan said. "But too busy to think about it. Hell of a thing."

"Hell, all right."

"You did right fine, Adrien."

"So did you."

"Guess we saw the elephant today."

"We surely did."

"Hell of a thing."

We ate beans, cornbread, and beef lifted from Yankee stores. I blinked away visions that kept appearing in the flames.

Young Lovell dug into his beans. "I was ridin' next to Doby, and I swear that horse of his let out a grand fart with every leap he took. Which prob'ly wiped out more Yanks than any of us." Chuckles and laughter rounded the group. J. J. Petty, a half-Mexican fellow as dark as me, whooped and slapped his knee, nearly sending his meal into the mud.

"Wonder they didn't pick you off with that flaming hair of your'n, Lovell," Bill Grissett said. His drawl was long and twisted up with the tobacco he was always chewing. "When Terry yelled for the charge and them cannon went off, I nearly soiled my trousers."

Lovell snorted into his coffee cup.

Thus began an unannounced game of how long we could keep laughter going.

Crane Forbes sat to my left, Ethan to my right. Near the end of the meal, Forbes pulled out a flask from his pack and passed it to me.

"Whew," I drove air through my mouth after I had swallowed. "That is some powerful."

"Brewed it myself. Saved for a special occasion. Figured this was it."

"I'll say," Ethan said, after taking a drink and passing the flask on.

The consensus prevailed that we had won. Then why leave the field to the Yankees?

December 19, 1861

Dear Papa,

Thank you for your letter and for Will's address. I heard there is not a better army than the Army of Virginia, so tell Berni not to worry overmuch as Will is in good hands.

I have been in my first battle and am relieved to say I did not disgrace my family. I am fortunate to have picked out a fine charger named Bandit, who did most of the work by keeping me out of harm's way. Our company was on the left flank of our glorious Texas Rangers and charged at the federals across a rolling meadow and along a fence. We made short work of them, and our entire squad is in fine fettle. The dismal news is our illustrious Colonel Terry was killed along with three other good fellows. Our company's Captain Walker and Lieutenant Morris were sent to the hospital in Nashville with Lt. Col. Lubbock, all of whom are gravely wounded. I cannot help but wonder if winning was worth the loss.

We took horses and supplies from the bluecoats; I have a new pair of boots, as my old ones were falling apart from being constantly wet. The folks hereabouts treat us most graciously, often inviting us for supper.

We have lost many men to measles, pneumonia, and the flux; eight passed away from our company.

It is pretty here in Kentucky when not raining. I have never heard so many foxes, and it was strange to hear them barking at the full moon last night, like our coyotes. We ride among rolling hills of oak, ash, and maple, and get our water from little singing creeks underlined with streaks of white marble. One morning we awoke to sun on frost—a sparkling lace fairyland. I wish Berni could have seen it.

Would it be possible to send a little tobacco? I have taken up a pipe, as it is a fine thing to smoke around the fire at night and drink coffee whenever there is a moment's respite. Everyone here either smokes or chews, and I find a pipe easier than trying to roll my own. It reminds of our family evenings in the parlor. I think of each of you every day. I hope and pray you all have a most enjoyable Christmas.

Your Loving Son, Adrien

Papa had been in war. Surely, he knew how it felt to see a man explode into red and white pieces of bone when pellets tore into him at close range.

Chapter Ten
1862, News

Ethan

First Lt. Ethan Childs was almighty wet and cold. He was tired of the squish of his saddle, tired of constant mud, wet trousers and socks, and chapped thighs, tired of the little stream that flowed from his hat and trickled down the back of his neck and on down his spine. The pervading odor of wet wool invaded his dreams. When he wasn't leading a scout, he spread his sodden underclothes on his half of a string line inside the tent at night. Before light he crawled out of the only dry, warm place in the world and, as rain fell, or likely would fall, pulled on freezing damp clothes and hoped someone had a warm fire going by the time he arrived—and coffee, or whatever stood for coffee. As long as it was hot.

He and Adrien now shared the slightly larger tent that had been used by Lt. Morris before he was mortally wounded in the charge at Woodsonville in December. No more whooping and hollering after battle, no laughing or congratulations. Captain Walker, newly recovered from his wounds, sent them out in small groups to scout for five days out of every eight. Upon returning to camp each man felt relief that he and his closest comrades had survived, felt relief for his grub and that he could crawl into his blankets.

Ethan had requested Adrien as one of his sergeants. Adrien didn't drink overmuch, act the lickfinger, or in any sense make himself disagreeable. Add top riding, excellent shooting, and dependability, and the men voted him in. Adrien had settled into the life since

Woodsonville. They all had. Any complaining included a grin or wink of an eye. They were the 8th Texas Cavalry, had a job to do and tended to do it their own way, regardless of army rules.

The sky turned a lighter gray, and the ever-present rain slowed to a drizzle. No one around the fire admitted to noticing, for fear of jinxing the possibility of sun.

"This outfit can't seem to keep its officers more than a coupl'a months," Forbes said. He was the best of them at tracking and snaring wild game, and was turning a sizzling rabbit on a makeshift spit of sassafras twigs. "You s'pose that's bad for you, Childs?"

"I got a tent that doesn't leak, that's good. I got a raise in pay, and that's good. As I've not seen the money yet, that's bad. I figure if I keep my head low and surround myself with you fellas in every battle, I may get by."

Terry's Rangers officers wore the same uniforms as everyone else. That sort of thing was kept for formal occasions yet unexperienced.

They were interrupted by whoops and hollers at arrival of the mail pouch, the only thing more popular than food. The more fortunate might receive coffee, tobacco, or homemade preserves, cookies, biscuits, as well as news—whatever mothers, sisters, wives and sweethearts found in their loving hearts to send, providing it got through the questionable mail service, which became more so each passing month.

The seldom-seen hazy winter sun had begun melting away the overcast as Ethan headed toward their tent with his mail. He spied Adrien heading in the same direction, a package under one arm.

"I believe I must get a game started tonight, with my luck running so high," Ethan said, signaling with his own package and letter.

"This from the man who does not believe in luck?"

"Luck's the word some use for skill and fate. Skill means you're ready to handle what fate deals you. Your philosophers have much to say about fate, don't they?"

"Not my philosophers. I only studied their words, and that was a lifetime ago. The more positive ones said fate represented opportunity."

Ethan's mother had always taken advantage of every opportunity. Now she hoarded everything she could get her hands on. If she were caught? She hinted at an American connection Ethan didn't care for. She was always up to something, and one day would be in trouble she couldn't get free of.

The two hunkered on a sunny log outside their tent, packages at their feet. Neither looked up as they conversed distractedly, cold hands tucked beneath armpits, elbows pressed to the pages at their thighs to keep them from blowing elsewhere in the breeze that had risen with the sun.

"Mother says hello to you, and she sent real coffee," Ethan said.

"Bless her."

"All New Orleans is worried about the Yankees blocking shipping."

Adrien folded one letter, freed another. "With good cause, I expect."

Ethan opened his package, closed his eyes as he took a long, slow whiff of the contents. "I can't believe this got through, likely due to her wrapping it three times." He meticulously folded both string and paper to stash in his bags for later use.

"Papa sent tobacco."

"Glory be. We won't need to trade any of this excellent coffee."

Adrien folded the letter, placed it on top of the first, rubbed his thumbs across the grease and dirt-stained envelopes. Ethan peered at his sculpted profile beneath the hat, where the turned-up left brim showed the Texas star, painted on more precisely than most. Adrien's jaw tensed, eyes staring.

"What news?"

Adrien took a breath, tucked his chin. "Nothing. It's nothing." He picked up a third letter from the top of the packet and tore it open.

What besides the local vermin had gotten under his britches, something in one of those letters? Adrien had been evasive ever since leaving New Orleans last September. Ethan had ignored it, hoping the youth would eventually come around. After all, they had been under fire together, shared their vittles, spooned at night to keep warm. They had both changed after Woodsonville, but this was something else.

"You've been offish since New Orleans, now this. We're pals, aren't we? Don't you think by now you can trust me?"

Adrien stared at his feet. "It's not important." He pushed up and shuffled off, tossing his package inside their tent.

Ethan snorted, stood, kneeled in the tent to tuck his own package and letters safely inside, then stalked off with a deck of cards in his back pocket. He needed a good game to exercise his mind. *I'm a gambler, after all, the son of a whore. I should have known better than attempt—whatever—with a plantation owner's son.*

Chapter Eleven
Available for Duty

Adrien

I had to get away, not only from Ethan, who asked so many questions, but from everyone. I headed off under the trees. At that moment, the sun broke through the last of the overcast as though to belie my current despair.

Lily had married that man. Of course, she had. Had I believed she might not? After all, I left so she would be safely free of my despicable nature. She as much as said goodbye when she walked away from me in the barn. So, why this sharp stone in my gut? I clenched the letter in my fist. I must forget her. The whole thing was impossible. Had always been impossible. *I am such a fool.*

I swallowed what felt like a lump of unsoftened hardtack. *Decide now, drown in misery and self-pity or go on with these good fellows who depend on you. We depend on one another for our very lives. Shit. If they knew who they've voted sergeant. I have never wanted that kind of responsibility. Shit. You have got it now and will do your damnedest, your damnedest, by God.*

I sniffed, wiped the back of my hand across my damp nose and mouth and wiped my hand on my trousers. Lord, Maman would have scolded me for such language. I stared at my dirty hand, filthy fingernails, and muddy trousers, glanced up at the hazy sun, squinted, took a deep breath, and headed back to camp.

Six weeks after Woodsonville, the regiment received word that Colonel Lubbock had died at the hospital in Nashville. John Wharton was made colonel and commander. Captain Walker was made Lt. Colonel, and Company K voted Augustus Montrose captain. Eighty-four rangers had died, five from the enemy, the rest from measles and its complications. Minus the sick and wounded, half the 1,100 men the rangers had begun with in September were available for duty.

I went down inside myself where I'll stay until . . . until it's safe.

Chapter Twelve
Texas Gallivanting

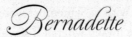

Papa hadn't wanted me riding alone, but I never dreamed I would bring Simon such trouble.

I needed a change, to get out of the house and away. For a little while I wanted to pretend all was as it had been, before Will and Adrien left, before everything went so topsy-turvy. After a week of rain, the sun shone, and it was a lovely morning for a ride. Or had been.

"He is my servant," I said to the stocky, dangerous-looking man on the buckskin horse. Pale gray eyes glittered at me from beneath a slouch hat; weapons of all sorts poked out from his waist, thighs, his saddle—like quills from a porcupine. The five men with him looked much the same way. "You cannot take him. He belongs to Blue Hills, and you cannot treat us so."

"You shouldn't be gallivanting around the country like this—ma'am. Specially not alone with this here nigger." The man mounted behind the one who spoke spit a wad of something dark into the wet grass along the side of the trail. All six wore filthy red neck scarves and sat their horses on the wide, muddy road before me and Simon. They appeared nothing like the appointed authorities they claimed to be, supposedly searching for deserters and runaway slaves.

My heart beat wildly beneath my linen blouse and wool jacket. They would take Simon with them over my dead body. I dug my heels in and forced my horse across and in front of Simon's, putting myself between him and the riders.

"I am Bernadette Hart, the daughter of Paien Villere, the owner of Blue Hills Plantation. Simon has been with us since he was a boy." I sat as straight and tall as possible in my saddle, chin up, glaring at the man. "And I am not gallivanting."

The first man's eyes narrowed. He seemed confused, then sat back and laughed. Two men behind him joined in, chuckling.

"You're entertaining, you are," he said. "And mighty handsome. Might be we oughta take you along, make sure you're who you say you are."

I must have done something without thinking because my gelding sidled sideways against Simon's mare, forcing her back a step or two. Certainly, my hands were gripping the reins tightly; my heart felt as though it were already fleeing down the trail.

Simon moved his mare out of my way and forward. He intended to get between me and those men!

Which is when two more men on horses came cantering over the hill behind us.

The first rode a big chestnut stallion. I knew him—mounted on one of Catchfire's get, obviously. Jacob Hart came up alongside my gelding and nodded, touching his hat, Colt Alvaro behind him on a bay. I had never felt so relieved to see Jacob Hart.

"Morning Mrs. Hart."

"Good morning, Jacob."

First man had a funny look on his face, surprised—perhaps, a little frightened?

"Mrs. Hart?" the man said, looking first at Jacob, then at me.

"Yes," Jacob said. "It appears you have met my brother's wife. I hope you have been polite to her and her servant. I'm sure you're aware how my father and I value courtesy and honor among our Confederate brethren. We leave poor manners and dishonor to Yankees and deserters."

"Of course, sir." The scarfed man nodded to her, "ma'am," and raised his reins. "We'll be on our way then. Nice to meet you. Mrs. Hart." Off they went, back the way they had come, little clods of mud flying in their wake.

I looked at my hands holding the reins then at Jacob. "Thank you, Jacob."

His lips crept to a half smile. "I've done nothing, just happened along."

"Did you? Just happen along?"

He stretched his long legs in the saddle, then settled. "I knew they were out here somewhere. Then I met one of your colored back there hauling staves, and he said you'd ridden this way with Simon. I was heading this general direction. They won't be bothering you again."

I leaned forward, ran my fingers through my horse's mane. "Why? I mean why did those men listen to you?" I risked a glance at his— what do I call him—friend? Retainer? The ever-present and silent Colt Alvaro, sitting his buckskin horse fifteen feet away on the side of the road.

I stayed leaning slightly forward against my horse's neck, my other hand holding the reins, and looked up at him. Handsome as ever, more so, perhaps, now he was older, unruly blond hair pushed back beneath his wide-brimmed hat. This year sporting a brush mustache similar to Papa's. It struck me then, how his bone structure appeared much like Papa's.

I had never fully trusted Jacob. But he had done me a good turn this morning.

"As ever, my father—keeps his hand in, you might say," he said. "He makes himself known to the people who hold power in this state. They depend on him for—things. I don't. . . ." He looked away, moved his jaw, as though chewing, considering whether to continue. Hesitant. A Jacob I had never before seen. He glanced down at me. "I don't want to presume, but you might mention that your father involve himself more, as well. Word is out. Those who aren't with the Confederacy are suspect."

"But I have two brothers and a husband fighting. And we provide supplies to the army!" I could not believe this.

"I didn't say what people believe made sense. All he need do is speak up. A few words to friends in town, anything. It's his silence that galls. And some think—some think he has helped colored escape, and that he has not sold his coloreds but set them free in New Orleans."

I felt color drain from my face. How dare they. Who? Who would dare? Did he? We could not afford to set our people free. My horse shifted; I tightly gripped the reins. This dratted war. Drat everything. Jacob was watching me, a worried frown on his face.

"Thank you, Jacob. I expect you mean well." How angry I sounded, not at all like I meant. Or did I?

I saw the old glint in his eyes. Here was the Jacob I remembered.

"You've never liked me, have you, Bernadette?"

"Me? Why. . . ." *Blather, I should have known he would do this. Very well.*

"No. I have never trusted you. Women's intuition, I suppose. I have suspected you have ulterior motives for everything, even for telling what you see as the truth."

He was definitely smiling at me now, eyes sparkling. "I should have waited for you."

"Waited?"

"For you to grow up. We would have made quite a pair."

The insufferable cur! "I am married to your brother!"

"I love my brother, so you needn't be concerned. Good day, Mrs. Hart." With that and a flick of his stallion's tail, he cantered off, Colt trailing along to his left.

Chapter Thirteen
Satisfied?

Jacob

Dear God, what was he thinking, flirting with Adrien's sister? What a mess that would be! If one believed in God, did thinking there was some supernatural power pushing their two families together mean one believed in the devil, as well? Just the sort of thing a devil would do.

He had promised himself change. Control. He was older now, not to be led around by libido or emotions.

Beauty, brains, candor—a combination he couldn't resist. Boys, women, a quick fix but don't get involved. Then Adrien. What a mistake. He would've done anything for that boy and instead had made a fool of himself. He had been a youth. Still, eight years older than Adrien at the time. If he'd only had more control over his emotions, if he'd waited. If.

Had Adrien loved Lily? How much of that affair was Lily's fault? He knew his sister. He and she were much alike. Christ. Too much alike, now she was grown. Part of that was his fault, concerning himself with her education the way he had. She hadn't been content with old man Garrison, no more than he would have been with some old woman.

He brought his horse to a halt in the middle of the trail. *I blamed the boy and he was right. It was partly my jealousy for his choosing her over me that had me angry, not merely for his ruining her future. Why didn't I see it before? Lily and I wanted the same thing.*

God, devil, or fate: See what you have done. You may have sent him to his death. Satisfied?

Chapter Fourteen
Give 'Em Hell Boys

Adrien

I woke in freezing dark to the sound of bugling. Ethan's arm slid from my shoulder. I had begun the night facing Ethan's back. Asleep, we tended to draw together for warmth and often woke curled tight as two pups. This morning Ethan quickly pulled away, silently gathered his gear, and headed for the sinks.

Ethan had lately been unusually reticent. But I suppose I had, as well. Hard going had been our lot since the third week of January: constant raiding in snow, freezing rain, once, a blizzard.

It was already February, yet we remained in the Bowling Green area. Each company took turns for two days of rest, then five days searching for Yankees and raiding. Company K's turn to ride came round again, and my turn came to down the tent. Snow swirled under my hat and collar and, *goddammit*, my fingers were already numb. I had ceased cringing with thoughts of Papa every time I swore. I had never imagined bruises on the inside of my thighs or that my legs would turn to water upon dismounting. Horses had gone down and not gotten up again. If they couldn't be replaced, their riders would end up in the infantry—a fate worse than death. No one complained. Not to one another. As far as I knew, not to anyone.

The same snow piled deep in the streets of nearby Bowling Green and clogged the rail lines. On our last ride through town the streets were crowded with wagons and boxes of stores and equipment. What would happen if Yankees decided to come in full force before that mess was cleared out?

No sooner had I hit the saddle than a couple of our own pickets came galloping out of the frosted trees and on by without a howdy-do, straight for the headquarters tent.

"What do you figure that's about?" Arch had been hanging close to me since a week after Woodsonville when we got word that his pal, Jim, had succumbed to pneumonia. Having turned twenty last August, I was closest to Arch's age, and he had looked so chopfallen that I had sat down next to him at the fire that night, offered him a cup of my share of Ethan's good coffee and told him about my best friend Will, who rode with Hood back East. And how Will and I had become pals when we were six and learned to ride and shoot together.

"Me and Jim are, were, like that. Knew each other's thoughts like. I reckon we got in some trouble now and then, but he always got us out. Nothing really bad, just cut shines a little. Don't know what I'm goin to do now, on my own hook in this here situation."

"You are not alone, Arch. You are a member of Company K of the 8th Texas Cavalry, and I believe I can say we all take care of each other."

"You think so?"

"Darn right. You ask any man here."

Arch turned away, wiped his arm across his nose. "Dang."

I wanted to put my arm around Arch's shoulders. Hesitant, afraid to risk that sort of intimacy. I stared into my empty coffee cup.

"Got to be trouble," I said, and risked a glance Ethan's way. Ethan was busy fiddling with the carbine at his saddle. He no longer caught my eye.

Sure enough, General Wharton, Major Harrison, a couple captains and aides came tearing out of the tent like bees out of a disturbed hive, heading for the companies and mounts.

Captain Montrose trotted his horse to our group and halted, his big brown mare arching her neck, mouth open, pulling at the reins.

"Boys," he said, loud enough so every man could hear, "it's up to us. Seems the Yankees have crossed the river and are lining up cannon, fixing to shell the town. We have to hold them until the railcars and the infantry can get themselves out of this pretty little village." With that, he spun his mare on her haunches and galloped off to the front of the line.

I later recalled nothing between then and our first charge. We rangers rode into well-placed cannon and learned never to do so again.

The enemy were emplaced across a field of pristine snow. A few drifting flakes fell, and to the regiment's right across a cottony blanket a half sun glowed pink and gold on the eastern horizon. Puffs of cloudy steam rose from the lines as horses snorted and tossed their heads, some pawing the drifts. Every tree, every bush and berry stood out in bright, sharp outline. I could practically reach out and pluck that Yankee soldier over there from his mount. Bandit stood placidly, ears forward, every hair keen as a well-honed knife. The cold air prickled my nose. I flexed my gloved fingers and booted toes to keep them from going stiff and numb. A perfectly formed flake drifted down past my face. I had the urge to catch it on my tongue.

Muffled thudding came from my left as Wharton trotted down the line, snow flying in sparkling puffs from his horse's hooves. He turned, the bugle and his "Charge 'em boys!" sharp and clear in the crisp air. Our flag, white stars on red crossed bars, swung with our fast walk, then bobbed at our trot, and whipped in the wind when we galloped across white snow that burst in fluffy gusts as high as our stirrups.

My heart pounded in my throat. Thank God the snow was dry and light—less chance Bandit would slip and fall. We began in ranks of four and the bugle sounded again and riders came up on my left and right and I dropped the reins to my bay's neck and lifted my shotgun in one hand and revolver in the other. A staccato thumping louder than our own thunder of hooves and something dark trailing hot air blew between me and Arch—a *thunk* behind like a mallet thwacking a giant watermelon. I heard horses fall but dared not look. The bugle told our lines to zigzag and we were continuously firing, reloading, firing. Bandit jumped a crumpled horse and rider. He stumbled, recovered, kept on, and I heard bones crunch and blood and bone flew fifteen to twenty yards every which way. Rapacious bursts of flame and gray-white smoke, hot whizzing, crashing, screaming. I ran out of cartridges. Someone's horse slammed into my leg and nearly knocked Bandit down and I leaned far over out of the saddle to keep him on his feet. Lt. Bouldin was on the ground, snatching his carbine out of the scabbard—his dead horse still kicking. I offered an arm, Bouldin swung up behind and we tore out of there barely ahead of the rest of the regiment as retreat sounded.

"Much obliged," Bouldin said when we got back in the trees. He swung down and didn't wait for an answer—as the quartermaster's boys had come running and everyone was scrambling for cartridges. We would more wisely advance on foot this time, like infantry.

I trotted from the trees with Company K, we were all running, leaping over bodies and pieces of bodies, diving behind dead horses, trying to get close enough to take a shot that counted. Steaming cannonballs flew through the air and rolled and bounced across the ground, sending heads flying, slicing off feet and slamming through bodies. Blood, bone, and body parts struck men who were still alive, knocking some to the ground. A volley of canister exploded over our heads, grapeshot spinning in every direction. The air was hot with flying metal and gray smoke. The land shook in migrating tremors, one following the other.

A Minié ball lifted my hat. The hot draft of a nearby explosion sent me flying and sound receded down a long tunnel. I lay where I landed, raised my head in ringing silence, and watched drifting snowflakes melt on my black-streaked hand until the *harump* of cannon again entered my consciousness. The next thing I recalled was spitting paper from a dry acid-tasting mouth and ramming cartridges into the car-bine I lifted from a dead Yankee, the man's foot yet twitching. "Sorry," I said, a dry whisper. The hot barrel burned my fingers. I could hardly see for tears from so much smoke. Acrid smells made my nose run.

The bugle sounded retreat and back in the trees, thank God, Capt. Montrose screamed in a voice that broke and cackled, "That's it boys, I'm told we make for Nashville. There's bacon and biscuits awaiting us there!"

I found Bandit, grabbed, missed, grabbed again at the stirrup and crawled up, heaved, into the saddle—*such a fine example of horsemanship.* My entire body felt like one large bruise. I loved this horse. *Please do not shoot him.*

Horses were missing, as were men. Holes decorated my hat; I poked my finger through one. Another through the outer edge of my jacket sleeve. Blood splattered here and there, a flapping rip in my trousers—my thigh ached and burned—a furrow of missing flesh. I looked for and saw Ethan riding just ahead, his horse's tail swinging. Beautiful. Arch came up on my right, his face filthy, his mouth black with powder. I wanted to say something, something that would make the world come right side up again.

"You are one marvelous mess, Arch," I croaked through a soot-filled throat.

"Take a look at your own self next time you get in front of a mirror," Arch grinned back, his teeth as black as his mouth.

Wet snow fell, straight and slow; the day as flat and white as one of Maman's china plates. I unbuttoned my overcoat and reached into my shirt pocket, curious as to the time. My engraved pocket watch, the same one Papa had given me at Christmas two years ago, still ticked. Lord, we had been at it over three hours. I couldn't recall half. A strange noise—my stomach growling. Breakfast had been a stale corn biscuit.

We destroyed the rail depot and any stores that remained, then became rear guard for our trailing Confederate forces. As the afternoon wore on, I lost count of how often we thrashed our way through fields of brown broom sage, dry, brittle grass, and Yankee skirmishers.

A rider came trotting back from the front of the double column and leaned toward Ethan. Ethan then turned to face the rest of us and yelled, "We gotta get to Nashville before the Yankees, before they destroy the bridges!"

Our regiment would be separated from our army and trapped on the northern side of the Cumberland River if we couldn't get across. Nevertheless, our duty was rear guard and we kept at it. By sundown word passed through the lines that our infantry had sent the federals fleeing Nashville. An hour later we heard the Yankees had taken over the city and we rangers would have to fight our way through to our own army. Glory be, I thought, what do you suppose we have been doing all day? I leaned forward and patted Bandit's wet neck, steaming with exertion despite the cold. Snow turned to sleet, then rain, as we rode farther south.

Late that night, cold rain falling as though determined to slowly but surely drown us, we caught up to our main army outside Nashville, still held by Confederate forces. I had heard how the Yankee infantry cared little for their own cavalry and often jeered them. Our regiment of rangers rode by our own infantry, men and horses dripping water onto the churned, muddy road. Men parted to let us through and cheered. I heard someone call, "Give 'em hell boys!"

We rode through the city streets after midnight, silent but for the creak of leather and the slow, syncopated clop of exhausted horses on cobblestone. Someone coughed. Many rode with raw, red hands tucked under their armpits. I dozed beneath my hat as freezing rain found its way through its holes, one stream over my left brow and down my nose, the other past the front of one ear.

Our line moved south of the city, drifted down through dripping white pine, ash, and dogwood. What remained of the regiment finally came to rest like scattered wet leaves in a tormented, dying wind. I got down stiffly from the saddle—the ground rose oddly to bash the soles of my boots. Company K sergeants gathered around Ethan.

"Captain says to unsaddle. We'll know more at daybreak, when our equipment and hot food will find us."

"Let us pray it be so," murmured Sarge Alexander. He turned and shuffled away through dribbling wet.

I passed the word to the men. We picketed our horses with the rest of Company K beneath a group of large pines, where I checked

Bandit's feet, tended to his sores and fed him the little grain left in my saddlebags. Someone started a fire, and I stood before it, oilcloth wrapped around my shoulders, in an attempt to warm up and dry out. "Check your feet," I said to the men around me. "Dry your stockings and put on dry ones if you have them." The cold wet had left my own feet white and wrinkled. They tingled and ached when I removed my boots and bared them on a rock near the fire, but what glorious pleasure when I shoved into warm, dry, wool stockings.

No one talked much, a murmur, someone threw on more damp wood. The fitful breeze blew smoke into my face. I backed up against a tree where my saddle lay, pulled the oilcloth over my head, slid down into the upturned saddle skirt and tucked my knees close out of the rain. I shoved a piece of hardtack between my teeth to soak, leaving a portion sticking out of the side my mouth like a flat cigar.

Eventually the piece ought to be soft enough to swallow. If I didn't fall asleep first. A dull popping of rain on the blanket drowned everything else out. I could be anywhere in this dark, makeshift little tent. A chill sent shivers up my center. *Do not think—not of cold, only of warm. A warm fire in the parlor at home, red and orange and yellow and crackling. Papa in his chair with his pipe. Berni. Lucien. . . .*

Chapter Fifteen
Hardly the Place for a Fight

Ethan

Ethan had prayed for warmth. Now it was here he'd not complain, despite how early spring sun beat down on his shoulders as though it were August and not the end of March. Dust from horses, men, and wagons rose into his nostrils and made him sneeze. Johnston's army and rangers were headed toward the Tennessee River and a place called Pittsburgh Landing where the enemy waited. Yankee General Grant had taken Forts Henry and Donelson on the Cumberland River and needed to be beaten down, and their army, having been joined by General Beauregard with his artillery, would drive those Yankees back from whence they came.

By nightfall Ethan recalled the heat fondly as, once again, it rained. They crossed back into Tennessee and reached the front where they were ordered to guard Johnston's left flank. No sleeping. At dusk the rain became a torrent; the torrent turned the night pitch dark. Still, they constantly rode to guard every bridge, road, trail, and opening.

The morning of April 5 arrived clear and bright, and the regiment was allowed to bivouac on Owl Creek, a tributary of the Tennessee River. They were close enough to the Yankees to hear their drums roll when the wind was right. Ethan walked with Sgt. Alexander as he distributed the usual fifty or so rounds of ball and powder. He wanted to check on everyone for whom he was responsible before tomorrow, not just those in his old squad.

"Blazes," Fields said, "I pray this here powder's drier than me afore we have a go at them Yankees."

An agreeing murmur circulated the squad as each man loaded his powder flask and cartridge box.

Forbes was loading his pistol. "Hell," he said, "I'm gonna make sure mine's dry." He'd no sooner rammed the cartridge in than several shots rang out. He wasn't the only one concerned about wet powder. He smiled, aimed his pistol at the sky and fired. "Guess it is."

Petty, not more than ten feet away, thrust his hand above his head and ducked. "Shit! Watch where you're aimin' that thing." He reached to the ground and snatched the spent ball from where it had bounced from the top of his hat.

"No foolin'?" Fields said, looked up, stretched his arm, and aimed his pistol at the sky. "Maybe I can hit my own self."

"Save it," Adrien said with a grin. "One for our squad is enough. We may need all we've got for tomorrow."

"He's right," Ethan said, and turned away, not waiting for Alexander. Adrien's glance when he'd agreed had made him look away fast, which was damn foolish.

Captain Montrose found Ethan shortly thereafter. "Pass the word. No more shooting and no fires tonight. The General says we're supposed to surprise the Yankees tomorrow."

"You serious?"

"Better believe it. Don't say anything, but Commander Wharton was just given a dressing down for all the noise we made."

"You mean the federals are so dumb as to not know this massive army is here? Don't they have scouts? Post pickets?

"Hell if I know. None of our scouts have seen any such."

"Christ." *If the Yankees keep that up, our side ought to win this thing hands down.*

Johnston had picked a hell of a place for a battle: second-growth trees, thickets, rambling ridges, potholes, scattered farmers' fields. Wildflowers everywhere. Peach blossoms from nearby orchards fluttered on the breeze like pink butterflies and stuck to the hides of their damp horses.

Ethan chewed on his supper, a stale corn biscuit dipped in bacon grease, same as yesterday and the day before. He had to nail another hole in his belt to keep his trousers up. Who cared about slaves or states' rights? He would fight tomorrow to get at Yankee stores.

Ethan took a last amble through the trees to check on his men.

"McKay, how they doin? Get some sleep, Weeks."

"Hey, Ethan, look at me here with the shakes. Don't know why, ain't never took on like this afore. Funny, ain't it?"

"You just aren't used to havin' so many generals about you, that's all."

"That must be it."

Adrien was huddled against a tree, hat pulled low, blanket around his shoulders, likely dozing, the way they all did whenever they got the chance. Ethan kept checking on him, in spite of a promise to himself not to.

Ethan checked on his horse, Bob, first and last, rolled himself into his blanket and lay down close to Adrien for warmth. At least the rain had stopped. He listened to the eerie *whirrr* of an owl, the muted voices of a couple men still awake, the snores of others. He drifted off, in spite of the chill, slept until his eyes popped open in the dark to a soft shuffling of fabric and Adrien pulling away. It was 4:30. Ethan's usual rising time. His bladder told him so.

⁂

Sunday morning came on clear and bright, and if he never had another cold corn biscuit, he wouldn't be sorry. He heard what sounded like skirmishing and more constant firing followed by bugles.

A couple hours later with the regiment mounted and ready, the battle began in earnest. From their far right came the sound of cannon, shot, and the eerie wail of a Confederate infantry charge. Because of rough ground, trees, and ravines, Ethan couldn't see anything but their own riders here and there among the wildflowers, buds, and new green leaves. As morning stretched on, a fitful breeze rose and blessed the riders with an ephemeral peppering of blossoming pink peach, flaming redbud and white dogwood trees. Their enchanting scent perfumed the air.

Christ, he thought, *this is hardly the place for a fight.*

He had felt the presence of this massive army around him more last night than he did now. He could barely hear the battle—they were so separated by this wrinkled and foliage-screened land. Rangers waited while a bird sang in a nearby tree.

I hope we go soon, or I, for one, will be too saddle-stiff to fight.

Colonel Wharton came cantering from the south on his bay charger, raised his hat high. "All right boys, let's do this for Texas and the Confederacy!" The bird, a little brown thing, took off with a wild flutter.

What they actually did for the next few hours was fight their way up and down ravines, slosh through quagmires of mud and grassy bogs of standing water. They were trying to get around the right flank of the Yankees and come at them from behind. Easier said than done in all this mire. Their companies became separated, and one rider got buried in muck to his stirrups before they decided to turn back and find another way around. At this point, the 38th Tennessee Infantry Regiment, part of Ketchum's battery, joined them. Having big guns with you in case you needed them was comforting, but getting those guns through such muck was next to impossible.

Finally, they came upon a halfway decent road and what remained of a recently abandoned federal encampment. Ethan hadn't the heart to stop his men from searching the tents. Hell, none of them had had anything to eat but those stale corn biscuits for days. He leaned from Bob's back, lifted a canvas flap from a wagon and, behold: crates labeled *sardines, ham, sugar, crackers, fruit.* Lord be praised. One of the Tennesseans used a bayonet to pry them open.

"Pack it up and let's move out!" Ethan hoped they'd do it and not hang around here eating; he didn't want to force anyone. Twenty minutes later, with bursting saddlebags, he munched an apple as they rode out. Rangers couldn't be responsible for the infantry, who were enjoying bread and butter.

They met up with Captains Montrose and Ambrose and Lt. Wallace at the side of a little creek. Montrose held a crude, penciled map against his thigh. "I believe we're about here." He pointed to a wavy line on his map. "Over there is Owl Creek, and over there a ways on our right is," he paused, held the map closer before continuing, "Shiloh Church and the center of our army. Colonel Wharton says we need to push forward as best we can, and swing around the federal right flank before nightfall." He folded the map and shoved it into his inner vest pocket. "That means we have to make better time than we have so far. Let us hope the terrain cooperates."

Colonel Wharton in the lead, it began to look like they might have a chance as they galloped through one farmer's field after another with no sign of the retreating Union army besides the constant noise of battle on their right. Midafternoon they came to a wide meadow with a deep ravine angling left to right across its entire grassy wet expanse. They had been riding hard with no sign of Union soldiers, and no one was sure how far they had to go. Only one narrow path led across the meadow, and they had to ride strung out in single file along the ravine until the path crossed at the far end, which was a good leap for a horse.

Ethan was nearly to the crossing place when a banging clatter erupted and a hundred hornets sung past—snapping at his clothes, buzzing his ears. Bob stumbled and went down. The racket continued and wet grass kissed Ethan's face. He tried to get at his shotgun but it was beneath Bob and Ethan pulled his pistol from his belt. Horses and men were screaming, and here came Bandit galloping at him, Adrien's arm out, reaching, "Ethan!"

Ethan was up from the squishy ground, lunging, and reached for Adrien's hand only his own leg collapsed, but Adrien had him. Then Adrien's hat erupted in red and they both plummeted to the long grass. Adrien lay spread-eagled on his back, his head all blood. Ethan croaked, "Adrien," and crawled, dragging his leg. A horse leaped over them; another bolted past, dragging a man by the stirrup. Ethan grabbed Adrien's hand, both hands, and pulled at him, hauled himself and Adrien over the edge of the ravine and out of brutal fire.

Leaning back against the muddy wall he saw a bleeding hole in his left thigh, which he had begun to feel as a sharp, burning ache like nothing he'd ever known.

Stupid boy. Why'd he do that? Now he was dead. What a waste. He shoved the back of his hand across burning eyes.

The bullet had come out the other side of his leg. Not too bad. Only he began to feel woozy. He ought to do something to stop the bleeding, and undid his belt. Scattered shots cracked the air, then silence, except for moaning, near and far, a horse thudding off into the distance. Someone yelled.

"Nnmmf."

"Adrien?" His chest lurched.

Adrien turned his head, palmed the side of his face, where blood bloomed brightest. "It hurts. My ear hurts."

Ethan leaned over for a closer look. "Your head is all blood! Christ, I thought you were dead. *Thank God.* Move your hand." He didn't wait, but moved it for him. "It looks like the bullet grazed your head and took part of your ear."

Adrien slowly pushed up, turned away and heaved. Wiped his mouth along the sleeve of his jacket. "Damn. Damn. That was the first ham I've had in weeks."

He's cussing about food and I thought he was dead! "You should have eaten the fruit."

"I did. Did you see if Bandit got away?"

"I think so."

"I hope no one empties my saddle bags before we return."

"You're optimistic."

"Why not? We are alive."

"That was a stupid thing you tried, Adrien."

"It is what we do for one another." Adrien cocked his head, thumbed his bloody ear, and scowled "Rangers, I mean."

"I wonder if the Yankees are still there."

"You want to stand up and find out?" He dropped his head between his raised knees. "God my head hurts."

"I'm thirsty; I may try for water before long."

"I'm also thirsty, but not *that* thirsty, yet."

"Don't drink this bog water."

"It does not entice me."

"At least wash your face. You look horrible."

Adrien gave him a toothy grin through the blood that had become globs and dark streaks around his eyes, nose, and mouth. "I will wait until dusk and scare the Yankees away."

Ethan lay his head back against the muddy wall, closed his eyes and carefully stretched his wounded leg, grimacing.

"Ethan, I didn't see."

Now he's worried. Ethan felt a hand above the hole.

"You need a surgeon."

"No hurry. It went all the way through. It's not so bad."

"Bad enough. You could bleed . . . .. I'll find a stick, or something."

He heard Adrien move off down the ravine somewhere. *Like a dog, here, boy, get the stick. Really am thirsty. Damn.*

Something was tightening around his leg. Adrien was fooling about down there. He made a better tourniquet with his stick, the belt twisted around.

Water, poured into his mouth, so wonderful. More. There was more.

"Ethan?"

He opened his eyes. The light was lower, late afternoon, nearer dusk. He must have fallen asleep. Adrien took his hand, placed it on a canteen at his side. Most of the blood had been smeared away from Adrien's face.

"This canteen is nearly full. The Yankees have gone, and I'm going to get help. I will be back. I promise. No matter what, I will be back. Do you hear me?"

"Yes." *That's what he wanted. Now let me sleep.*

A momentary hand on his shoulder and Adrien was gone.

It was raining again.

Chapter Sixteen
Texas
Mint Tea and Mail

The German-made grandfather clock had struck ten some time ago. Knitting in my left hand, I took another sip of mint tea from the cup on the table. We had plenty of mint from what grew along the north side of the house, but no more tea from China, as such was not deemed as important as guns and gunpowder. I have never knitted so many wool stockings. What if we ran out of wool?

Silly. There were always sheep. If people did not eat them. Thank goodness, Joanna's people raised sheep. I glanced up at her over there under the other lamp, knitting. Joanna was faster, her stitches so much tighter than mine. Much like Maman that way. Joanna had had her spinning wheel brought over from the farm along with piles of wool.

I sighed. I would much rather be with Papa and Lucien and the other men at their meeting over at Hartwood. Why must women have to wait while men made all the important decisions? I waited for letters from Will and Adrien and now waited for this.

I had not waited for anyone to tell me what to do at Blue Hills. I was learning to cook and grow vegetables for our table. And Joanna, thank goodness, knew all about canning vegetables and fruit, and was teaching me. Everyone had new jobs, including Simon, who no longer had time to sit around in the hall waiting for someone to come to the door. Charlie was teaching him to be a cow hand, and how surprised everyone was at how well he took to it.

The sound of horses out by the barn—they had finally come home! Papa and Lucien rode directly to the barn to put their horses away, as we could no longer afford an extra person to do so for them. Everyone worked all day in the fields or taking care of remaining stock: cattle, three milk cows, pigs, and chickens. So far, the military had taken eight of Papa's horses and left us enough to run cattle, which included a couple geldings, his stallion, a couple mares, and one old fellow too old to be of any practical use. The mares had been in foal, or they might have taken them, as well. We had been paid in Confederate script, which I supposed was somewhere in Papa's desk.

Joanna put down her knitting and stood. "I'll put on more tea," she said, and left for the kitchen.

No point in pretending I could keep on knitting. I was too anxious to hear what had happened. I stood, walked to the front window, moved a corner of the drapery aside, and peered out. Nothing much to see, as there was no moon. A strip of yellow light at the barn door was all. Marcus was likely down there. He would wait up, though he need not. It was like him to do so, and Betta, as well. She would stay up until Marcus returned to their cabin. No word from their son, Isaac, but then none was expected. How could there possibly be? Adrien had sent word they had parted safely. It was all we knew. I prayed every night Isaac was free in Mexico. Drat this war. Drat it all.

The light was gone. Here they came, three dark shadows—Marcus with them, as I had suspected. I dropped the drapery.

"Well," Papa said after carefully hanging his hat and coat on the hook in the hall, "that went about as expected."

Lucien followed him into the parlor. As Marcus had not come in, Papa must have told our overseer what he needed to know before entering. They settled into chairs, Papa in his favorite by the fire, as Joanna entered with the tray of hot tea.

"Bless you, my dear," Papa said, leaning forward to take up his cup. Joanna and I sat on the green sofa, anxious and attempting not to show it. Practically everyone in the county had been invited to the meeting, at least everyone who owned property or a business.

Everyone who might be concerned about raiders, be they white or Indian, or any sort of lawlessness while so many men were gone to fight in the East. The Comanche and Kiowa, in particular, had begun raiding in west and north Texas and could conceivably come this far south and east.

Papa blew across his tea, took a sip, and placing it in the saucer, sat back. "We have formed a state militia and elected officers. Jacob Hart and Lucien share a small company they will head alternate weeks. They will report to Judge Hall in town. That way plantation responsibilities shouldn't suffer too much."

My heart dropped. Dear Lord, how would we get along? Papa was still strong, but not as young as previously. I would tie up my skirts, if necessary, and wear gloves. Pull those dang weeds. I had done so in the kitchen garden. The fields, the corn, oats, were merely larger. More rows. Of course, we still had most of our people.

"We will manage, Papa. We always do."

He smiled at me. Then . . . "Oh. I nearly forgot. Glen Hawkins was there and brought everyone's mail. Papa was up and walking to his coat before I could exclaim.

"One from Will, and one for us, plus another for you inside," he held another to me.

Adrien often sent a special note for me inside his family letter. I would listen to the family letter first, then read mine later.

March 27, 1861

Dear Family,

> *I have taken this time to write as we have been given a couple days rest and were issued bacon and flour this morning. Forbes, I believe I mentioned him previously, showed us how to add water to our flour, knead it on one of our oilcloths, wrap it around a ramrod or stick and hold it over the fire until it becomes bread of a sort. I like using a stick, and leave sprigs on mine to keep the roll from sliding down and off onto the coals. I also tried wrapping my bacon around the bread, which is dandy with a couple sprigs stuck*

through to keep it attached if I am careful not to let them catch fire. Necessity breeds self-sufficiency. I believe I read something like that somewhere. I am afraid my former ability to quote the classics is suffering quite horribly due to lack of what Maman would have called polite conversation.

Survivors of measles and other scourges have joined us along with new recruits, including Terry's two younger brothers.

I applied hot poultices to my mount's legs (Bandit, if you will recall). It is a caution how he stands unmoving, with lowered eyelids, his lower lip trembling in satisfaction.

Earlier this month, our doughty rangers assisted our troops to Nashville. The next morning riding back through that city, I heard a high wail—it was women who came outdoors and onto balconies braving the winter cold, shawls and blankets about their shoulders, to cheer our cavalry as we rode by. Troops in the city joined them. A chill ran through me, not from the cold.

Those women stirred thoughts of home, of all of you.

In Charlotte we found escaped troops and Nathan Bedford Forrest's cavalry. After a tentless frost-laden night of four hours sleep, Ethan met with us sergeants under an ash-white sky. We were ordered to ride as fast as possible to Mufreesboro where our cavalry units were camped. Every rider had to take a man on his horse. We had heard of Forrest, and our riders had to prove we were every bit as good as him and his men.

Immediately afterward, we covered the retreat of Johnston's army through Tennessee with Major Tom Harrison leading. Without tents and little sleep, on furious, wild rides in freezing rain, we collected stragglers, horses, mules and supplies—Confederate and Yankee—but lost many of our men in the effort.

That ride with two in the saddle was a misery, especially crossing ice-crusted rivers and streams, and wore us and our horses to the bone. Colonel Wharton and a few others had to be taken to Franklin to recover.

I have never been with men as worthy of admiration as these.

I pray all of you are well and send my love,
Adrien

    Papa sighed and lowered the letter to his thigh. My brother had never written a letter quite like this before. The others had been so positive. He must have been exhausted to let slip such feelings.

Chapter Seventeen
Corinth

Adrien

I sat cross-legged on the end of the bed and watched rain trickle down the window panes. Wrapping the bed quilt around my shoulders and tucking my bare feet, I fingered the tiny, even stitches of the quilt and drew its soft, worn folds closer about my ears—the left ear, along with the top of my head, was wrapped in bandage.

A sparrow nested on one of the white blossoming branches of a tree close by the window, feathers fluffed up and huddled in the rain. How fortunate to be warm and dry in this second-floor room of whitewashed walls and polished pine floors scattered with rugs.

Ethan lay sleeping in the bed behind me, and three more injured rangers occupied a room down the hall. The Culpeppers had graciously opened their home to all wounded from the battle that had taken place farther north, the same our army had won one day and lost the next to reinforced Yankees. Both days the bluecoats had fought hard, harder than anybody expected. This war would not be over soon, after all. The Yankees insisted they fought against slavery, yet few in my regiment owned slaves. What mad irony—being Negro, myself. I clutched the blanket closer.

I had nearly lost Ethan, and had watched over him every waking hour since we had come to this place. I memorized the lines in the corners of Ethan's eyes and mouth, the tiny mole on his left cheek. I watched the way his long, thin hands and fingers lay in repose, the way his eyelids rolled and fluttered while dreaming. I brushed unruly hair from his forehead, lovingly stroked that forehead the way Maman had when I was ill.

"Adrien?" A whisper.

I turned. "Welcome back." I slid from the covers, stood and carefully perched on the edge of Ethan's bed.

"Water?" Ethan's voice came raspy from cracked lips.

I poured from a white pitcher sitting on a nightstand between the two beds. I held Ethan's head in one arm and lifted, held the glass while Ethan drained it, then fluffed his pillow.

"Is it still there?"

A moment for me to catch what he meant. "Your leg? Yes."

"I feel it, but fellows have talked of phantom pain." He closed his mouth and eyes, turned his face away.

"We had the devil's time finding you in the dark. We were ambushed, if you recall. Yankees hid in the woods waiting for us to string out like one of those carnival pot shoots." I took a deep breath. Stated the result out loud for the first time. "We lost twenty-five men in that meadow, including Captain Montrose. Are you up for the rest?"

"Yes." Ethan swiveled his head, looking at me, ready for the worst. "The whole thing, and where are we?"

"Back in Corinth. Our army beat them roundly the first day. But another Union army crossed the river that night and beat us back on Sunday. Our regiment lost a lot of men, maybe fifty more than at the ravine. We lost Terry's brother, and Colonel Wharton was wounded." So much bad news, I had to find something good. "Harrison took command, and he did all right. He truly did, in spite of what everyone thought of him before." Then the worst must be told: "General Johnston was killed."

"Johnston?"

"Yes."

Silence, but for the ever-constant rain pattering the roof. The papers called the battle Shiloh, because of that church. The church neither me nor anyone in our outfit had seen. I would forever think of the place as "the ravine." Didn't matter. I would not be going home any time soon. Not even by Christmas. Maybe never.

"We are going to be at this a while," Ethan said.

"Yes." I was gazing down at my hands, palms on my bare boney knees where the linen nightshirt had pulled up when I sat. I hardly recognized those hands: so cut and bruised, black under the ragged nails and defining every crevice.

"Why are we in this house?"

"Most of the wounded abide in the Tishomingo Hotel, but there are too many and some have been sent to homes like this one. Mr. and Mrs. Culpepper have two boys in the war and we are in their room. Their daughters live in Richmond; one is married." I managed a smile. "I believe we get much better food and care here than we would in the hotel."

"That's a strange crooked turban on your head."

"I expect it keeps what is left of my ear from falling off."

"How is it, your head?"

"I have headaches, but fewer each day and less severe, a little dizziness. I expect they will send me back before long. Why the smile?"

"I just wiggled my toes."

"You did not believe me?"

"I did. Still, it was rather splendid, to feel them moving."

I stood, lay out my quilt and crawled into bed with a sigh.

"How long have we been here?" Ethan said, once I had settled. We gazed at the ceiling while continuing to speak.

"Three days. Plus three days getting here."

"Lord."

"Be thankful you do not remember the trip."

"Bad, was it?"

"You cannot imagine."

"I'm tired. I'm going to sleep, but later, since we're stuck here together, there's something we need to settle."

The rain slowed enough to hear a wagon, the clopping of horses passing in front of the house.

I felt old, as though all energy had drained from me after the search for Ethan. A familiar pressure clawed its way over my eye from my left temple, and I also wanted to sleep. I was not sure I wanted to wake up later, to hear what Ethan had to say.

The following morning, shortly after Mrs. Culpepper left with our breakfast dishes, Dr. Hill visited us and changed the bandage on Ethan's thigh. Dr. Hill's slave stood by with a pan of water, clean bandages hanging over one arm. Ethan had a look at the puckered pink hole going in, and Dr. Hill assured him the one going out beneath wasn't much worse, considering.

"You are fortunate it was a Minié ball and didn't hit bone," he said, carefully prodding around the edges while Ethan grimaced. I wanted to strike him for causing my friend pain. Except the surgeon had dark circles under his eyes and pulled himself off Ethan's bed as though his bones ached.

He removed my turban and replaced it with a single wrap. "Stay in bed until I return in a few days. I don't want you getting dizzy and falling down those stairs."

After the surgeon left, we dozed off, until a tap on the door announced Mrs. Culpepper and a slave girl entering with wicker trays loaded with bowls of hot chicken soup and what looked and smelled like fresh-baked wheat rolls.

"Ma'am," Ethan said, "it is nearly worth getting shot to be treated like this."

"You boys are much too thin. I only hope someone will care for my sons the same."

I paused, spoon in hand. "Folks such as yourself have treated us royally wherever we have been. If I had not realized what I was fighting for previously, I surely do now."

How she smiled and folded her hands in front of her apron, bobbing a little. Her skin sagged like someone who has lost weight too fast, yet her smile was cheery and her gray eyes shone. "I'll leave you in peace and be back shortly to collect the dishes. Lord knows, you both deserve a little peace." She turned and hustled out the door, closing it quietly.

"When this is over, you should go into politics, Adrien."

"That is not funny, and I meant what I said." I surprised myself with my bitterness, and Ethan had likely noticed. The sounds of spoons in bowls, subdued slurping, chewing filled the otherwise silent room. No longer rain on the roof. *Why no birds singing or dogs barking? Come to think, that one in the window is the only bird I've seen for days . . . or longer. Is it the battle, all the way down here?*

Ethan put the tray on the bed at his side, leaned back against the pillows, and closed his eyes. "Why did you risk your life for me?"

I cleaned out my bowl with a last piece of bread. "I answered you before." I would not look at Ethan. Not for asking such a stupid question. Twice now.

"I can't figure it. It's been pretty damn obvious that I'm not up to the exacting standards of a wealthy plantation owner's son. I don't blame you for not trusting me, being in your eyes a whore's son and a gambler. I only wish you'd been honest in the beginning, rather than make me believe you considered us equals."

"What are you saying?" I could feel the blood rushing through my body and quickly put the tray on the floor, almost dropping it. Here came the pressure of another headache.

"Don't play stupid with me. My mistake, thinking you were someone with whom I could be totally honest and who'd be the same in return."

I grabbed the quilt in my fists. This was the man I had risked my neck for? The one I thought was my friend? Why had I insisted on being in the same room with him? The bureau drawer held my clothes—I had seen Mrs. Culpepper bring them back washed and mended. I threw the quilt aside and scrambled out of bed to head across the room. Only my ears hummed the room away, blood pounded my head and I grabbed the side of the bed, pulled at the quilt and dropped to my knees.

"Adrien?" Ethan's voice spun from anger to concern.

The pounding was a little less each second if I breathed deeply, made myself relax. *I got up too fast; that was all. And tried to run from the truth—again.*

"You are right, Ethan. But only partly." I stared at my knees, now encased in someone else's woolen drawers—one of her son's? "I am not the man you thought, whoever that may be. It is me who is not worthy of our friendship. Any tobacco my father once had is gone, and was never mine anyway, but my brother's. That is the truth. The other truth is I nearly ruined a girl."

"These are the horrible secrets you have been hiding?"

"Some."

"You think such things make any difference to me? You should have known that your financial or social position has no meaning for me by the state of my own. I assume the girl is Lily."

I lifted my head, turned toward Ethan, "How?"

"You mumbled her name when you were feverish with measles. From that and what I do know of you, I doubt the affair was lightly done."

I rested my palms against the bed, raised slowly, and sat on the edge. I inspected my folded hands, thumbs rubbing the fingers. I could not tell Ethan the rest—that I was Negro, and depraved. I could not lose this man's friendship.

"I loved her. And had to leave to save her reputation."

"Give me your arm, fool." Ethan's right hand was reaching toward me.

I leaned forward, and Ethan took my hand, then moved up to clasp my entire forearm.

"Don't anger me again, or I will put a notch in your other ear."

I should not have taken Ethan's hand. That I did only proved me weak and deceitful. Yet I grasped his arm tight. I would do anything for Ethan. Anything but tell the entire truth. Anything but that.

Chapter Eighteen
Texas
Entirely Unexpected

Jacob Hart had been waiting in the Hartwood library for twenty minutes. The first ten minutes he calmly listened to the trill of tree frogs outside the French doors, slightly ajar to let in a cool evening breeze and scent of jasmine. Determined to remain undisturbed by the old man's whims, for the last ten minutes he had begun to ruminate on a possible reason for the summons.

Due to his exertions, Hartwood continued in excellent condition, as his father spent most of his time hobnobbing with his cronies—which meant lurking about Brenham, Austin, or Houston more often than at home. This suited Jacob. He had made an excellent profit on the sale of his horses to the cavalry, proving his father wrong on that score. The old man had formerly believed raising fine horseflesh a gentleman's avocation, not a way of making a living. The war also meant cotton prices rose, as long as they managed to get their cotton past the Galveston blockade.

Indeed, this war could prove a godsend to his family's endeavors. While Will survived. So far the Texas Brigade under John Bell Hood hadn't fought in any major battles, but that didn't mean they wouldn't—and soon, according to his brother's letters. This new General Lee, under whose command Hood's brigade had recently been assigned, didn't sound like the sort to run like those western generals. At least he hadn't yet.

Which reminded Jacob of the recent Conscription Act passed by the Confederate States Congress: All healthy white men between the ages of eighteen and thirty-five had to serve for a term of three years. Was this meeting about his father buying him out? Such a thing was allowed by the Act, but Jacob wouldn't allow it. He wouldn't be able to look any of his companions in the eye if he did, let alone live with himself.

The door opened behind him and Randolph Hart strode in and sat behind the oversize walnut desk.

"I won't waste words," his father said, "I'm sending you to Galveston."

Jacob couldn't help but inhale and stiffen in surprise.

"I talked to Senator Wigfall, and you'll be more useful down there making sure our cotton gets past the blockade and returns with war supplies than fighting in some regiment."

"I don't know anything about ships."

"You won't have to. I've purchased an English ship and hired a captain and crew. I've found a Galveston runner bound for Nassau where you can pick them up, and you leave tomorrow morning.

"Captain McNeil and his men will take care of the sailing and loading; you'll do the rest. There's a lot of money in blockade running, and I don't trust anyone else not to fleece us. Certainly not those fools who are attempting the run to Galveston at present. Some are trading in perfume and fancy doodads instead of arms and equipment for our soldiers, and with Will fighting, I won't have it."

Family being the one thing he and Father agreed upon.

"Take Colt. You'll likely need him where you're going. You'll have a couple days to see your sister. She sent a letter and she's already in her confinement, and I want to know how she's doing."

"If she'll see me."

His father slammed a fist on the desk. "Make her see you. I don't know what went on with you two last fall, but fix it. She's going to have my grandchild, and she's down there in Houston and needs to know she can depend on her family. I can't take the time from our concerns here, but you'll be nearer Houston from now on. I'm depending on you to take care of your sister."

He hadn't seen this sort of responsibility in his father before. Was it advancing age, war, or the idea of another grandchild that brought this on? Maybe all three.

Speaking of which, he wasn't looking forward to telling his own wife and children that he was leaving for who knew how long. On the other hand, Lucretia would likely be happy once he left. Duty ruled their marriage more than pleasure, though she had gained higher position and wealth than she might otherwise have expected. He was satisfied with the two children she had borne him as, so far, neither showed signs of being weak or spoiled.

The next morning the tenderness that nearly overcame him surprised and even threatened his sense of masculinity. His wife and children gathered before the veranda for a final farewell. He fell to one knee to better face his four-year-old daughter, and Louisa grasped him round the neck with her chubby little arms and held on, sobbing.

"What's this?" he said, taking her tiny hands in his.

"Unca Will went to war and he's been gone forever," she managed between sobs.

"Dear Cricket," he said, "you'll see me again as soon as the cotton is fluffy balls. I promise."

Her teary eyes blinked at him. She might be only four but, knowing her, she would watch for the cotton to turn if she did nothing else all summer. He lifted her high in his arms for a hug before handing her over to her nanny and mounting his horse. The boy was three and stood as stoic as his mother, holding her hand. Turning his horse away, he caught sight of his father upstairs in a window.

So, the old man had seen him off, after all, in his own way.

The end of May, Houston was already showing signs of hot, humid summer. *The sooner this baby arrives, the better.* Never mind that a birth in May, any day now, could mean trouble. According to when she married Andrew

Garrison, a birth now would signal an entire month ahead of schedule. Lily hoped her husband would remain absent on business in Charleston until after this baby was born. Long after, if at all possible.

Ah, well, first babies were known to come ahead, weren't they? Or late, or however they might choose. *Oh, God*, she thought, turning to her side and pushing a palm against her lower back. *I don't care what anyone thinks, get this over with.* She had thrown every cover away and the sheet beneath her was damp with perspiration.

"It's so hot up here already," she said to her maid, Mae, who was waving a large bamboo fan back and forth from the side of the four-poster where Lily lay.

"You must try to relax, Missus. All dis turnin' and movin' about is makin' you hotter."

"Sakes alive. I cannot bear this much longer." Lily spread her arms and lay across the bed, staring at the ceiling.

Agitated voices at the door. It flew open and there stood her insufferable brother, her husband's butler half-hidden behind his tall form.

"I tried to stop him, Missus, but he wouldn't—"

"Never mind, Abram. Leave us." She managed to raise herself onto her elbows.

"Confound it, Lily, if you don't look like a beached whale lying there," Jacob said.

"Thank you for such an astute observation." She held herself up while Mae stuffed a number of pillows behind her. "You may leave us, Mae. It seems my brother has forced himself into my presence even though I made it clear I never wanted to see or hear from him again."

"I came to see what I can do to help," he said as Mae left and closed the door.

"Help? Can you have this baby for me?"

His brows lowered. "You're due any day, aren't you."

He wasn't asking her, he merely wanted confirmation, and she was hardly in a position to deny the obvious. She folded her arms and glared at her brother.

"It's his, isn't it."

Still not a question. Would he strike her? She didn't like to think of how he had likely struck Adrien, how Adrien would have fought back, to no avail. Adrien was alive, though. And well. Berni sent her letters so she knew he was, even after being wounded, which had frightened her so when she heard.

Jacob moved toward her and she couldn't stop herself from flinching. He hesitated, then came on and sat on the bed next to her.

"You're afraid of me?" he said. "Have I ever done anything to hurt you, Lily?"

"Don't you think hurting Adrien hurt me?"

"Not really," he said, regarding her. "Look at you, in this fine house. Hasn't Garrison given you everything you've ever wanted? He'll probably give you more once this child is born, early or not. The man is making money hand over fist in this war, moving goods on his railroad, buying and selling like so many others. Play your cards right and you'll be independently wealthy, with or without him, when this thing's done. Then you can do as you please."

"In God's name, how? At present, I am his property as much as this house and everything in it."

"Why do you think I made sure the marriage contract was set up the way it was. Haven't you read the small print?"

"Of course, I read it. But I get nothing until he is gone."

"You didn't read the small print, did you?"

"I did. Well. Most of it. I'll allow a good deal of the reading got rather tiring and I always meant to get back to it."

"I hoped he would think that being a woman, you wouldn't take advantage of what's available to you. The wording appears simple, but it's not. There's a trust for you and your children, which is common. But this one you can add to whenever you please from any gifts he might present to you, or from anywhere you might receive funds on your own. Most importantly, you can take funds from it for certain special reasons—that's the important part that we must discuss."

"You mean I can start now, even before he's gone?" Be her own person, dependent upon no one, not her husband, her father, no one.

He smiled. "Certainly."

"Oh, Jacob." She threw her arms around his neck and gave him a hug. Then leaned back, still holding on, and said, eyes wide open. "Why didn't you tell me?"

"You weren't speaking to me. Remember?"

"Of course, I wasn't. You were being terrible, and I was all in a muddle because of it, and—Oh!" A terrible clutching at her insides. She bent forward, jerked up her knees and grasped at her oversized tummy. She gasped.

"Lily?"

Thank God, it was gone. She relaxed. "Nothing. For a moment there, there was this. . . ." A loosening, an immense wet warmth beneath her. "Oh, dear, I'm—you better get Mae."

"It appears I arrived just in time," he said on his way out the door.

How relieved she was he was here. Someone from her own family, and he had been through the births of two children of his own. As much as a man could experience a birth. She nearly giggled. She could always depend on Jacob.

Mae arrived just as the next pain clawed her.

Adrien's child. Adrien's child is coming.

Lily stood in her bedroom window gazing at the people passing by on the street out front. She had told Mae she would have breakfast in the little garden out back. It would be her first excursion out-of-doors, her first venture out of this room in over a month, only eight days since the child was born. But she could not stand being shut in here for one more hour, despite the fact she was still a little tired. A nap this afternoon would suffice.

The birthing had been difficult, though the doctor said he had seen worse. She hadn't liked having to say goodbye to Jacob two days ago, but he said he had already stayed longer than business allowed. Father's ship business, of course. He had promised to return as soon as possible, no more than a few weeks. The people who had visited and left cards were all her husband's friends and business acquaintances. She had made no real friends here in Houston, and she was lonely. At least—

A cab pulled up out front, its horse sweaty and blowing. The door was thrown open and, *oh my God*, it was Andrew. He practically ran up the walk to the door. She backed from the window, lifted her skirts and spun, *what do I do?* "Mae," louder, "Mae," and Mae hurried through the door, leaving it open and she could hear voices below, her husband bellowing, his tread on the stairs.

She pushed at her hair. "Do I look all right?" Thank God, she had washed and had Mae do her hair first thing. Mother always said to make yourself presentable upon rising, before breakfast, even if you had it in bed, for you never knew. Mother had been right, as usual. She didn't wait for Mae to answer but bent over for a quick look in her dresser mirror. The dark circles beneath her eyes were gone; she pinched her cheeks, stood straight, faced the door and smiled—just in time.

He halted in the doorway, taking up its entire space but for the top foot or so. "Where's my son? Is he healthy?"

She nearly lost her smile. *I suppose I shouldn't expect him to ask how I feel.* "He is fine, and healthy for having been born a month early." *I must allude to an early birth, but not over-often.* "Mae, will you bring in Joshua?" She took a step forward. "I named him Joshua after your first son and father, as we once discussed, if you will recall."

He smiled, one of his seldom-seen good smiles, and relief flooded her. "I do," and he stepped forward and took her hands when she lifted them and kissed her lightly on the mouth, tasting of cigars, as ever. She had to fight the urge to scratch her chin because his beard tickled. "I am content you are well," he said, looking down at her. He stepped back as Mae entered the room with the baby in her arms.

Joshua was tiny, as all babies barely a week old were. "My God, look at that dark hair."

At Garrison's exclamation, the sleepy baby opened his eyes and puckered his face as though about to let out a mighty wail. Instead, he smacked his lips and waved his tiny pink fists.

"He has your blue eyes."

She took her husband's arm. "Yes, and your determination, else why arrive into the world so early? He already has everyone at his beck and call." She turned to Mae. "I believe he's hungry, will you take him to the nanny?" She urged Garrison toward a settee. "He doesn't cry unless he's hungry or needs changing. He is such a good baby." She had begun prattling, and her husband resisted sitting.

"You must realize I only rushed here when I heard and can't stay. This was entirely unexpected and interrupted some important negotiations I can't leave to chance. Of course, I had to be sure for myself that you and the baby were fine. Now that I see you are, that he is healthy . . . I'll stay the night but will take the train back to Galveston and on from there first thing in the morning."

Thank God. "Oh, Andrew, must you?" She had to sit, herself, for her knees were trembling—bless all these skirts.

"Yes. But I want to see the child again, later, after he's eaten and not so sleepy."

I'll get through this, somehow. It's only one night.

Chapter Nineteen
Tennessee
Prayer of Some Sort

Ethan

Rangers camped at the foot of Lookout Mountain for a much-needed rest of men and horses. On a glorious May afternoon after recovery, Ethan had just hung a pair of socks on a twig to dry when Adrien ambled up with a hangdog look on his face.

"New Orleans has been taken by the Yankees," he said.

A stone lodged in the middle of Ethan's chest.

"Here," Adrien pushed a canteen into his hand, "try some of this."

He took a sip and liquid fire chased over his tongue and down his throat. He opened his mouth wide, blew out what he supposed was hot air, sucked in cooler. "Dear God." A tingling warmth spread to his fingertips.

"Got it from Sergeant Schimmel. Nothing but the best for our Lt. Childs."

"And why did you refuse an offered commission?"

"I don't care for that much responsibility. Being a sergeant is enough of a cross to bear. There are no end of fellows who aspire to be officers, and I shall leave them to their destinies." Adrien tipped the canteen up and threw back a deep swallow, bent over, coughed. Straightened, tears in his eyes. "Well. Rather splendid. A noble start on a magnificent evening, I should say, as our company is only on the first day of a three-day rest period. What do you think, Lt. Childs?"

Ethan took the canteen, held it up. "Excellent. Here's to 'O Be Joyful,' which we are about to be." He took a hearty swallow this time, which made him cough.

Ethan had a darn fine voice, and Adrien was not bad either, at least they thought so less than an hour later as they sat around the fire singing, "The Girl I left Behind Me," "Eveline," and whatever else came to mind. Most of their company joined in. Someone appeared with a banjo a little out of tune, but no one minded. More 'O Be Joyful' was passed around. "Lorena" was sung in the late hours, and who would say the tears shed were from liquor only? The fire was left to die and many slept where they found themselves over logs, stumps or behind them, and Adrien and Ethan struggled back to their tent and fell arm-in-arm onto their bedrolls, mouths open, drooling. They did not snore in harmony.

As usual, any word of the eastern theater passed quickly among the men. The latest was that President Davis's new general, Robert E. Lee, chased McClellan's army across the Shenandoah and took "right smart" prisoners and equipment. This news was cause for celebration. They had finished off the last of their spirits, but the men created their own warmth with music and dancing. The youngest were chosen to play girls. Adrien caused a minor ruckus by refusing to do so, and Crane Forbes, one of the oldest, despite his beard, covered it by volunteering to play a jolly good matron and twirled his skirts and lifted his knees higher than anyone, much to the delight of all.

In June, General Beauregard put Wharton's rangers under the command of Nathan Bedford Forrest. The rangers were pleased that stern, six-foot-two Forrest, though a former slave trader, had the reputation of a good leader who didn't run from the enemy.

The rangers returned to Middle Tennessee with the newly formed brigade to do what they did best—scout and scare the hell out of Yankees by appearing out of nowhere, creating havoc, and disappearing with as much loot as they could carry or drive before them.

"So," said Ethan, patting his belly, "now we're raiding again I can let my belt out a little."

Adrien shoved his foot into his third pair of boots since leaving Texas. "I have learned to count on nothing until I see, smell, touch, or taste it upon my tongue." He stood and took a few steps in one direction, then the other, looking down at his shiny Union boots. "I found these in a supply wagon with new uniforms. Maybe if I roll my fresh pair of stockings in the toes, they will fit properly. It will be a handy way to carry clean stockings."

"Then they'll likely stink as bad as your old ones."

"Ethan, you do not care for the smell of my fine feet?"

"Not when you haven't washed them for a week or more."

"I wash every day, when there is water available and we have time."

"Precisely the problem."

"C'est la vie."

In July they rested near Chattanooga, Tennessee.

Ethan retained a slight limp which, so far, hadn't affected his riding—until he joined a gander-pulling contest played for the amusement of soldiers and civilians alike.

He and Adrien had devised a plan for seizing the goose. Adrien was to ride up on one side of the rider and hold his attention while Ethan came up from his opposite side. Adrien rode hard on their victim's right—a private from Company A who clutched the goose's feet and swung it away to the opposite side of his horse. Ethan came tearing out of nowhere on their victim's left and leaned far over to snatch the bird away. Only his right leg no longer served him as before, and he tumbled from the saddle, rolled through a cloud of dust and sat there hacking, while his horse ran on after the goose. Folks from nearby towns and countryside, particularly the farmer who had provided the goose, thought it was grand fun. So did officers and men, including those who from earlier play had sprains and broken bones.

Adrien walked Bandit up as the dust settled and held out Ethan's hat. "You all right?"

Ethan wiped dirt from his mouth with the back of his hand. "All but my pride."

Adrien turned Bandit's withers around a couple neat side steps closer, inviting Ethan to mount behind. He slowly stood and swung up.

Adrien held Bandit to a smart, tight trot past the lines of onlookers, and Ethan raised his hat with a grin, prompting louder whoops.

"Better to know now than later, or my goose would be cooked."

"God," Adrien declared with a pained expression.

They chased the Yankees from one town after another, constantly on the move because their army ran from the bluecoats, always losing the big battles. They retook Murfreesboro, where the citizens welcomed them back with cheers and plenty of good food. Winning would not always be so easy. Ethan began to enjoy the hot rush of excitement, of blood coursing his veins after he came through another skirmish alive and uninjured. He began to feel invincible, and he wasn't the only one. Fellows would come together from another skirmish, another victory, and laughingly pound one another on the back, brag on their fearlessness, joke on how one ranger could whip ten Yankees. If the western army were made up of the 8th Texas, why, the Yankees would have surrendered by now. Ethan feared they were too confident.

When their regiment suffered one hundred eighty killed or wounded charging a Yankee stockade, that danger was confirmed. His own company lost nine men, including an officer and sergeant. Adrien came through with merely a few bruises and scrapes. Ethan again tried to put him up for lieutenant and he again refused.

No one in the squad said much that night around their campfire, finishing up dinner and what stood for coffee. "The war will be over by Christmas," mumbled Bob Fields through his new blond mustache. Arch closed his eyes, moving his lips. Ethan figured it was likely a prayer of some sort. No one believed the statement as they had this time last year, but some still said it, hoping saying so might make it true.

Good news arrived from the East. The Confederate army had chased the Yankees back across the Shenandoah and captured thousands of prisoners and nearly a hundred cannon. Ethan couldn't figure why the North didn't surrender.

In August the exhausted rangers made camp in an ash grove near McMinnville where they and their horses got much-needed rest. They sent out scouts, posted pickets, and made dry, smokeless fires over which they cooked suppers of cornbread, greasy bacon, and canned pork and beans they filched from Yankee skirmishers. Those with tobacco smoked or chewed while frogs chorused from a nearby creek, and the day's adventures were told and retold with embellishment.

Adrien had turned in early, and his breathing was deep and even when Ethan lay down carefully on their blanket so as not to wake him. He had been too long without a woman. Despite the warm night, he wanted to spoon—more than spoon.

Many fellow rangers had formed attachments. A few had declared love for one another. Only it was chancy to take affection too far into the physical, even once. Though he would be surprised if such a thing hadn't happened. With death at your shoulder, with what you saw and did nearly every day, you took comfort where you could.

He rolled over, faced away from temptation and toward the next two fellows sleeping no more than fifteen feet away. In any other regiment he would be tenting with another officer. Few in this outfit wore a full uniform, and fewer cared.

He must approach this . . . seduction, with as light a hand as he would setting up a mark, and be careful not to get as involved as he had with Louie. It was the same as overly caring about the results of a card game. Caring too much could affect your concentration, the outcome. Problem was that in this case, the stakes were damned high. What he might lose was more valuable than money. He had become practiced at shutting his mind off and sleeping in all conditions, and did so now.

The following morning Adrien rolled out from under their blanket and dressed, though he didn't speak until offering Ethan his first cup of "coffee," such as it was.

"I'm afraid we are back to chicory for coffee."

Ethan took a sip. "At least it's hot, which is about all I can say for it."

Forbes stood across the fire from them, scumbling biscuit into his cup. "I got some extra corn biscuit, either of you want some."

"Thanks." Adrien sidled over the log they sat on to the older man and held out his cup.

Ethan watched, wondering how Adrien's family would react to their son having chicory coffee with scumbled corn biscuit for breakfast. Unimaginable, he expected. This whole business was unimaginable.

Adrien took a little bottle from the inside pocket of his coat and poured a drop from it into his coffee. Forbes stood up, stretched and ambled off, pretending not to notice. Ethan had seen Adrien with this bottle before and had suspected what it was since April, but here it was the middle of June.

He made his way over and sat down on the log. "You still having headaches?"

"If you're asking why the laudanum, I only take it for the bad ones, and then only a drop. Less and less. We were riding hard there for a while and I couldn't make do without it."

"That's why you slept so sound, huh?"

Adrien lowered his head over his empty tin cup. Their fire was nearly out.

Ethan rose, lay a hand on Adrien's shoulder. "Be careful is all. Don't want you falling off your horse." He strode off, gait a little uneven.

Chapter Twenty
No Longer a Game

Adrien

"I believe we have been here and done this before," I said.

Once again in Georgia, our evening firelight cast soft dancing shadows onto the dusky trees behind us. The rangers had acted as rear guard of the retreating Army of Tennessee. "Those Yankees keep getting reinforcements." Ethan stood next to me scratching his head. "They multiply worse than fleas on a hound."

"Don't speak to me of fleas." I bent over and scratched where my trousers met the top of my boots, mumbling, "Gol-blamed," jerked off my boot and furiously rubbed, louder, "damn." Chiggers had latched onto us, and some other crawly thing no one could get rid of without total immersion of self and every piece of clothing and bedding in the nearest river—to no avail if your bedmate did not do the same. We picked critters out of beards and hair and flicked them into the fire. Ethan was pretty good about keeping clean, but no one cared for dunking himself into cold water as much as Bob Fields and I, and we got teased plenty about it.

Bob was close to my age and sported a neat mustache and beard the color of hay long in the sun. The beard and his thick wavy hair were his pride and joy. He kept both free of vermin by washing in every halfway convenient pool and stream, even if he had to break through a thin film of ice. His most precious possessions, besides his rifle and horse, were the bone comb he passed through all that hair morning and night and little scissors with which he kept himself trimmed. "The ladies appreciate my locks," he said. Under sunlight, candlelight, or by kerosene, he shone like an angel come down from heaven.

The two of us had been in the habit of sneaking off and lowering our entire selves into cold water whenever possible. Often our only chance was at night, which, although colder, was safer. The first time I dipped my bare feet into near-freezing water I had nearly backed out on the idea. Except my head itched—my entire body itched and smelled, though I had gotten used to the smell, somewhat. My clothes were stiff with dried, salty sweat that rubbed me raw in too many places to count.

I learned to slip out of my clothes in record time and ignore feet that went numb in three or four fumbling steps. Three frantic breaths, a dunk and I came up gasping. Again! The entire process was a matter of moving fast and not stopping, even once I dressed. I slapped myself silly and pranced back to our fire, even when Forbes or someone else gave a chuckle and a knowing grin. My squad vied with one another for the most clever comment.

"You look a might chilled there," or "You been off scarin' them Yankees again?"

"Fellows, I feel so tremendous right now, so tingling with warmth and goodwill, that nothing you can say will make me feel the tiniest bit less." I held my hands out to the fire and gave the biggest, most satisfied smile I could manage, meaning every word. Getting into the freezing water was hell, but getting out was heaven.

"You know that little drummer in Preston's Brigade?" Grizzled Forbes sent a gob of well-aimed spit at a spindly mutt sniffing around our campfire. "They woke up and he was gone. Found him over by the supply wagons. Them graybacks'd carried him off to munch on at their leisure."

The only positive thing about coming winter was that the vermin died off, for the most part.

That night frost settled on our tent. I felt Ethan close behind me, my friend's steady breath on the back of my neck, breath that became a soft, rumbling snore. The warm, damp breath on my nape kept me awake. I could move, but was unable to. One of Ethan's hands curled against my back, an arm draped over my shoulder and a knee pushed into the back of my thigh. I must have been too tired, or asleep first, not to notice such things last winter. How I had to fight merely to stay in the saddle day after day sometimes frightened me.

Last winter contact with Ethan had been pleasant in some ways, in another way had made me think of Lily and try not to think of her—to little success. What would it be like to turn and hold Ethan; how would his cheek feel against mine? Would our bodies fit together face-to-face? I should not think this way.

I wanted to hold someone and be held. It had been so long.

The rangers liked following Forrest, a regimental commander as game as we were. But that fall, when Braxton Bragg replaced Beauregard as commander, Bragg transferred Forrest out. Bragg gave the command of the combined cavalry brigade to Joseph Wheeler, leaving Wharton head of the 8th Texas. The Army of Tennessee headed for Kentucky where, despite several successful charges, capture of over two hundred prisoners and weapons and retention of the battlefield, Bragg retreated to Tennessee. Rangers were assigned, once again, to cover the army's withdrawal. On October 8, Bragg finally made a stand at Perryville.

Was it laudanum, insufficient food, or hopeless repetition that gave me such lack of enthusiasm. We had lost three regimental commanders in twelve months, one in the last charge. What horses and supplies remained we took from the Yankees. Men could not be replaced.

At Perryville, it was enough to sit my horse behind the waiting infantry while artillery on both sides fired away; enough to hold my hand steady on the reins while Bandit mouthed the bit and tossed his head; enough to clench the inner muscles of my thighs, my shrunken genitals, whenever a closer, louder, round boomed and shrieked the air. The ensuing hours I saw and heard everything from the end of a hot barrel, until the air was quiet enough for my ear drums to stop reverberating from the crash of battle and rumble of artillery.

In darkness that night, both armies remained near where we had fought, the battlefield silent in gathering mist. I and other rangers who were practically barefoot searched for boots and found some of our own exhausted riders asleep among the dead.

That damn artillery had given me another headache.

October 21, 1862
Dear Papa,

May you never see me as I am at present, not having bathed or shaved for a week. Our fellows find me great entertainment when I bathe in any pool or stream we find. I expect our smell and looks could frighten the Yankees away. Considering the incompetence of our generals in this army, why else should they run? I am thankful Will found a place with the Army of Northern Virginia, where they can be proud of their victories. The duty of our rangers is to keep the Yankees off the heels of the Army of Tennessee as it retreats from another battle through no fault of the common soldier, for they are as willing as any cow to the slaughter.

If I had any sense I should throw this letter into the fire, but it is the last of my paper. We are at the last of nearly everything: ammunition, food, clothing, shelter.

Do not concern yourself; I do feel slightly better now, having vented. In truth, our rangers are more fortunate than most. I would not be in the infantry for all the coffee in the Union, which is considerably more than we have in the Confederacy. We run and steal and skirmish to survive and lose men and do it all over again. I am sorry, Papa, but you said you wanted to hear the truth. I often wonder what you wrote to Maman during the war with Mexico. Likely what I write to Berni.

On October 8 we made a stand at Perryville.

The batteries were still smoking when we rode through the infantry. Nearly one hundred guns had been firing at one another while we waited. We charged down a valley and formed columns of four to cross a bridge over a creek at the bottom. A wonder the Yankees did not blow us apart then, but the earlier bombardment pretty much emptied their cannon. We formed into five lines and charged up the hill at the federals in the woods beyond. They could not hold before us. Lt. Col. Mark Evans was mortally wounded, as well as other gallant comrades. After Perryville, Wharton was made Brigadier General.

I must stop frequently to warm my hands at the fire. The ground is white with snow. We are again covering Bragg's retreat, and the federals keep coming. Our wagons have gone ahead, so there is nothing to eat. It is always feast or famine. You should see how Southern Ladies greet us when we ride into towns. I cannot decide which is better, the food or the kisses.

A new day. Alas, self-pity does not become anyone. I shall write positively from here on.

To have such a friend as Ethan is worth everything. I have never had nor imagined such grand comrades as the men in my company. Any one of us would die for one another, and often do.

Tell Berni I love her, also Joanna and the children. Every day I pray Lucien and Will are faring well. I do not forget Betta and Marcus.

Your loving son, Adrien

What happened was preordained—like so much else that did not bear consideration.

The raids, the charges and killing had practically become routine, but the rush of adrenaline through body and mind remained strong. After so many months, individual experiences began to run together. Yet certain ones would be remembered forever.

One of our important tasks was to stop the flow of men and supplies to the federal army, the major part of which was done by rail. We had become accomplished at blowing up bridges and engines, as well as twisting rail ties so they could not be reused. In response, the federals added more and more soldiers to their trains to protect their precious cargo. Their determination and ability to resupply themselves with men, animals and weapons was as endless as Tennessee rain.

On a dreary, wet afternoon the end of September, Company K destroyed the rail fifteen miles west of Murfreesboro. We had a grand fire going in spite of the misty rain, laid the rails across the flames until red hot, then twisted them beyond use. Such a large fire was bound to attract attention, and there was barely time to complete the work before our pickets tore from the trees screaming, "Yankee cavalry!" We were outnumbered and low on ammunition, so those who weren't already mounted ran for our horses.

Bandit broke into a full gallop after Lovell's big sorrel mare, then staggered, heaved, staggered again. I kicked from the saddle to avoid getting caught beneath as my horse went to his knees and rolled. Blood pumped from his neck with pernicious regularity, and he kicked and tried to rise. I foolishly took time to caress the velvet nose and murmur in his ear what a fine fellow he was. I set my pistol behind that same ear and fired. I stood up and walked away, daring a Yankee ball to hit me. Forbes galloped by with a second horse, barely slowing so I, shotgun in hand, could swing up and gallop off with the others.

That evening in camp the sky cleared and a full, yellow moon rose between a last, few, trailing clouds. I slipped off while Ethan and the others huddled around the fire, its unsteady light making their shadows dance. I notified the picket I would return shortly, then ducked beneath dripping trees. My ramble served no purpose beyond a peculiar impulse that caused me to seek solitude, to be gone from human association, despite the cold and wet.

I wound in and out, avoiding the densest thickets, memorizing the patterns of small, open glades where moonlight fell on last year's dead grasses, weeds, bent flower stems. I followed a deer trail where it crossed my path, smelled the pine, heard the scutter of something small in the underbrush.

If it were not for the exact angle of moonlight, I would have missed it—white caught my eye, so out of place among blacks and grays. The object glowed against the dark background. I walked closer to investigate, had to pull apart a few leafless stems to see, wetting my hands and the sleeves of my wool jacket. In summer I would never have found what lay there: the skeleton of a tiny fawn. Curled up, the little skull rested upon tiny hooves as though asleep.

How was it possible the fawn was not discovered by some predator, even after death? Why weren't its bones scattered? To lie here in perfect repose through summer and half of winter until now, when I should happen to find it, the moonlight just right at this particular moment.

I froze. Held my breath, trying to understand, eyes darting among the white bones partially covered with green moss and twisted vines.

God would not speak to such as me—if there is a God. My eyes filled with tears. Images charged through my mind: a horse I had cared too much for, men blown apart, men I had killed, faces, uncounted moments come and gone.

Berni playing Chopin.

I dropped to my knees, sobbing, clutching at rotting leaves and mud.

No idea how long I huddled there. I was cold and stiff; my legs were wet to the knees and my feet were numb. Drawing a damp sleeve across my face, was I strangely lighter? Chopin would never sound the same.

I rose and stumbled, feet tingling, made my way back through the trees to camp, somehow managed the password, went straight to our tent and quickly undressed to wool underwear.

"Where were you?" Ethan said from the blankets.

"In the woods." I crawled beneath, wrapping my arms about Ethan.

"Are you . . . all right?" Ethan didn't pull away as I'd half expected, but enclosed me in his own arms.

"Yes."

Ethan's arms tightened.

"I hope you don't mind, Ethan, if I love you."

"I don't mind. I feel the same. I'd better, because you're damn cold."

"Sorry."

"Go to sleep."

❧

Adrien had dealt him a surprise card in declaring love that way. *Damn. I said as much, myself, didn't I. Did I mean it?* Adrien meant more than comradely love, and Ethan hadn't counted on that. What did he feel, besides what drew him by having Adrien's body close against his own: soaking in the smell, the growing warmth of him, the smooth muscle beneath his hand? This play had been for one thing when he started, was it something else now that Adrien had changed the game?

Ethan feared this was no longer a game.

❧

December of 1862 was the best cold month since the war began because the rangers spent the first weeks within the warm hearts and homes of Tennessee citizens—plenty of food and pretty ladies who treated them as heroes. Six hundred and ninety remained of nearly twelve hundred who had left Texas.

As Christmas neared, Federal Major General Rosecrans decided to confront their own General Bragg west of Stones River. Fortunately, volunteers arrived from Texas to fill the ranks. The rangers were again sent around the enemy's flank to create as much damage as possible.

"That is quite a fancy blue line of cavalry coming our way, Sergeant Villere." Ethan raised his voice to be heard over the hooves and firing of charging federals.

❧

I kept a firm hand on my horse as the gelding arched his neck and pulled at the bit. "They should be in range shortly, I believe, Lt. Childs." As if to prove me correct, a Minié ball whizzed past my undamaged left ear, and General Wharton screamed, "Have at 'em!" followed by simultaneous caterwauling down the line.

In seconds, our shotguns did more damage at close range than did federal rifles in the entire Yankee charge. What a rout. We took wagons, cannon, cattle, supplies, and were chased off only because so many of our own force were occupied in taking prisoners and loot to the rear.

Ethan came tearing up to Company K on his hot and lathered bay mare carrying Yankee gear, and yelled as the horse spun in a circle, "The army's falling back and we're covering the right flank."

Bob Fields spit to the side of his own mount in disgust. No other comment necessary, as one we headed off, horses pounding the earth.

I limited my thoughts to the survival of my squad and our mounts. No more speculation, judgment, or worthless self-absorption. Reflection was no way to get through this mess.

Four days after Christmas, our company was bivouacked beneath blackened, cannon-topped trees when word passed down that Lincoln had issued what he called an Emancipation Proclamation that would free all slaves on January 1.

Sergeant Alexander stretched his legs, sliding his boots closer to the fire. "I wouldn't worry much about it. Just a nice bit o' propaganda, something to get the abolitionists and slaves fired up cause the Yanks are losing so badly back east."

Most stared into the fire. Lovell was trying to write a letter by firelight. I figured we were likely all thinking the same—Yankees were winning here in the west.

Ethan hunkered next to me and sipped at what was left of our supposed coffee. Lincoln's Proclamation meant if the North should win this thing, Negroes were free. Our people were free. Or was this merely a political maneuver? Only time would tell.

Chapter Twenty-One
1863, Texas

Bernadette

L ate Sunday evening after another rainy day, my family sat in their usual places enjoying warmth from the fireplace. For the first time after Sunday dinner the children had been sent to bed without dessert, as there was no sugar, honey, or molasses. Previously when the chickens laid what I considered "extra" eggs, I had traded them for whatever we were short of. Thank the Lord our two remaining milk cows were healthy. Cotton grown on mine and Will's section was sold and gone, and I prayed the cats would keep critters out of our few remaining grain bags. Nearly all our grain had gone to supply the Confederate cavalry.

We were mostly living off what I, Joanna, and Betta had put by last fall, and I hoped that would last until new crops came in. What little passed the blockade went east to the armies or never got farther north than Houston. We still had a few beeves, but the wonderful herd that Charlie, Adrien, and Isaac had built up was nearly gone. Papa had sent three beeves and two smoked hams downriver to the military hospital in Galveston. He was determined to hang onto the bull and a few heifers so we could make a new start once the war ended.

If it ever did. I must not think that way. I mustn't.

"This morning I picked up a letter from Adrien and a copy of the *Galveston Weekly News*," Papa said from his chair by the fire.

"Papa, how could you not tell us?" Joanna said.

"I thought you both could do with a nice surprise." He opened the paper first, making us wait for the letter. "General Magruder retook Galveston on New Year's Day."

"What grand news." Joanna lay her sewing in her lap.

"I suppose you have already told Marcus, so Betta and the others know," I said.

"I saw Marcus on the way in."

Papa's behavior encouraged me to practice patience.

"Did you have any trouble on the road?" I wished he would take someone with him on his trips to town.

"No trouble. I did run into Walter Perry. Someone ran off with his milk cow and I said he could borrow one of ours as long as he needs her."

"That will leave us with only one," Joanna said.

"I believe Perry's granddaughter's child is only two," I said. "We shall manage. Perhaps with Galveston ours again, conditions will improve."

"Don't count on it," Papa said. "Union ships will likely patrol the coast outside the city."

"They had better stay out of range of our guns, hadn't they?"

"As long as we have something to fire at them."

"Oh, Papa." There were times when Papa neglected to hide the way he felt about our chances in this war, especially as it wore on. His cheekbones were more pronounced and the gray had spread farther back on his temples. Still, his dark eyes retained their sparkle, especially when his grandchildren bounded through a room and into his arms.

There must have been nothing more of note in the paper, for he had set it on the carpet and was unfolding Adrien's letter from his lap. A dark streak of something ran across the back of the last page. As usual, the writing was small and crammed into every corner of the paper, two pages this time, written on both sides. Will's and Lucien's letters were written the same way. If only Lucien had been able to stay with the militia and not been conscripted last May. *Damn those Yankees for having so much of everything. But they don't have our courage. Our determination.* I had to relax my hands which were clasped so tightly together my fingers hurt. Papa began reading.

"Adrien says they're under General Polk and received new tents and uniforms so they're ready for winter." Papa looked up. "This was written last November." He looked at the page, squinted, pulled spectacles from his inside coat pocket and put them on. "Aah." He held the page a little farther away. "Wharton's been promoted to General and Thomas Harrison is their regiment's commander." Papa smiled. "It seems that while they were outside Nashville in December, *several of the brave ladies from town slipped through Union lines with supplies.*

"*This whole month has reminded me of home for being among so many warm-hearted Tennessee folks who provide us with meals. Early in December President Davis reviewed the entire army. General John Morgan was married in nearby Murfreesboro and we had horse races, parties, and visits with hospitable citizens who opened their doors to us. Such wonderful holiday spirit among all until General Bragg returned and issued an order that accused the entire army, officers and soldiers alike, of loitering and marauding. He said parties were pernicious to discipline, efficiency, and command, and citizens must aid in suppression of the evil.*"

As Papa switched pages, I could not restrain myself. "I do not care for this General Bragg. He runs from the enemy whether his army wins battles or no, then he is sallow and hard-hearted when the men under his command find a moment to relax and enjoy themselves."

"He may have had a point, as we shall see." Papa said.

So, Papa has already read Adrien's letter.

He lifted the page in order to continue. "*On Christmas Day the main army was enjoying themselves in Murfreesboro while most of us rangers were enjoying eggnog in camp near Nolensville. Near noon a Yankee force surprised us and drove in our pickets. We quickly mounted to meet them.*"

Part of me saw the joke, the other part was angry at those few, terse words for what must have been a frightening situation.

Papa scanned the letter and began again. He was skipping parts.

"*Thus began another period of skirmishing and holding back the Union army.*"

"There's more," Papa said, "about the armies fighting at Stones River. Adrien says the rangers captured four cannon and horses one day, then the following day General Wharton and the rangers took artillery, more than two thousand prisoners and supply wagons." He scanned again. "At one point the entire regiment dismounted and faced a major federal charge with sabers drawn. Adrien says they did nothing until the enemy was nearly upon them since the only ammunition they had was buckshot for their shotguns. The Yankees stopped a few steps away and just stood there."

"Why, Papa?"

"Surprise? That the rangers didn't run? Who knows?"

"What happened?"

"The rangers fired. Adrien says the men swore at their prisoners afterward, for being so stupid as to come at them with sabers.

"He ends here, saying the paper's getting wet in the rain. He sends his love to everyone."

Papa folded the pages, stuffed them back into the envelope and sat back in his chair, closing his eyes. Silence, but for the crackling fire. I wondered about all the words Papa had skipped; words he didn't think I should hear. Words much too harsh for my delicate ears to hear, my delicate mind to encompass. I could imagine though, sitting here in front of this nice warm fire, how awful it must be in wet and cold Tennessee. I might imagine things too awful to write about.

"That's quite enough for me," Joanna said, placing her sewing into a basket next to her chair and standing. "Goodnight."

"Goodnight," we answered.

I knew Papa was limiting himself to one pipe a day, as there was not much left of his dwindling supply of tobacco. He waited until after Joanna left the room before lighting his pipe, as she didn't care for smoke. How strange to think that good tobacco had been the one thing of which we previously had plenty. A year ago, our last tobacco field had been given over to the production of grain for the army's horses.

I could talk to him about what he had left out of the letter, but what would such a thing accomplish? Papa would be upset, and I would likely feel worse knowing how awful the situation was for Adrien and, subsequently, for Will. Could my imagination be worse than reality? The last months I had seen chickens and pigs gutted and prepared for our dinners. I had never seen a man shot, though I had seen both my brothers and a few of our people bleed from cuts and other injuries. I did not like to imagine what explosions, what cannonballs, shotguns, and rifles did to a person. Not when I thought of my own brother and husband facing them.

No. I did not care to know what was in the rest of the letter.

Chapter Twenty-Two
A Baby, a Ship, and Brandy

Afternoon sun parted a few last rain clouds and poured through the lace curtains of the second-floor nursery. Jacob hoped the day would be a little less cold and damp by the time he had to leave this nice, fire-warmed room.

"Isn't he beautiful?" Lily turned and looked up at her brother, flashing a curiously vulnerable smile. "I wasn't sure at first he would be, you know, all red and wrinkled. Then you ran off so soon after."

Jacob stood next to his sister peering down at the bundle wrapped in gauzy cotton and white lace within the crib. His sister's blue eyes gazed steadily back at him from above the serious round face of her son. No one in his family had hair like that, soft and black as a raven's wing. From the photos he'd seen, neither did Garrison's. As though finding Jacob's thoughts humorous, the eyes widened, the little mouth puckered and tiny bubbles poured from between the baby's lips.

"That's his new thing. I swear, there's something new every day," Lily said, a smile in her voice.

The baby waved his pudgy little arms and kicked the bed clothes in glee.

"I think he likes you, Jacob." Lily bent over the crib. "You like your Uncle Jacob, don't you, Joshua?" More bubbles. Lily reached in to pick him up, when his face took on a startled look and a decidedly rank smell rose followed by a lusty cry that repelled Jacob a step backward.

"Mae?" Lily backed up, as well. "Mae?"

Mae must have been right outside the door, for she was quick to enter, to take up the wailing baby and retire to a rear room.

"He's got quite a pair of lungs, hasn't he?"

"He is a Hart, after all," Lily said, sitting in the nearest chair.

"Yes." Jacob said, one eyebrow raised, hands clasped behind his back. "Half Hart."

"Don't."

"Does your husband suspect?"

"I don't know. He's said nothing." Lily clasped her hands together, lowered her head. "He's been at me practically every night he's home. I think . . . I think I'm carrying again."

"The devil! Already?"

"Yes." He barely heard; she had spoken so quietly. Then she raised her head, clutched the arms of her chair and fixed her eyes on his, daring him to say another word. "I must deal with where you and Father have placed me, mustn't I. You say one day I shall be free and have power of my own. I can only hope that day comes soon."

After a decent supper of roast chicken and dumplings, nothing so extravagant as might have been expected before the Yankee blockade, Jacob and Andrew Garrison departed to the study to partake of a couple of after-dinner cigars and brandies. Garrison made himself comfortable in a leather-bound chair at one side of the unlit fireplace; Jacob stood at the opposite side, nursing his brandy. He gazed into the glass as he swirled the contents, as though hoping to foresee what might come of the next moments of this meeting. Uncanny how Garrison reminded him of his own father. He never had before. The man was too portly. His father had been adding weight until the war and its lack of sumptuous eating had slimmed him down.

The war didn't appear to have affected this man.

"That will be all, Abram," Garrison said. The ever-present servant who had lit their cigars left, closing the heavy walnut door behind him. The room suddenly felt thicker and heavier than the velvet drapes and closed windows suggested. Jacob stubbed his cigar in the nearest ashtray.

"You don't care for the cigar?"

"I must've gotten used to not having them. I suppose the sea air has cleared my lungs."

Garrison took a good puff, let the smoke roll from his lips and nostrils. "I wanted to discuss that very thing. You've become quite successful, I hear, with that ship of yours. I want space on your next return trip. Not the whole ship, mind you, merely twenty percent of your total haul. Small items, mostly. Say, perfume, silks, fine liquor, items that bring a high price for their size and weight, hardly noticeable along with what you usually bring."

"But that *is* noticeable. I would have to remove military supplies to make room. I can't do that."

"My dear boy. You can and you will. Unless you want Houston society and the entire state of Texas to suspect your sister is a whore."

A stone lodged in Jacob's throat. He would not drop the brandy glass or squeeze it too tight and break it. Or let his hand tremble. He stared at the man, aching to strike that smirk from his face. Made himself blink. Carefully placed the glass on the mantel. "You wouldn't. You would be cuckolded."

"At my age? I would not care for such a thing, but neither would your family. Which is why I ask for only twenty percent of your entire ship, something we can both live with."

"You can prove nothing."

"I wouldn't need to. Suspicion is enough. Do you think I got where I am by being a fool? I have ways of discovering what I must and learned of your two families up there in Washington County and how close you were. I even know who probably fathered her child. No matter. I'll get a son of my own on her and plenty more children before I'm done, regardless of your little family trust." He took a swallow from the brandy glass, finishing it.

"Now. Do we have a deal? Say, yes, my boy, and be done with it."

Jacob, of a sudden, needed the privy. Swallowed. "Yes."

Chapter Twenty-Three
The Safe Path

Adrien

That spring was the coldest I ever experienced. I cleaned ice from my horse's fetlocks after crossing streams and crashing through rime-covered puddles. Men huddled around campfires trying to warm their hands and feet. Arch nearly caught his stockings on fire from holding his feet too close to the hot coals.

We rangers continued raiding Yankee supplies, volunteers only, because raiding was more dangerous without a supporting army. Nevertheless, we were often successful, ambushing federal trains and removing as much track as we could. One raid resulted in thirty thousand dollars in federal cash with which Commander Wharton purchased much-needed mounts. We used Confederate script to start our fires.

I had missed that mission, but cared not.

Politics eluded me. My fellow rangers, my company, the men with whom I shared the campfire, the men next to me in battle were important, particularly the man with whom I shared warmth at night—Ethan. New Orleans and Kentucky were long ago, a different life. No one knew the truth about Papa. Or me.

My aunt had never written. Any written word from her would be dangerous. I had begun to wonder about them. She had been kind, more than kind. They all had. If I ever got back there, again, I might look them up. Would I dare?

"Soaking up the May sun?" Ethan came upon me lounging on my back in the sun on one of our two blankets.

"Caught me," I said, squinting up at my friend's face. My slouch hat lay upturned on the blanket at my side where I hoped it would finally air out, like my shirt and the rest of my damp clothing hanging from a tree nearby.

"Mind if I join you?"

I moved over to give Ethan room on the now-warm blanket. "You don't have to ask, you know." My heart fluttering at the sight of his long-limbed lanky self standing there in the sunlight. As long as we were busy playing soldier, everything was fine. But give us a little time to relax, to be ourselves, and my heart raced.

Ethan made himself comfortable. "I could've shoved you aside, I suppose."

"Just don't block my sun." *Christ, I wish he had shoved me.*

Ethan leaned back on his elbows, raised his face to the sky and closed his eyes. "Wouldn't think of it." After a moment, "Want to tell me what's in your letter? You know how nosey I am since I hardly get news of my own. I'd like to give that 'Beast Butler' what for right now."

"I'll bet your mother has found a way to do that for you." *I have no idea what I am saying.*

"I hope she's held her tongue. From what I hear he'd throw her in jail and throw away the key. The man has no manners and is certainly no gentleman."

"I mean, from what I saw of her, she'll likely have him wrapped around her little finger." *In spite of this war, or because of it, I'm caught up again and no longer care I swore I would never be.*

Ethan's lips crept up into a half smile. "Now wouldn't that be something?"

I lay back flat and raised my letter above my face. "Let's see. Papa says my brother's a lieutenant with Sibley's Brigade. That's the same man that served under Magruder to retake Galveston last January. They're in Louisiana now under General Taylor. Papa's growing food and grain for the army and is paid in Confederate currency."

"Lord," Ethan said, "I suppose he'll use that to start his fires come this winter."

"He says they're managing mostly because they grow their own food, which is scarce for most folks since Yankee gunboats are still in the Gulf attempting to blockade any ship that tries to get through. He says plenty do get through, though any supplies are taken by Galveston and Houston or sent east." My arms dropped. "We haven't seen any of it." I stared at a passing cloud to avoid looking at him, for the fear of revealing this fluttering fluster inside.

"Nope. Rangers are so tough we live on air and leather."

"I thought it was air and gumption."

"That, too."

Arch Lovell trotted up, throwing his shadow across our feet. "You fellas heard? There's been a battle back East at a place called Chancellorsville. We won, but dang if 'Stonewall' Jackson ain't been killed. Shot by his own pickets."

Ethan sat up. "You sure? This isn't some rumor?"

"No rumor. Got it straight from Major Harrison."

"Damn."

Chapter Twenty-Four
Advance and Retreat

In June the rangers again protected General Bragg's army as it retreated from Middle Tennessee. Ethan thought if he ever wrote a memoir about his war experience, he would call it "Advance and Retreat."

"Wake me when something happens." Adrien pulled his hat down over his eyes and slumped in the saddle. It was not long before fitful snoring could be heard from under there.

Ethan pulled his horse up to watch his men ride by, and nearly half of them were dozing in the saddle. They'd been up for three days and nights chasing Yankees. If he wasn't first lieutenant, he'd join them. He was too exhausted to do anything but sleep whenever he had the chance.

In the middle of July, they camped on Silver Creek near the pretty little town of Rome, Georgia, where the earth was so red it appeared the blood of the armies had already soaked it.

They were down to four hundred twelve men and finally eating well, though local farmers squeezed whatever they could out of the rangers for provisions. They supplied themselves, as next to nothing came from the Confederate government. Many resorted to buying local horses whenever available. They bought with cash and traded with loot taken from Yankees, including clothing, footwear, arms, ammunition, food, tobacco, liquor, even spectacles. Though the men had seen little or nothing of their pay, they took up a collection and presented General Wharton with a brand new thousand-dollar Mexican saddle.

The rangers made the most of their fine camp near town, visiting, relaxing, and eating heartily while they could. To top it all, a tent revival was planned that Sunday afternoon between camp and town. Revivals were nearly as popular as horse racing, minstrel, and variety shows. Ethan, after a cool wash and swim in Silver Creek with the rest of the company, shaved in front of a mirror perched in the fork of an ash. "Come with me. Revivals can be fun."

Adrien, clean and pink-faced from his own wash and recent shave, was buttoning up a fresh shirt. Ethan and the men had finally convinced him to accept a Second Lieutenant's commission, as long as, like the rest of them, he needn't wear any bars or such. "No thank you. I am Catholic, remember? We are much too demure for all that fire and brimstone stuff. Haven't you had enough saving from Reverend Buntline? Besides, I am going to see that barber in Company C for a haircut." His hair was down to his shoulders, which did make him look a mite wild.

"There will be ladies there." Maybe the sight of a lovely lady or two would take Adrien's mind off whatever had been at him for the past months.

"I wondered why you were going and getting so handsomed up, as well," Adrien said with a smile from one side of his mouth.

"And what is your excuse?"

"The war between the graybacks and the fleas is keeping me up at night, and I want no more complaints from you as to my odor—not if you are going to smell so sweet."

Later that afternoon, Ethan found Adrien reading beneath the shade of the same ash. The revival had been fine, a grand way to let off steam because the preacher had been one of the positive ones praising God's love in these hard times. He wished Adrien had been there. Afterward the ladies had been more than happy to meet the Texas heroes.

"Her name is Katherine Wheatley, and she has invited both of us to dinner tonight. She has a sister." Katherine was also pretty—and so clean she sparkled.

"My, you have been busy."

"It's all very proper. Her mother and father will be there, as well as a younger brother."

"How old is this sister?"

"I don't know. We'll get a home-cooked meal."

That decided him, as Ethan knew it would.

The house was whitewashed clapboard with a front porch, and the sister looked about eleven years old. Adrien didn't seem to mind. In fact, he and little Marjorie appeared to have a fine time. The girl was small, pale, and delicate, but precocious, and had the energy of a busy bee. It was obvious the whole family adored her, including the shy little brother, Harry. Katherine took after her mother, self-assured, dark, and lovely. Ethan realized after this second meeting that he could be in trouble for how much he already admired her. He had never been so taken with a person of the opposite sex, certainly not on such short acquaintance. Was it possible this was why he had so stupidly joined up? Was he meant to meet this young woman?

Theirs was not a fancy plantation house, but neither was it poor. Mr. Wheatley made a living from minor investments in cotton and sugar, and a small additional income from writing articles and texts on biological science.

"Bugs and buds, as my dear wife likes to say, and I do study the little things." He was nearly six feet, large-boned and stocky with thick hands and fingers. It was difficult to imagine him handling such small objects as insects and seeds, until they saw him pick up a tiny spotted beetle from his collection and hold it delicately in his fingertips.

Riding back to camp, Adrien admitted he had nearly asked Wheatley about their own problem with vermin.

"I'm glad you didn't," Ethan said. "He'd likely never let us enter his house again."

"That was precisely why I said nothing. There must be a way to come at it in a round-about manner so that he will not suspect we often carry the little devils on our own persons, although we take care not to bring them into his home."

"It's not worth the risk. Do you find washing our equipment every other day that much of a problem? Or is it showing off your manly physique in the creek you dislike so much?"

"The only reason you have not yet made major is because you are so irritating."

"I thought it was because of gambling."

"As if such a thing mattered in this outfit."

What matters to me? Ethan thought, gazing somewhere a foot past his horse's nodding ears. Is my head trying to keep me from getting into trouble again by steering me toward the safe and proper path of involvement with a young woman? Is this real, or am I fooling myself? A life with Katherine would be so much easier. He refused to let himself look toward Adrien, who remained silent for the rest of the ride.

※

August in Georgia was a time for dozing away hot afternoons beneath large, shady trees or soaking in the nearby river. On cooler mornings Ethan and Adrien took care of their horses, mended clothing and equipment, and attempted to solve problems among the men. Usually, such problems had something to do with too much to drink the night before, whether it be a tender head, stomach, or broken toe from tripping over a rock.

Evenings they were in camp for barbecues or joined the Wheatleys for dinner.

Ethan had previously accepted the possibility of going through life alone. Since the war, he had not imagined anything beyond the day at hand. He had recently begun considering "when this is over," whatever that might mean. Because of Katherine Wheatley. The whole family, really. They made him believe in the possibility of something more. Something he wanted. Was it too much to ask for a fine woman, a home and family? Maybe children one day? He would be happy to give up gambling to make something of the peach orchard behind their house or raise beans and cotton. All he need do was ask her. He was pretty sure she would accept him.

They were riding over there when Adrien woke him from his dreaming. "It is your turn to tell me what is going on in your head, Ethan, although I believe I know."

"Then why don't you tell me." He'd been more desperate to hear what Adrien thought than he'd realized.

"You have strong feelings for Katherine Wheatley."

Ethan tucked his chin, rocked forward in the saddle, back. God, why did he feel fifteen?

Adrien laughed. "I never thought to see such a thing." He reached over and slapped Ethan's thigh. "Have you told her how you feel?"

"Not in words, exactly. I am thinking on it." He was half relieved and half disappointed by Adrien's reaction.

"Rangers are known to be men of action, Ethan. *Carpe diem*."

"It's difficult, when I don't know. . . . What if I don't survive this thing. It wouldn't be fair to her."

"I think she is the kind of woman who would like to make that decision for herself."

Ethan turned to look at him. "I thought you weren't paying attention."

"I always pay attention to pretty women."

Ethan watched him, his profile nodding slightly with his horse's gait, and Adrien turned, dark, liquid eyes on his. "What?"

"Nothing." Surely, it was nothing. He hadn't expected Adrien to be aware, to be so, accepting. What a strange notion. Why wouldn't he? They had never discussed the future, as though it might bring bad luck. Although he had daydreamed more than once while riding along in silence or before falling asleep at night—and dreaming mad, lustful dreams.

That evening he and Katherine slipped away onto the back porch. He had earlier asked her father and received permission—now he must ask Katherine, before he lost his nerve. She stood with her hands resting lightly on the porch rail, gazing toward the yard, he wasn't sure at what. The breeze changed; he smelled peaches too long in the sun. Wisps of loose, dark hair lifted from around her left ear.

"Katherine," he said, and she turned, dark eyes catching his, making his breath catch in his throat. He could love her. He would love her more as time went on. "I have saved enough back home in New Orleans to get us started," he said. "To fix up the orchard, and your father approves." *I'm not saying this in the right order.* "I mean . . . I haven't much, but enough for a start, I think. Once the war is over. We'll have our own place. Here. In town. If you'll have me, that is." He took her hands. "Will you marry me, Katherine?"

"Yes," she said.

Simple and direct. *His* Katherine. He kissed her, more lightly than he had kissed any other woman and, after a moment, her lips pushed more firmly against his. He thrilled a bit at that.

On a Sunday afternoon, Mr. and Mrs. Wheatley gave them a rousing engagement barbecue that spread its joy from the back porch onto the lawn and into the neglected peach orchard. General Wharton attended along with Company K and friends of the Wheatleys. Neighbors and rangers supplied the victuals, libations, and music, which consisted of a banjo, a fiddle, an overturned bucket, numerous spoons, other homemade contraptions, and Alfred Peercott's coonhound. Old Barney was the last of the pack, and no one had the heart to drag him away from such pure enjoyment in his own sound.

Chapter Twenty-Five
My Friend

Adrien

Nearly everyone danced with everyone else, including the children. I recalled all the fancy steps I had learned and gave the
ladies, young and old, a thrill, especially little Miss Marjorie. She lured
me out to the back porch for lemonade and declared I should marry
her after the war.

"You are too young to think of marriage, Miss Marjorie," I said,
taking a long, deep drink of Mrs. Wheatley's lemonade, nice and tart
the way I liked it.

"In two years, I will be fourteen, nearly the same age as my mother
when she married my father. The war may last until then. This way, we
can all stay together, all four of us."

She innocently looked up at me, both hands on her half-empty
glass.

"Let us not believe the war should last so long."

"I will wait for you, no matter how long."

"Do not wait for me, Marjorie. So many young men more worthy
will want your hand."

"But they shall not have it, for it will always be yours, forever
and ever. You will see, when you return with Ethan." She flounced off
toward the others, glass in hand, black curls bouncing.

Why did I attract such strong-minded females?

I stood there awhile, lemonade in hand, and listened to the music
and happy voices inside. Ethan was to be married. Ethan had found

himself a lovely young lady and a family, home, orchard . . . a future. *I am happy for him. Why this numbness, this sense of isolation beneath my smiles and good humor? I am going through the motions. I must. He is my friend.*

Chapter Twenty-Six
Texas

Details

Jacob and Colt left Houston at dawn by rail and four hours later arrived in Chappell Hill where they unloaded their horses, had a quick bite to eat and rode fifteen miles home. Not so long ago the trip would have taken all day by riverboat, which would have been more comfortable and given Jacob time to think. Though having more time to think was questionable. He would rather sail *Sea Hawk* into a federal artillery barrage than face his father with his current news.

His father expected Lily and her baby, but anyone who had known Adrien as a baby would suspect him as the true father of Lily's child, despite the blue eyes.

Jacob dismounted in the yard where the grass had been worn away by previous horses and handed Colt the reins. "Get yourself dinner. I won't be needing you for the next few days." He removed his hat as he went up the wide steps to the veranda, ran his fingers through his sweaty hair and turned to gaze at the scattered oaks and rolling hills spread before him, picked cotton fields defining more than half the horizon. To his right were the stable and paddocks, the few horses left grazing, their tails swishing at flies. So much had changed with the war, but the land hadn't. Anxiety he had carried for days settled. This was his home and always would be.

The door behind him opened and Henry stood beneath the arched glass portico. "Suh?" he said. "We all's heard you ride up. Masta be waitin' in the library."

Father's impatience hadn't changed either. No time to clean up. Get right on in here and answer for yourself.

He went. If they heard him ride up, where were his wife and children?

Father stood behind his desk in stark profile against the afternoon light, gazing out the French doors, an ever-present cigar in his mouth. Its rank smell permeated the room.

"I wasn't expecting you until week's end. Where is Lily and my grandson?" He had removed the cigar but still faced the glass-panel doors.

"I wanted to discuss an important matter before they arrived."

He did turn now, a lower eyelid trembling. "Could this matter have to do with the fact that our profits haven't risen with the price of cotton, but lowered?"

"Yes."

"This had better be good."

No acceptable reason, and there was no way to make one sound so. "It's Lily's husband, Garrison."

"By God, what's he got to do with a loss in profits?" His father crushed the cigar out as though he'd like it to be someone's head, maybe his son's. Jacob noticed how stubby his fingers were and the weight he had regained since he'd seen him last March.

"Garrison used blackmail to take twenty percent of our space on every return voyage."

"Blackmail! How blackmail? Are you mad?"

He was relieved there was a large desk between him and his father. "Lily's child. It's not his and he knows it. He's threatened to expose her."

"Not his?" Louder, "not his?" His father leaned forward, stiff-armed, both fists on the desk. "A month early, but how dare he? How can he possibly?"

Jacob watched his father slowly straighten, his eyes seeing nothing, his mind seething with possibility. "Whose is it?" He jerked, as though shoved, face reddening. "No, don't tell me." His entire body bristled, virtually swelled like a balloon. "I know whose it is." He pounded the desk, making inkstand and pen jump. "God damn him," he spat, face twisted and running with sweat. "That insufferable, skulking, son of a bitch. I knew he was trouble." He stood still, as though to quiet himself, but lost the attempt. "All my plans, God damn him." He grabbed, picked up the heavy desk chair and slammed it down. "I'll kill him. I'll hang that goddamned son of a—"

His father went rigid, clutched at the left side of his blouse, coat askew. He staggered, fell forward half on the desk, flinging an arm and knocking the cigar and ashtray to the floor. His face went entirely red, then paled as he pitched to the Aubusson rug. He lay there on his back, gasping, all but head and shoulders hidden behind the desk.

Jacob hadn't moved, disbelieving what he saw. This power, this master of all before him, down there, eyes bulging, grimacing mouth sucking air, right hand clawing at the left side of his blouse.

I should do something. But Jacob stood, watching. He had been ten, the first time his father had slapped him in the face; twelve, the first time he realized the man beat his mother; the first—so many firsts. He didn't know if it was fear or rage that kept him where he stood, frozen to the floor.

His father's body suddenly came to a shuddering halt, relaxing, one hand dropping with a soft *thuf* to the carpet. Jacob crept over, as though the man might jump up and thrash him. He slipped around the edge of the desk so he could see his father right side up, all of him lying there, from his black shoes to the top of his head. He went to one knee and hesitantly lay two fingers to feel for a pulse—he couldn't recall the last time he had touched the man. Nothing. Placed his ear near his mouth. No breath.

Jacob rose to his feet, gazed out the doors as his father had done moments before.

What did he feel? Relief. Shouldn't he feel something more for a father who had died? Nothing more but slight trepidation for what he now faced. He thought of his mother, hoped there was no afterlife so she wouldn't have to put up with the man again.

Lots to do. Colt wouldn't get his three days off, after all.

"Mistress Hart be under the weather and gone to see her mam, and took Nell and the children with her." Nell, the children's wet nurse, went everywhere the children did, Henry told Jacob the moment he found the servant waiting outside his father's study. He would check on his family after completing his duties here.

"Have a man fetch the doctor, Henry. You may as well tell the others: my father has . . . expired." The only response from the man was widening of his eyes. Jacob expected there would be little wailing for this master's death, and damn if he would pay out coins to make such wailing happen at the graveside. "Find someone to help you carry him down to the cellar." Fortunately, a cool cellar had been dug under the back section of the house when it was built years ago.

Jacob couldn't leave now. He'd send Colt to fetch Lily and the child, as he'd have to fetch his wife and children, or see if she was able to return for the funeral. There would have to be an announcement, as people from all over the county would want to attend. What a bother. He would have to make certain that everyone understood he was now master of Hartwood Plantation. Which also meant a thorough search of all of Father's papers and a meeting with his lawyers as soon as possible. He should have been kept apprised of everything all along, but Father never expected to die so suddenly. He had likely thought himself immortal.

Jacob returned to the library, went behind the desk and sat down. The cleaned ashtray and humidor sat on the right corner. Daguerreotypes of himself, Will, and Lily sat in the front middle of the desk, which surprised him with a momentary risk of dampness to his eyes, a slight clutch in his chest. *That's all you'll get, you old goat.* A lamp, inkpot, and pen to the left. Jacob placed both hands on the edge and glanced around the room at a view he'd never seen, natural light coming from behind him. The morning sun would be in any visitors' faces, as he well knew from experience. The old reprobate left nothing to chance.

There had to be something in his files he could use against Garrison. Old Randolph would have checked Garrison out before accepting him as a son-in-law. Elbows on the desk, he stroked his chin with his right hand. *A man who used blackmail will have at least one skeleton in his closet, and I will find it.*

❧

"I can't believe he's gone," Lily said. The funeral had been over for some hours and everyone had left except for Paien Villere and Bernadette, whom Jacob had asked to stay for dinner. Joanna had remained home at Blue Hills with her children, and his wife was still with her parents. He would head out there tomorrow to see what was keeping her. The four were in the parlor sitting at the coffee table with cups of tea, the afternoon sun diffused by drawn lace curtains.

Jacob placed his cup on the table. "Why don't you have Joshua brought down, Lily? I expect he's had a long-enough nap. You'll never get him to sleep later if you don't wake him now."

Lily smiled. "Jacob thinks he knows more about babies than I do because his wife's had two. Men assume a great deal from little actual experience."

Jacob gave her a smile.

"I would love to see him, Lily," Berni said, eyes sparkling with enthusiasm.

Lily glanced at Jacob, then ordered a maid to bring down the child. Jacob suspected she knew what he was up to, but didn't know why. Berni would likely be clueless, but Paien would surely notice. Jacob was counting on it, for what he had in mind.

The maid brought Joshua down and placed the silent baby in Lily's arms. She sat in her chair while Berni made her way to Lily's side. "He's lovely," she said, beaming and raising her hands as if to catch him rising above Lily's lap. "I've never seen such a beautiful baby. I do hope his eyes stay that wonderful blue. Your eyes, Lily, they're yours. And such dark hair and long lashes. My goodness. He's smiling at me."

Jacob watched Paien navigate the coffee table, stand behind Berni, bend and look over her shoulder. He saw Paien stiffen, clasp his hands behind his back, hard. Paien swiveled ever so slightly and caught his eye. There was nothing else on his face to show he'd noticed anything, but the keenness in his eyes was enough to pin Jacob to his chair. That look said: You were waiting for this, now dare to tell me what you mean by it.

Paien's was not the blustery anger of Jacob's father, but one seldom stirred and possibly all the more dangerous. Jacob hadn't counted on this. But his plans would be all the better for that sort of strength—if he played his cards right. He wasn't much of a gambler, so he was going to do everything possible to stack the deck in his favor.

Jacob rose from his chair. "Paien, why don't you and I retire to the library and let the ladies coo over my nephew. I've something I'd like to discuss with you that I'm sure they would find utterly boring."

"Lead the way. I would like to hear what you have to say, and I'm sure I won't find it the least boring."

Jacob felt Paien at his back the entire distance, as though a knife might slice him any moment. How dare Paien make him feel this way? It was Paien's son who was at fault. Jacob had merely pointed out the transgression—with Paien's daughter present and unknowing.

He didn't close the door. Paien did. Jacob hastened to the sideboard where Father had kept his liquor. "A whiskey? My father kept a fine bourbon. There's also—"

"Bourbon it is. Straight."

He poured two, turned and gave one to Paien. Each drank.

"You need not say he's Adrien's son," Paien said. "Come to the point."

"I want nothing but what's best for the child and Lily. The problem is Lily's husband. He knows who the true father is. Garrison is blackmailing me with exposing Lily. I need to find something on him, something to keep him quiet. It'll take time and maybe money for an investigator if I can't find what I need in Father's papers." He took another drink and the few steps to sit half on top of the desk, one leg dangling.

Paien stood in place, brows furrowed, boots planted. The glass of bourbon remained half full and steady in his right hand.

"If I do get something on Garrison, I don't know how he will react. I never thought he was the sort of man. . . . I made a mistake. So did Father. I don't want Lily to pay. If she has to—leave him, I want her to have a safe place here, for her and the child.

"My wife is ill and at her mother's. I may have to bring the children home to Hartwood. But I can't stay here all year, Paien. I have to make sure our cotton gets through; there is no one else. It's why my father sent me. You're the only one in this entire county I trust." He paused, took a breath. "I want you to take my father's place here at Hartwood."

He had surprised Paien with that one. The man swallowed and remained silent, slowly turned the glass in his hand.

"Consider what I ask." Jacob set his nearly empty glass on the desk and stood up. Keeping his gestures strong, never begging, he continued in a firmer tone. "I can afford to send men to help at Blue Hills. I'll pay you and them. That will help keep Blue Hills running, too. Once I get rid of what Garrison's costing us, I'll cut you in for ten percent of whatever we make on cotton, and we're making a lot. You'll come out of this war better than you went in. Think of your grandson, and what you're leaving Lucien and Adrien."

"Do not presume to tell me who to consider, Jacob."

"No, sir." Never push this man.

"Twenty percent and you will put this in writing."

He hadn't expected bargaining from Paien, but he should have. "Of course."

"You are exchanging gold and war goods, not Confederate currency."

"Absolutely."

"There are details to work out." Paien looked into his glass of whiskey, as though the details might be found there.

"There are."

"All right."

"Thank you." Thank God. Everything had depended on this. Jacob felt breath go out of him, breath he hadn't known he'd held. He held out his hand.

Paien took it. They finished off their whiskeys.

Chapter Twenty-Seven
Fine as Cream Gravy

Bernadette

They were waiting when I entered the Hive, with a complete stillness that struck me as odd considering the usual activity that took place there. An old man and a boy, barely sixteen by the look of him, with a pistol hanging backward on his left hip that appeared so huge on him it might slip with a thud to the floor. Someone had pounded an extra hole in the belt to make it fit. He held his hat in his hand, the other hand clutched the barrel of a rifle, its stock on the wide pine floorboards. The old man, his grandfather I'd been told, held a larger rifle in the crook of his left arm, hat also in hand.

"Pleased to meet ye, Mrs. Hart," the grandfather said. His eyes were a sharp, steely blue, and belied his age. "Mr. Jacob Hart said we was to look out for ye and yours while Mr. Villere ain't about. We may not look like much, but me and my grandson here muster up else he wouldn't've sent us. Name's Tainter. Ye can call me Amos. This here's Gid, short for Gideon. He a mite shy so don't say much, but he been handlin' firearms since he was knee high to a grasshopper. Jus' show us where we lay our bones for shut-eye now and then, and feed us what you do your nigras and I reckon we be fine as cream gravy."

I hardly knew what to say. Bernadette Villere Hart, at a loss for words. "Thank you, Mr.—Amos. Betta will show you to one of our cabins. Or the bunkhouse, if you prefer."

"What's closer to the house be better for our purpose, ma'am."

"A cabin then."

I discovered later they chose the cabin closest to the house, the one with the stain on the door.

Chapter Twenty-Eight
Ride Like the Devil

Adrien

I found dissembling expedient.

Maman used to say that if you truly love someone you want their happiness, even above your own. Katherine will make a perfect wife for Ethan, and he will have the orchard and another smaller house and property to the west. *I am happy for him.*

"We're breaking camp," Ethan said. "Rosecrans is on the move." He had come from the headquarters tent, and I noticed other officers hurrying beyond our little group. The sun hadn't risen but most of Company K were huddled around fires for breakfast. What had been a quiet early morning was now an anthill stirred by a stick.

"We'll hold them." I gulped down what remained of my coffee. Empty words and I knew it. The rangers might hold, but General Bragg had done nothing but retreat since he had taken over. Ethan was worried about Katherine and her family. We saddled up beneath a copse of fluttering birch trees before Ethan revealed what was on his mind. He shoved his shotgun into its scabbard, picked up the reins and slung one long leg over the saddle. "Mrs. Wheatley has a married sister near Columbia, South Carolina. They're prepared to move the entire household there for a while."

I figured my friend was under considerable strain regarding his new fiancé, and was assuring himself as much as anyone that the Wheatleys would be safe. My recently acquired temperamental Yankee mare was tossing her head and spinning as I mounted, or I might have said something more to reassure him. Though I had no idea what.

We joined the regiment as it swung out ahead of the infantry, drumming the air and trampling dry grass.

From that day on we 8th Texas Rangers skirmished with Rosecrans's troops in Lookout Mountain passes in an attempt to keep the federals from following Bragg into Georgia. In mid-September, we sideslipped around the federal right flank near Chickamauga Creek to meet newly arrived Longstreet's Corps of the Army of Northern Virginia.

Longstreet had a reputation—he didn't run. How he would do under Bragg was anyone's guess. Along with Longstreet came Hood's Texas Division, and I wasted no time seeking my friend from home.

"Captain William Hart? That's his regiment over yonder. He rides a large brown gelding."

"Captain Hart, *sir*, may I have a word with you, *sir*." I saluted from the back of my black mare.

"Adrien, I'll be!"

We dismounted in order to clasp arms and pound one another's backs.

"What a fine beard and mustache you have grown upon your face, Will."

"Keeps me warmer in winter." Will stroked his beard with the palm of his right hand and smiled. "You are still clean-shaven."

"Mine did not come in so thick and curly as yours, and all that hair only leaves more hiding places for little critters. I would cut off the hair on my head, only I fear the ladies would no longer smile my way."

"The only worry you ever had from the ladies was keeping them off, you miscreant."

I took a step back and cocked my head. "How are you? You look healthy and handsome as a peacock. The fur makes you appear quite distinguished."

"I'm fine, though not so fine as I would be if I had the company of my wife. I have not had a furlough since this thing began."

"Me neither."

"We've heard the 8th Texas is unruly. Though you're the only western regiment the Army of Northern Virginia considers worthy."

"Worthy, are we?"

"Longstreet wants you with us. Everyone knows how you've been all over Tennessee and Kentucky protecting Bragg's army and harassing Yankees."

"The men in the lines fight as hard as anyone. Give them a commander like Longstreet or Lee and see the result." I shifted my feet. "We would welcome fresh horses and those new guns."

"The repeaters? So would we."

I grinned and lay a hand on Will's shoulder. "I'll let you know when we latch onto a few."

"You're different, and thin as a rail."

"I'm older, as you are. And you've got little meat on your bones." A wisp of melancholy dragged at me. "I expect war changes a man."

Will looked at me as he would at a stranger, or as if I'd risen from the dead. "I expect it does," he said.

Momentarily drained of emotion, we stood facing one another, arms dangling, as though mesmerized by some thought neither could speak.

Someone shouted a sharp order to move on, and the brigades began to separate and move away. Will straightened, as though waking. "The war doesn't wait for us."

I squeezed Will's shoulder. "Take care, Will," and added a quick hug.

"I will. You also—take care." Will mounted, leaned down for a hand clasp, and I watched him ride off, his horse kicking up clods of red mud. Ages ago, another time, Will had ridden off in the heat, after asking for Berni's hand—and asking me to meet with Lily.

Lord, I hope she is happy. The raw despair when Lily had first entered my thoughts had been replaced by residual sadness, which I suppose was progress of some sort.

The following day, we rangers charged the enemy's right and either wounded or captured over one hundred members of Crook's brigade. We joined Bragg's army and chased Rosecrans and his army through McFarland's Gap back to Chattanooga.

"We cannot rest on our laurels," Captain Freeman said. "Our duty lies in keeping the Yankees from supplying Rosecrans."

The rest of September and into October, under 8th Texas Commander Wharton, we repeatedly crossed the river and raided into Tennessee and Alabama, capturing and destroying supplies and resupplying ourselves with food, horses, ammunition, and, as I hoped, a number of the new Spencer repeating rifles. By the end of nearly two months of fighting, seven hundred men of Wheeler's entire cavalry command were lost and over thirty rangers killed or missing. Among those killed was fellow Washington County volunteer Ludus Grubb from my squad. Grubb had been a quiet sort, unnoticed for the most part and no one's particular chum. Though any one of us would have risked his life for the young man. Now his absence was noticed as the first one of our squad to go. The rest, men and horses, were worn out.

In November, we landed in Ringgold, Georgia, joining hundreds of refugees from Tennessee and Kentucky, mainly starving women and children. By late November, we bivouacked back in Chattanooga. In all the previous months, I had not seen Will, as Longstreet and Wharton had been deployed in widely different directions.

She is so lovely, the sun in her hair, reflecting on her creamy complexion—

"Wake up sweetheart. You have the most appealing look on your face."

I squinted, wiped the gumminess from my eyes with the back of my hand. Ethan, grizzly with frosted three-day beard, a lock of greasy hair over one eye, grinned down at me.

"Up, or I'll pull the blanket. We've got orders to move out." His words trailed steam in the frozen air.

"Huh?"

"You didn't really think we were going to rest here for long, did you?"

Rest. I had one definition before the war, now I had another.

I threw my saddle onto my horse, a gray with dark mane and tail, bad luck. I would stand out among all the darker horses. I pushed my knee against the gray's ribs and pulled hard on the cinch. Politicians, civilians, ranted about morality, the union and states' rights. For me the war was simple: What is for breakfast; is my horse shod and healthy; how far do we ride today; when do we stop? I ambled over to a stump, picked up my tin cup and knocked it upside down against my hand to remove whatever might have settled inside overnight, and joined the others at the fire.

Doby pulled the end of his nose between thumb and forefinger. "Say, Slick, you know him best, that a grimace or grin on Childs's face?" They'd all taken to calling me Slick, ever since I'd let slip it'd been my childhood nickname. Ethan came ambling up to the fire, and it sure enough looked like a grin. He'd been at the officers' meeting and I wondered what he had to grin about.

"Bragg's ordered us out from under Wharton, boys. We're to join Longstreet and attack Knoxville."

"Son of a gun!" J. J. Petty slapped his hat against his thigh. There was murmuring all around, as though bees had joined our squad.

Along with us went parts of the Texas Brigade, including the 1st Texas with Captain William Hart.

Longstreet made quite a ruckus heading north into Tennessee. I thought it would be a fine thing to write Berni that me and Will had made a charge together, but things didn't turn out that way. Instead, we rangers led a charge with the 11th Texas, and fought forward through cannon until exhausting our ammunition. The federals ran and kept running right on into Knoxville where Fort Sanders protected them.

All day we rangers were put to chopping trees in an effort to blockade boats supplying the city. It would have taken better woodsmen than us horsemen to chop down enough logs to block the wide Tennessee River.

"I could have been wasting time better than this." I slumped down on a stump and watched a loaded barge push its way past floating logs. As far distant as the boat was, the nearly full moon made for clear sighting of the goings-on. "A few good marksmen could do more damage," I added, and picked at the new calluses on my left hand.

Ethan sat on the ground next to me. "Wouldn't stop them."

I sighed mightily. "Shit."

"You're in a hell of a mood."

"The 1st Texas was in camp today, while we were chopping trees."

Ethan put a hand on my knee. "Maybe in the morning."

In the morning, Longstreet sent wave after wave of willing men against Fort Sanders. The Texas Brigade and the 1st Texas advanced over broken terrain and felled timber, piling up dead and wounded in a watery ravine before the few left alive managed to plant their flag at the fort's wall before retreating.

I rode in from a morning scout around the outskirts of the army when a sergeant from Company D jogged up. "An orderly's been askin' after you. You know a Captain Hart from the 1st Texas?"

"Yes." My heart jumped.

"He was brought in to the field hospital."

I ran, asking, this way, that way, then I saw the hospital tents, smelled them—made me recall the ride in the ambulance wagon with Ethan. *Don't think of that now.* "Officers, 1st Texas, where?"

"The charge?" someone said, his blouse covered in fresh blood. "Too many. That tent, officers, I think. They're a bit mixed up, though maybe. . . ."

I was already running.

Men lay lined up like corpses on the ground outside tents, despite the cold. Other men were sitting about holding themselves stoically, or rocking, healthy ones rushing back and forth carrying things: pots of water; linen—some clean, some stained bloody; a fellow in baggy clothes pushed a wheelbarrow full of tangled body parts; a nurse in a gray dress, her white starched apron splashed bright red and brown. There was ragged screaming farther along.

I ducked into the tent. Darker in here and the odor stronger. Six cots, all occupied—the man in the far right one was mumbling.

Will was first on the left, his cot above a pool of blood, right boot missing, wool sock halfway off and dangling. Two neat holes the size of gold buttons breached his chest. Slack lips had drooled bright red into his new beard. His once warm brown eyes stared up as though seeing through the canvas to heaven.

I dropped to my knees and took Will's hand. Breathed in deep, shuddered out. With my other hand I stroked Will's forehead once, kissed him there—he was still warm—and closed his eyes. Started to recall . . . no, I wouldn't. Couldn't bear the past. I would be here with Will, right now. No past. Only now. *Dear God, why Will and not me?*

"We got to ride like the devil, boys," Captain Freeman said. "Rosecrans has whipped Bragg and chased him from Chattanooga, and General Sherman's army's between us and Georgia." This time we were surrounded by the enemy, and we and our horses were exhausted.

Ethan and I rode with forty-three men out of originally over a hundred. Our squad of ten was nine. Rangers acted as scouts, rode around the infantry as moving pickets and foraged, night and day. At night it was sometimes below freezing, yet we crossed and recrossed streams and rivers, sliding and breaking through ice.

By December we had foraged the valleys to emptiness and scoured colder mountain trails where local Yankee sympathizers could pick us off from trees or cliffs. Since losing Bandit, I had had three horses killed under me and no longer named them. When had I last slept for more than three hours straight?

Freezing dry cold was better than rain. Wet cold seeped into my bones even when I rode, making them brittle. One must get close enough to a fire to singe one's britches, creating wafts of steam. There was nothing like the pleasure of drinking chicory coffee while steaming a damp sock over a hot fire, my frozen foot inside, tingling out of numbness. Only now we practically never camped, seldom got a fire, and generally slept on horseback. We napped when we could, unless we were on point or scouting along the sides or rear of the column.

I was dozing in the saddle, one eye half open to gray early morning light from my left when I felt a poke from my right.

"Happy Christmas." Ethan.

"Happy Christmas." I opened both eyes and saw the brown rolling rump of Forbes's horse over the nodding ears of my own mount. "Happy Christmas, Forbes."

"Yeah? Happy Christmas. Happy Christmas, Fields."

Happy Christmas, repeated, fading, on up the foggy line.

Early morning the day after Christmas we joined the 11th Texas and 3rd Arkansas in a cold rain to face two Union brigades. Four times we charged to draw the fire of the Yankee battery and received four wounded. By some miracle none of us were killed. Little was accomplished. Three more skirmishes finished out the month, yet the bluecoats kept pushing Bragg's army south.

Chapter Twenty-Nine
Texas

Guilt

Jacob's wife wasn't merely ill, she had been carrying his third child.

The darkening sky threatened rain as he left his horse and hurried up the front porch steps where the house man opened the door before he could knock.

"They're in the parlor, sir."

Mr. Neal stood when he walked in; Mrs. Neal was on the sofa with her other daughter, Vivian, Vivian's husband in the chair next to them. Both were distraught—eyes red, lace hankies clutched in their hands. Jacob's throat tightened.

Mr. Neal reached toward him, "I'm sorry my boy. My daughter, Porscha, and the child, both, passed away late last night."

Jacob began to lift his right arm but got no farther than a couple inches. His breath had left him. He was no longer on solid ground. *Who? What?*

"Porscha. Your wife. She passed away last night."

He must have asked that last out loud.

"Thomas, get that whiskey out of the cupboard. Here, come sit down." Mr. Neal guided him over to a chair. Jacob let him, as though he were a child. Child? He popped up from the chair. "What child?"

"You didn't know?" Mr. Neal, again. Aghast, this time, stepping back.

"He didn't know because that horrible man wouldn't let her tell him." Mrs. Neal from the sofa this time, bursting through her tears.

"He let her come to us only if she swore never to tell you she was with child because it might interfere with your duties to your blasted cotton deliveries!"

"Oh, God." His father had managed to ruin his life even from the grave. *No, not my life, my wife's life. My children's lives. And I let him.*

He took a gulp of air and, stifling a moan, turned to Mrs. Neal. "You don't have to concern yourself with him any longer. If it's of any comfort, he died of apoplexy three days ago."

❧

He sat next to her bed, the bed where she yet lay and so recently died attempting to bear him another child. He saw the signs of that attempt on her face, the dried tears beneath her eyes.

Life has a way of playing with a person. His father passed on unexpectedly, then he learned his wife was not merely ill, but carrying his third child. She had left the comforts of their own home three months ago to come here to her parents' house, to the dubious care of her mother's physician, an old goat who didn't know one end of a stethoscope from the other.

If he had been home this never would have happened.

But he had been in Galveston seeing to his father's cotton interests.

He should have known she was carrying his child when he was last home, but he hadn't paid attention. As always, he had been concerned with "weightier" matters.

Could he blame her for leaving his father and coming here with his children to a place she felt more secure? Less lonely? Perhaps, loved?

The guilt was nearly unbearable. *I must find a way to pay for this, to make the rest of my life worth her sacrifice. Hers and yours, Mother.*

Chapter Thirty
1864, Western Theater

Adrien

"We will never quit, never, not so long as an armed foe dares to tread on our sacred soil, never while he threatens the glorious state of Texas!"

We were all hurrahing and throwing our hats in the air, not a few fellows shooting their pistols and rifles into the gray, overcast sky. Ethan and I were caught up with the others.

Right after the new year, the question of re-enlisting had come down from higher authorities. Unlike most of the army who had signed on for three months or a year, we rangers had signed on in Houston for the "duration of the war." No one believed it would last so long, and many wanted to return to Texas to protect homes from the Union army assembling on the Rio Grande, but not a single ranger would be called a quitter. In response to our declaration of re-enlistment, fifteen furloughs were granted. No one blamed the fellows who temporarily went home.

I scratched at my ribs, feeling how they protruded, and recalled the wealth of food last August. We were all on the brink of starvation, skin drawn tight on ropy muscle and bone. Mounts were not much better for lack of forage.

Happy New Year.

The end of January word passed around that one of our favorites, young Ephraim Dodd, had been captured and hanged by the Yankees as a spy, all because he wore Yankee trousers—which most of us did out of necessity—and wrote in his journal about Yankee pickets, whom he was attempting to pass in order to return to his regiment. Many of us wrote journals. I wrote sporadically of our exploits in the margins of my copy of *Les Misérables*.

Two weeks later we were crossing another river somewhere in Alabama when my horse slipped. My own legs and feet were numb. I couldn't get them out of the stirrups before I and the horse went under, as freezing water took my breath and I saw a hoof plunging at me like an underwater cannon ball.

When next aware, hard stones riddled my back, Ethan was pushing me into them and yelling, "Adrien, God dammit." My lungs were frozen, I was choking and coughing up water.

Ethan helped me sit, head down between my thighs, shivering and dripping water onto smooth, rimy river stones, tongue and throat numb. Words faded in and out. Ethan grabbed at my clothes, peeling my coat away and, God, my head throbbed. If I didn't already have enough headaches. I was on my feet being held under my arms. Someone pulled my shirt, my trousers, everything, off. Let them. Didn't care. Shoving dry long johns up my legs. My head dropped against Ethan's shoulder. Grabbed at Ethan's shirt but my fingers wouldn't work. Sliding down, away into darkness.

I was three days with the hospital wagons before they let me go, before the purple swelling over my eye—the same side of my head as that dang gunshot—turned yellow and I felt strong enough to walk straight without getting dizzy and weaving as though soaked on 'O Be Joyful.' Lying under rolling canvas dozing in and out of laudanum dreams, I tried to recall every second of grasping onto Ethan, the feel of Ethan's ribs and back, the warmth of his wool-covered shoulder and chest against my face. It had been months since we spooned in a tent. We never slept facing one another. Loving him, being loved by him, had been enough. Now I wanted to grasp Ethan in my arms, grasp him so that every inch of us touched. To feel his strength, to kiss him the way I had kissed Lily. Everything would be different with Ethan— he would be strong and hard where Lily had been soft and gentle.

This war changed everything. Me, it changed me. All that stuff that worried me is now trivial. Intimacy with death and slaughter has changed my perspective.

"Lucky that horse landed a glancing blow. Straight on would likely have killed you. Cold water helped, too." *Gol-danged cold it had been.* Dr. Hill handed over another blue bottle. "This is to tide you over till the headaches settle down."

"I know," I said, tucking the bottle into my shirt pocket.

"Might be able to get you a medical pass. You could go home. Least for a month or so."

"I can't." Company K, the whole regiment, was denuded of veterans, of men who knew what they were about. I was needed.

I couldn't face going home without Will.

Chapter Thirty-One
Instincts

Ethan

The rangers crossed and recrossed the Tennessee River six times to get around the federal army, and for the next few months raided, captured supplies and prisoners, always falling back, moving south across North Carolina, South Carolina, never stopping long enough to put up tents.

By middle April in Dalton, Georgia, they found their old commander, Joe Wheeler, and Wharton was promoted to Major General and sent farther west. Terry's Rangers finally landed in one place long enough to put up tents for the first time since fall, and those wounded during the winter returned and replenished their depleted ranks. Captain Freeman was made Major and popular Jim "Doc" Matthews was made Captain of Company K. He'd previously been captured, escaped, and risen in the ranks. Only a year older than Adrien, his dark beard gave him maturity and authority.

Late afternoons might turn hot and sultry, yet nights were cool. They spent two days washing months of rain and mud off themselves and their clothing in a nearby creek. Most sat around trying to put on much-needed weight with whatever they could forage from the woods, fields, or local farmers. The men didn't care to forage with Lt. Villere—one crying child, and a bag of corn would be left behind.

"We're fighting for them, aren't we? Protecting them from the federals?" Ethan said.

"Are we?" Adrien stood in late morning sun, an accusing look on his face, and said nothing.

Too damn tenderhearted, Ethan thought. What about their own who were starving and dying for those same civilians? He knew what Adrien would say, though. Ethan had seen the devastated fields hereabouts, old folks, women, and children left behind to fend for themselves. Damn. None of this was his fault.

❧

Two people can be around one another for years and still not know the other or, more to the mark, themselves. When Adrien went under the water, time stopped for Ethan. He was on his mount, then in the river diving from his horse at Adrien's back floating downstream, then holding him up, swimming.

Ethan watched him as though he would disappear at any moment. Something to do with the fear of loss. Death might easily have come to either of them at any time these last years, but seeing Adrien floating off downstream like that—Ethan hadn't been prepared. An empty bedroll. No more silly jokes. A big hole as though part of the air had been sucked out of his life. Regret? You bet. He had plenty experience with hypocritical preachers not to take their word for anything, certainly not who to love. Only what made a thing pass from simple desire to this aching fear of losing someone?

Adrien was asleep—a dark lump on the ground. Ethan was damp and cold, and stripped out of his jacket, boots, and trousers. He lifted the blanket and fit himself to Adrien's back as usual, lifted his arm up and over, and lay his hand lightly on Adrien's chest. He pressed himself in closer, pulling Adrien in. He was pretty sure he heard a break in breathing, a sigh. He let out his breath slowly into Adrien's hair, inhaled the leather, the familiar horse and woodsmoke muskiness of the two of them.

He considered the differences between man and woman, Adrien and Katherine. What was the same that made him love them? Both were beautiful but, more than that, he liked himself around them. Katherine made him want to be a better man. So did Adrien.

He loved Katherine, but he might never see her again. She knew as well as he did what his chances were. Adrien was here, now. Besides that declaration of love, the youth had given him no signals of wanting anything further than the warmth they now shared. No sly smiles or tender looks from his eyes, nothing like Louie had expressed when he desired more than mere companionship. Not being experienced, as he obviously wasn't, Adrien likely didn't know what he wanted. *What if I'm wrong? Might he look upon me with horror and expose me?*

His instincts told him he wasn't wrong, and he had become an excellent card player by following his instincts. He'd been comparing the games of cards and seduction all along. He had better play his final hand at the next opportunity. Or get out of the game.

He hadn't asked for this war any more than Adrien, but here he was, risking his neck like the rest.

The following morning Adrien had gathered a pile of clean clothes and headed off toward the creek, the upper end likely, where there was a bit of a pool and privacy. As if they hadn't all got the dirt off days ago. Maybe Adrien washed so often because he was trying to get dirt off that wouldn't wash. Ethan watched him ramble off through the trees.

What might get his thoughts off food? A trickle of anxiety but a lot more of something else propelled him forward. He knew what he wanted, and he was sick of waiting.

Chapter Thirty-Two
Texas

Paien

Every time he rode into Washington for mail, Paien Villere hoped for two things: letters from his loved ones and, please God, that they remain in good health. The Eastern Front, where Will fought with the Army of Northern Virginia and General Lee, was usually good news. Then they learned Longstreet and Will's regiment, the 1st Texas, was sent west to join Bragg. What twist of fate had sent Longstreet's men to the Western Front? Paien could not help but curse the day Adrien had joined the 8th Texas which, from the news, was in the thick of every battle protecting the long-suffering Army of Tennessee from advancing federal forces and losing countless numbers of their own. Every night he went down on his knees and prayed God would not punish his sons for his own transgressions, one, in particular.

In January a letter arrived from Will's commanding officer informing the family Bernadette's young husband had been killed outside Knoxville. She appeared to bear her grief well, though she lost weight and gumption for weeks afterward. Six weeks later, she received a letter from Adrien stating he had been with Will when he died and saw him buried, which was some consolation. The letter put a tiny spark back into her eyes, to know Will's best friend had been with him. A miracle, that. Jacob said he had begun what was necessary to bring his body home to rest with his family.

Thank God for Jacob's children. Since Jacob's wife had passed on, Bernadette had taken them under her wing and spent time at

Hartwood almost as often as he did. Lucien's Joanna brought her three to Hartwood, and all five children crawled and ran about the house and gardens at Blue Hills. Amazing how five children underfoot brought hope into one's life in the midst of disaster.

There was a new letter to wait for—from his oldest son, Lucien. He had joined the 4th Cavalry with Sibley's Brigade months ago and was posted somewhere in Louisiana. Paien had considered speaking to his son of his own transgression before Lucien left, but hadn't been able to do so. He had not wanted the thing to weigh upon Lucien's mind at such a dangerous time.

Paien urged his horse, Max, to a faster walk. *I must thank Jacob for the help of those two fellows he sent over.* At first, Paien had been dubious about the old man and his grandson, but they brought no trouble and turned out to be excellent shots, bringing in plenty of game for the table.

Riding to town for mail was his one chance to be on his own and make connections with neighbors and other Washington County folks. He took time to have one short drink and savor his own letters at Robert's Hotel before heading home. Sometimes he ran into an old friend and they drank together and caught up on family news. He took Bernadette's suggestion and, in an offhanded way, mentioned one son or other in the war—or made a positive comment about General Lee's exploits. No matter his personal feelings regarding this war, he was resigned to do whatever necessary to keep his family safe.

The late afternoon cool enough for a canter, he urged Max on; the old fellow was getting on to push him for much more than that these days—they had both seen their best years. The county was not as safe as before the war, what with all the no-accounts who took advantage of the fact that most law-abiding menfolk were absent fighting. Plus, he didn't trust the local Confederate militia. Ever since last August when a gang of rowdy outlaws executed a bunch of anti-slavery German-Texans who supported the Union, the militia had been roaming the countryside hanging anyone they suspected of being a Union sympathizer. Bernadette had once mentioned running into Jacob Hart on the trail. *If I hadn't cornered Simon, I'd never have discovered the whole truth. Lord, I hope Joanna's family keep their views to themselves. If word gets out about their eldest fighting for the Union. . . .*

What the deuce is that? The lowering sun cast long shadows, and he noticed movement far ahead on the road. He put his hand on the stock of the rifle at his thigh and slowed Max to a walk, eyes scanning left and right. Along this section of trail, the oaks were spread out and, for the most part, set back some fifteen feet or more from the road, not the best place for an ambush.

A buggy lay canted on one side with the wheel lying next to it. A woman—no—two women, stood on the grass between the road ruts next to a somnolent bay in traces, its head hanging dejectedly.

"Thank the Lord," the taller of the two said as he rode up, one delicate gloved hand on her chest. The shadow of her hat hid most of her face, but he could still see her delicate features. She had a fine figure and appeared little affected by the heat or her situation beyond that single exclamation. He dismounted, noting the more plainly but well-dressed mulatto next to her.

"I am so relieved you came along when you did, if nothing but to assure Flora I was correct in assuring her that some gentleman would."

Her speech as well as her appearance was that of a lady, though he had never met her before, which was unusual in such a small town as Washington. He nodded and touched his hat in greeting. "I'm Paien Villere. I'll take a look at that wheel and see if it's possible to get you on your way before long. Though riding about the countryside by yourselves is foolish and unsafe."

He could see her bridle at this last. Perhaps he should not have said foolish, but foolish is what it was, and he had enough to worry about without this. Upon closer view, he could see she was no silly young chit, but well into her womanhood, though she held it well. Exceedingly well, he must admit.

"I'll have you know we were visiting Mrs. Silas Bunting over by Miller Creek. Her menfolk have all gone to this stupid war and she is ill and all alone but for one loyal Negro. We took her soup and fresh fruit."

Not only her chin was up. She might fly at him like some angry hen whose last egg you had just filched from beneath her feathers. He nearly blushed at where that thought led.

"Excuse me," he said, touching the brim of his hat. "I'll see to that wheel." No one had given him cause to blush since, Lord, since the day he met Madeleine over twenty years ago. This was absurd.

He immediately saw the problem. The hub was cracked—no quick fix here. Standing up and turning back around, he faced the two of them. "The wheel can't be fixed out here. Maybe not at all but by a good blacksmith. I'll unhitch the horse for your servant to ride and mine will carry the both of us."

She stood stiffly while a hawk wheeled high in the sky behind her, then said, "My name is Maryanne DeLeon and this is Flora. I thank you for your service, Mr.—" a moment's hesitation, "—Villere."

He unhitched her mare in short order and Flora climbed the buggy to mount without his help. His own black, Max, behaved himself, and stood quietly while he held his hands so Miss—he saw no wedding ring—DeLeon could step up, one leg over the cantle. He supposed that's where it went, beneath all those skirts. He swung up behind her, something he could still easily accomplish, thank God.

No way he would get home before dark, now.

They rode the first quarter mile in silence. He had not been in such close contact with a woman, besides his daughter, in years. The end of the feather in her hat repeatedly tickled his nose, but that wasn't what he was most aware of. At first, she was stiff before him, then began to relax into the circle of his chest and left arm. He carefully kept his right hand on his thigh. The warm scent of spice drifted from her, not flowers like most women with whom he was acquainted. Who was she?

"I hope you will excuse my earlier unbecoming behavior, Mr. Villere, but my maid and I have lately come under some stress from the, might I say, disagreeable attitude of most so-called gentlemen of Texas."

Deuce, I think I know what she's about. Still, he straightened a little in the saddle, made sure he wasn't holding her too tight. "I hope you haven't found me . . . disagreeable, Miss DeLeon." He wasn't sure that was said the way he meant.

"Why, not so far, Mr. Villere. You have been most helpful." The sun to their left dropped below the horizon, turning the sky a soft pink-gold. They rode beneath the dappled shade of oaks casting long shadows across the rutted road. As the cooler evening came on, more and more birds sang.

"I believe I should have known better than to speak even remotely of politics in the present climate. You may as well know, I am not enamored of this war, as many are. There. If you wish to leave me and Flora in the road, I am sure we can find our way from here. We have only a mile or so to go, I am sure."

"As I have three members of my family fighting in it and would rather they were home, I am not enamored of the war, either. I will see you home, Miss DeLeon."

"I am obliged, sir."

"Don't be." He let out a great sneeze. *Damn that feather.*

"Bless you," she said.

He could swear he heard a withheld laugh.

Her white clapboard house with green trim was only a little over a mile farther this side of town. He had seen it before, but never paid it much attention, as there were plenty town folks with whom he wasn't acquainted. He mentioned he would spend the night in town, and she offered him breakfast on her little veranda the following morning. He accepted. It would have been impolite not to.

Such a beautiful morning. He stayed longer than intended. He learned she had wanted to leave before the war began but, because of one circumstance or another, had been unable to. She was intelligent and easy to talk to. She made him laugh. Eventually, they exchanged confidences: Her maid, Flora, was a free woman earning wages; he would free all his slaves if he could.

The sun was high in the sky and he had to leave or the folks at home would worry. She gave him cold ham and cornbread to eat on the way. Before he mounted, he took her hands in his and kissed them, intending to be the gallant gentleman. But as he looked into her brown eyes, he was a little afraid at what he was doing.

"Goodbye," he said. But suspected he didn't mean goodbye at all.

Chapter Thirty-Three
One Never Knew

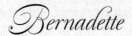

Bernadette

"**P**apa, we were beginning to worry." Silly to worry about Papa, but I could not help it. Here he was, striding in the doorway with the biggest smile on his face as if he had been told the war was over.

"You needn't. I was held up, was all. Had to help a lady who lost a buggy wheel on the road."

"A lady? Do we know her?" Joanna was right behind me, and we had just put the children down for their afternoon naps.

"I doubt it. Here's a letter from Lucien." He held up another bundle. "I've got the newspapers, too, which I'm going to enjoy reading after supper. First, I'll get the road dust off me. Will you ask—"

Betta appeared down the hall. "Simon put water to boil soon's he hear your horse, Marse."

"Thank you, Betta." Off he went, following her. Well, that was that. He would likely get an early start for Hartwood in the morning.

Joanna had already turned away and headed for her room to read her letter. It was her habit to share what she found appropriate later. I had received a long letter from Adrien only last week, so had not expected another so soon, though one always hoped. Adrien wrote to Papa then to me, back and forth, which was only right as we shared his news. Though Papa didn't share all Adrien wrote. Neither had Will. Men were like that, protective about horrid reports they thought their women too delicate to hear. Though I was not so delicate as my men thought. My brother ought to know better.

I went to my room, sat on the chair at my dressing table, and looked in the mirror. I looked the same. Thinner, Maman would say a little peaked about the eyes, my mouth set too firm. I blinked, fast, several times. I would not let tears come. There had been too many tears. Too many thoughts of what had been, of what might have been. Certainly, with that particular line of thought. Something else, then.

I had given Papa such a surprise the last full moon. Papa and Marcus had been up late with the difficult birth of a new foal. Tired as I had been, the light from the moon in my window had woken me from fitful dreams. I had loved the full moon ever since Maman read of fairies when Adrien and I were little, and we had gone looking for them in Maman's flower garden and an especially promising place along the creek where wild ferns grew. How delicious to wander about in the night sounds and moon shadows.

My pumps were under the bed—a quick search and I set my shawl about my shoulders. The recent newspaper articles of Comanches raiding further west made me take the rifle off the wall on my way out. These days it was always loaded.

The panther was lurking about the horse barn. Marcus said afterward it was likely drawn by the foal's birth smell. The main door was closed and latched at night, but the loft door was open, and the cat might have leaped up there and got the colt or hurt the mare. Its tawny form low to the ground, tail twitching, it crouched lower, turned its head my way as it scented me. I killed it with one shot to the heart. It looked smaller in daylight than it did when alive in moonlight.

"When did you learn to shoot like that?" Papa said after he and Marcus came running from their beds.

"Adrien taught me."

"I might have known," he said, and what began as a smile of relief turned to a broader smile of pride.

Practically nothing was the same as it had been before the war began. Along with the two fellows Jacob had sent over, I felt safer knowing I could shoot that rifle, and would be sure to take it along next time I rode anywhere. I would teach Joanna to shoot, as well. Especially with Papa over at Hartwood so often, one never knew when such would be needed.

Chapter Thirty-Four
Tired of Waiting

Ethan

Ethan stepped into a small, sunlit clearing where gold air buzzed and sang with spring. Adrien must have had a mighty fast wash in that cold stream, for he was already beneath a flowering dogwood and reaching for his underclothes. Linen hanging from both hands at his hips, hair dripping, he froze when he saw Ethan.

Seeing him alone and unclothed, still damp and vulnerable, Ethan couldn't help but be drawn in, as though the moment were inevitable. If he had arrived a moment sooner or later what happened might have been different, even avoidable. As it was, Ethan's forward motion forced Adrien back against the tree hard enough that a few white blooms drifted down upon them like snowflakes, one landing in Adrien's dripping hair. Ethan grasped his shoulders, took his mouth in his own and poured every bit of the past year's longing there.

For a frightening second Adrien was unresponsive, then his lips pressed onto Ethan's with unbridled intensity, his hands clutching at Ethan's sides hard enough to hurt. Ethan felt possessed by fever. He pressed his entire body on the youth, tongue aggressive and probing. Adrien's slight resistance, as though he would test his muscle against Ethan's, sparked something deep inside that made Ethan grab Adrien's wrists and slam them above his head against the trunk. Before Ethan could react, Adrien slipped a leg behind Ethan, sending him off balance, dropping him to the ground and landing on top. Ethan had to catch his breath, as much from surprise as from Adrien's weight across his middle.

"I hoped you would follow me. I didn't know if you would, but I hoped," Adrien said, perched there and totally unaware of what the position was doing to Ethan—or was he?

"The devil! You mean you planned this?"

One side of Adrien's mouth turned up. "I got tired of waiting."

"But you—"

"This war. I figure caring for a person is not the worst thing a man can do."

Ethan saw on his face when he took in the entire thing, how they both were, how he was, and that beautiful vulnerability made Ethan reach up and take Adrien's face in both hands and haul him in for another kiss.

Chapter Thirty-Five
Nice to Know

Adrien

The Army of Tennessee was retreating, and I cared not a whit. Many rangers complained when Bragg's replacement, General Johnston, didn't fight. I kept my thoughts to myself, even from Ethan. Better to retreat than throw ourselves uselessly at artillery and well-emplaced infantry the way Longstreet had done with the 1st Texas and Will.

The 8th Texas stopped running at Kennesaw Mountain. Captain "Doc" Matthews trotted his black along our front line, the horse's head and reins held high. "It's our old friends, the Indiana cavalry. Seems we got to hold them long enough for the infantry to clear out." His mount turned forward, arched his neck and blew. Matthews settled himself in the saddle. Out of the corner of my left eye I saw our flag raise, faded and ragged, but the proud cross and circle on blue lifted in the breeze and waved.

I screamed and charged with the rest. Once smoke-rancid air blew through my teeth amid buzzing, bone-shattering shells and clattering muskets I stopped thinking and became a crazy thing of stones, shot, steel, and rampant destruction. The stones were in my heart.

I saw the horse through dust and smoke and bluecoat riders—a goal in all the confusion—a beautiful, rearing, spinning chestnut stallion. I did not care how many Yankees I had to mow down to get to that horse. It was something to focus on. I fought through three soldiers and leaped from my gray to the chestnut's back, my knife at the throat of this dandy officer.

The rangers took more than sixty prisoners, including the brigade commander, Colonel LaGrange, the officer whose stallion I had taken.

Back at camp my back was slapped and pounded, I was shoved and told what a devil on horseback I was. Not a word from Ethan who kept his back turned while rubbing down his horse. He mumbled something at his mount's shoulder.

"Say it so I can hear, Ethan." My blood was up, and I felt foolish, wanting to throw something.

Ethan turned, face dark and body tense. "I said you're a fool, Adrien. That was the stupidest stunt you've pulled, and if it weren't for the men who followed and saved your neck, you'd be dead."

"I wanted that horse." It sounded inane, even to me, which made my blood boil. Ethan sent me an angry stare, jaw muscles churning, then threw down the curry brush, spun and strode away, as though he couldn't stand another second in my company. Forbes was a few paces away rubbing down his own mount. "Pull in your horns. He's got the worrysomes, is all."

"We all take chances, any day, any one of us. . . ." I didn't know why I felt so wrathy; I just did.

"Don't gimme that shit, boy. Even I know it's different with you."

I looked at my boots, heart thudding. The idea frightened me, that we were so obvious. No one minded such a romantic notion as long as it hadn't gone too far. Now it had. I had made it so and lost whatever armor I had previously built up over the years with Grace and Lily and damn, damn, damn. I got out of there into the surrounding dark as fast as I could go.

May 12, 1864
Dear Papa,

I write this from a fallen tree downed by a Yankee artillery shell. Seems all we do these days is slow down the bluecoats. Our general has again been replaced, this time with John Bell Hood. I feel none too comfortable under this man, who has been known to waste men for his own glory. The 8th Texas is, again, part of Wheeler's cavalry, and we chase down the enemy and abscond with prisoners and horses, yet there is no end of Yankees. I talked with a Mississippi infantryman the other day; they call the Yankees Strangers. Perhaps because in Mississippi they never saw a northern man before this war? The bluecoats are much like us and yet unlike us. They resupply themselves with everything so much faster than we can.

General Sherman attacks civilians while we do nothing but inconvenience his soldiers. It is horrible what war has done to the families hereabouts, to see old folks, women and children starving for lack of food that the "Stranger" army has either carried off or destroyed, leaving nothing behind. Sherman has set fire to homes and entire towns. I have never felt hate for those people, as I expect they believe in what they are fighting for just as we do, but when I see how they have left these poor citizens, Papa, a terrible rage at them comes over me.

The Wheatleys left Rome to stay with Mrs. Wheatley's brother's family in South Carolina. Hopefully, they will be safe there.

We are constantly on the move. Just north of Dalton, Georgia, on May 9, we were ordered to charge a force of the enemy, which proved to be an old acquaintance, La Grange's Indiana cavalry, and took more than sixty prisoners, including Colonel La Grange. At Cassville we saved a wagon train captured by Wheeler when the enemy tried to retake it. You could hardly see a thing for all the red Georgia dust. I thought I would choke of it. General Wheeler surely loves to collect wagons, and likely has as many wagons now as he does men. Thankfully there was a mighty storm afterwards which laid down the dust, though the mud is worse for the wagons, those we have not burned, that is. I got blisters from wielding a pick axe with the fellows to build a breastworks that we abandoned before it could be used. On May 29, we charged the entire Yankee line at midnight, and the charge was a mess. I do not like pushing a horse

*in the dark, and thank God I no longer ride that gray that would
have stood out like a full moon in a black sky.*

    Give my love to Bernadette and all,
    Your loving son, Adrien

I babied my new horse and cleaned my recently acquired Spencer
rifle, wondering how long I would be able to keep it supplied with
ammunition. I stayed clear of Ethan, which made a wreck of me. For a
while after our "meeting" I had felt like nothing could stop me, and he
had brought me down so fast with his unreasonable harangue I didn't
know whether to be angry or sad.

Near the end of June, it rained. Neither army moved because the
artillery went nowhere in so much mud. The rangers were able to put
up tents and, after scouting all day, I followed Ethan into our tent,
both piling wet gear at the entrance. I waited there while Ethan made
his bed and settled himself. I had felt like a snake in the grass ever
since the argument, but didn't know how to tell him so.

"You're not going to sit there all night, are you?" Ethan said.

"I want to be sure of my welcome before removing my boots." I
rubbed my hands on my thighs and looked down at those same boots.

"Get on over here."

I crawled closer on top of the ground cloth, removed boots,
overshirt, and trousers before pulling the blanket over our laps, heart
beating furiously.

"You didn't need to hide for three days, you know."

"I was not hiding. You galled me, Ethan." That damn snake was
rising again.

"Galled you."

I looked at him. "I am no child to be admonished, no matter what
you think."

Ethan stared back, then lowered his eyes. "I thought you had
more sense."

I leaned forward, arms crossed, elbows on knees. Raised a hand
to rub my forehead, fingers tangling my hair. "Sense. I have no sense

once we begin. It is all instinct. Long ago, it seems, I decided I was already dead. How else kick my horse into artillery and musket fire. I am not the person I was, not sure how exactly. I'm afraid I have lost something . . . valuable." I stared at something invisible a foot away. "I was ashamed before this war, but that shame is petty considering what I feel now. I thought I would prove myself a man, but I feel even less so. If this is what a man is, I'm not sure I want to be one."

I had not planned on saying so much. I was surprised, definitely grateful when Ethan took me by the shoulders and pulled me close. I felt the old fear for only a moment, then slid my arms around him. There was no use in fighting this. No use at all.

"Thank you, for listening to my rant," I said, and slipped down under the blanket.

"You can thank me by taking better care of yourself." He slid under and turned toward me.

I should tell him everything. But if he knew I was Negro and hiding it, would I lose him?

"It's raining so hard, if we're careful no one will hear us." Ethan's fingers were unbuttoning my underclothes and reaching underneath, making me shiver.

"I can barely hear you now." I caressed Ethan's left buttock, drawing him in. *I love him. Isn't that all that matters? I'll make him happy while we're both alive.*

"Shush." A whisper, as Ethan nibbled down my neck. "When we're making love like this you can't let loose and forget where we are." He kept licking, nipping, and murmuring in my ear.

I took Ethan's head in both hands and murmured back. "You mean what we are, as well as where, don't you. I know well about keeping silent, more than you know. Don't you forget, either, old man, for I may not be able to see you in this dark, but I am going to explore every part of you all the same."

My heart, my entire body, throbbed like a drum. What I said to Ethan was true, but saying and believing were different matters, according to jumbled thoughts that rushed through my head with

Ethan's every touch. Ethan was stronger, used his heavier weight to roll us over so he was on top. His kiss proceeded down my neck to my chest, drawing my hands away to Ethan's back, his hair. This was not my memory of Jacob, kissing, licking and biting lower and lower, and what he was doing, what was happening was fine, but it wasn't what I wanted. I ached to pull Ethan close, feel his flesh against my own, run my fingers and hands over his face, ribs, and chest and down the soft trailing hair of his belly to the most intimate part of him.

"Ethan." I pulled his hair, his head, until he was looking up, a little dazed, to be sure. "I want you." I hadn't felt this shy in ages, not since well before this war we were in. "Remove your shirt, won't you? And your trousers. And come up here where I can feel all of you?" Ethan actually looked a little abashed, which gave me more courage. "I've done this only that one time."

Ethan, somewhat comically I thought, to my relief, elbowed his way up to my chest.

"Don't fret. It's one of those things that come rather naturally, much to preachers' regret."

Opposite of regret, how quickly Ethan got his shirt off and trousers down. Like most things, he was right about the rest.

Afterward, the rain beat a constant staccato rhythm on the canvas and Ethan lay warm and soporific in my arms. I had not been so content since leaving home. How many thousands of men were at this very moment spooned together in how many hundreds of tents? Out of those thousands, wasn't it possible, even likely, that some of them had found solace from the horrible reality of this war the way Ethan and I just had? "Earlier, you said we were making love."

"What did you think it was?"

"It's nice to know, is all."

Chapter Thirty-Six
Texas
Galveston Bay

The Sea Hawk was a long, low side-wheel steamer, schooner rigged with a rake in her masts and smokestacks and painted grayish white—common to all blockade runners—to make her undistinguishable against the foggy horizon that prevailed in the Gulf. She had a light draft so she could sail in shallow waters where Yankee gunboats could not—namely, sail through the bar outside Galveston Harbor. The bar was a strip of land that lay like a long wall between Galveston Harbor and the Gulf. One shallow channel through this bar allowed boat traffic into the harbor.

Jacob spent more time on deck than in his cabin. He didn't like the cooped-up, tight feeling quarters below gave him, or being below the waterline with only a few inches of bulkhead between him and the sea. He was a good swimmer, but he generally swam on top of the water, not below it. He and Colt had learned sailing lingo fairly quickly, had to, in order to get along on board.

The third night after leaving Nassau, the sea was calm with no moon. He was again on deck with Captain McNeil. "We've run our distance," the captain said, "and by the lead we're within a few miles of shore. Now to find Galveston Bay before federal ships find us."

Jacob nodded in silent agreement. After all these trips, he yet felt like a student. He had learned plenty from sailors on previous trips, but the last couple crossings he had kept close to McNeil where he learned what it took to make a good captain. Whatever Jacob didn't like about his old man, he had always known how to pick the best men to work for him.

Sea Hawk crept slowly up the coast until their lookout made out the topmasts of the blockading squadron ahead. As they were about ten miles from the federals, Galveston must lie a little farther off the starboard bow.

"All hands on deck," McNeil called. Quietly he added, "Let go the anchor. Be ready to unshackle at notice." The men immediately responded as though waiting for such orders—as they had. They also built up steam pressure as high as possible without having to blow it off, as such would expose them to a prowling coast patrol.

Jacob watched from his position at the rail. *What might I do if I could run Hartwood like this, with men as willing and responsive?* He had waited off the coast plenty the past months, but this voyage was the most important. In his cabin below lay a strongbox containing information that would give him and his sister freedom from Andrew Garrison's manipulations. What he had discovered made all the months of investigation worth every penny of the investigator's fee.

He rested his left hand on the rail and peered across the water. Something lurked out there. "Quiet," McNeil hushed. A man stood ready to loose the anchor as a cruiser steamed toward them. Silence reigned on board but for water lapping at *Sea Hawk's* sides. She rocked as the cruiser passed by to starboard, her engines raking that silence, and continued on south. They had been saved by the darkness of the coast behind them.

He must have dozed a while, for he woke with his back against the port bow with the smell of fishy sea in his nostrils. They were moving—he could barely make out Captain McNeil standing on deck about six feet away, staring into the dark. Jacob shuffled to his feet and McNeil said, "Two hours till daylight. If we're lucky, by then we'll be inside the fleet and opposite Galveston where we'll make a dash for the bar."

As daylight came on, Colt, looking fresh and eager, joined Jacob topside. "I suppose you had a good night's sleep," Jacob said.

"Like a baby," he said with a ghost of a smile.

"Damn," McNeil said. Enough light to see now and, instead of the fleet being off to starboard, the blockaders were right off the bow. "Up to you, Hart. We don't have fuel for a second attempt. It's either turn tail back to Nassau and risk capture, or dash for it and take fire."

Risky, but he'd always taken risks if the payoff was worth it. "Commence this thing, captain."

"Full speed ahead and hard to starboard," McNeil bellowed. "We'll make for a cul-de-sac along the beach. There's shoal water and heavy breakers, but it's our only chance. The blockaders can't get close to us there."

They took fire from every ship they passed.

Captain McNeil calmly walked the bridge between the wheel houses, both hands in the pockets of his pea jacket, smoking a cigar. The giant wheels to port and starboard spun around, leaving a track of boiling, foamy water astern while thick black clouds of smoke poured from both funnels. A flash and puff of smoke from a Yankee ship announced that a thirty-pound Parrott shell flew toward them, arched over the bow and exploded in the water beyond. Another exploded at the stern.

Less than two miles distant, they opened fire on the nearest blockader with an eleven-inch pivot gun, exploding a shell under her bow and deluging the federal ship with water.

At a mile-and-a-half, McNeil put Sea Hawk's helm "hard-a-starboard," and ran across the bow of the Yankee ship, running for shore.

In under five minutes, the other ship had shortened sail and turned on her heel. That ship had five guns on Sea Hawk and rapidly neared.

A shell from the federal ship's rifle exploded over the port wheelhouse; a shell from the eleven-inch pivot burst close alongside, and six-inch guns fired thick and fast as enraged hornets. Half a mile separated the two ships when Captain McNeil changed course and ran down along the beach, directly across the bow of the federals. The air smelled of cordite and made Jacob's nostrils burn.

The leadsman at the bow called out their depth: "By the deep three fathoms."

"Hard-a-port, quartermaster," shouted Captain McNeil; and as *Sea Hawk's* head swung to port, he said, "By God, we'd been ashore in another minute!"

They ran for it, nip-and-tuck, the bar between. Their only chance was to get out of range.

Shot, shell, grape, and shrapnel shrieked before, behind, and over them, or struck the water and ricocheted over the decks. A shell exploded a few yards from the ship. A ten-inch shell shrieked over the rail and out the other side, narrowly missing three men. The shrouds were slashed from under another man as he ascended the rigging, and he grabbed a line above to keep from falling. A large piece of exploding shell cut a metal pipe above the deck and sent shrapnel flying everywhere.

A six-inch piece spun into the meat of Jacob's thigh, driving him to the deck.

Colt was the only one who noticed. He shrugged out of his shirt and used it as a tourniquet while Jacob gritted his teeth to keep from screaming. He lay against the port bow, the same place he had fallen asleep earlier. "Help me up," he said, gasping. "I have to see." Colt always did as he was told.

The channel widened; if *Sea Hawk* could only hold her own for another twenty minutes.

The entire Yankee squadron belched fire, smoke, steam, shot, and shell, trying to tear *Sea Hawk* to shreds. McNeil kept her close in to shore, while two pursuers, forced to remain in deeper water, stayed alongside, firing broadsides as fast as they could load.

Jacob saw the white water ahead, creating the cul-de-sac. Their only chance was to bump through. If she stuck fast, he would lose the ship and all lives. *Sea Hawk* approached her fate, taking no notice of the bursting shells and round shot—it was not a question of fathoms,

but of feet—twelve feet, ten, nine, and McNeil put her at it as a horse
at a jump, and as her nose entered the white water, the leadsman sung
out "eight feet." They touched and hung. All was over when a big wave
rolled in and lifted the stern and the ship with a crack which could be
heard a quarter of a mile off. Her back was broken!

No! She burst ahead and, after two minor bumps they were in the
deep channel, helm hard-a-starboard, leaving the blockaders astern.

Despite every effort to prevent her, *Sea Hawk* sailed into three-
mile-wide Galveston Bay and, as the channel through the bar was
perilous to vessels drawing more than ten feet of water, the federals
had to give up the chase.

Galveston Bay: white sand dunes in the distance; the city of
Galveston to the south, its piers filled with sympathetic spectators;
Fort Jackson flew the Confederate flag, its ramparts crowded with
men praying for their success.

Captain McNeil hoisted the Confederate flag and dipped it three
times, took off his cap and, bowing, waved it toward the federal ships.
One crying gull spun overhead.

It was the last thing Jacob saw before he passed out.

❧

Someone was over him holding him down and it wasn't Father. *Father's
dead, you fool.* This man was in a white coat. With stains on it. Damn
it was hot and his leg was burning fire.

"You must hold still. You aren't doing yourself any good thrashing
about like this."

"Where is it? Where's my sea chest?"

Colt appeared from beyond the man, thank God. "I've got it.
Right here with the rest of our things."

"You can't worry about that right now," the man said. "I'm Dr.
Campbell. You're going into surgery to get that thing out of your leg.
I'll be frank with you. You may lose the leg or you may bleed to death,
but I'll do the best I can. That's a big piece of metal in there."

"Wait . . . wait." He grabbed Colt's shirt to pull him close. "Send for

Lily. Get her down here if you can. She has to see what's in the chest. Only Lily. Not Garrison. Don't let him near it. Promise me. Promise you'll guard it with your life."

"I will. You have my word."

He could depend on Colt. Always had.

Chapter Thirty-Seven
Cargo

Lily rocked in a chair on the front porch watching every sort of rider, wagon, and carriage pass by on busy Sabine Street. Though there weren't so many passersby as a year ago. She enjoyed the houses on the opposite side the street, most pastel or white-washed with all colors of trim. Their house was set back about fifteen feet from the street so visitors could leave their horses tied up at the hitching post and out of the way of traffic. Spring rain this morning had made the outside air cooler than inside the somewhat stuffy house, at least until the sun turned it to hot vapors. The welcome rain also kept down the dust. Rose bushes along the porch subdued the odor of horse dung in the street. One of the riders turned and trotted into their drive, bringing his horse to a halt at their iron hitching ring.

Their visitor flung his horse's reins through the ring and came up the steps to the porch. Lily had never seen him before and automatically placed a hand over her stomach as though to protect the baby within. She was alone, as Mae was inside with Joshua.

The man was wiry and fairly young, maybe late twenties or early thirties, and wore a derby hat. He put two fingers to its brim and nodded. "Ma'am. May I ask if you are Mrs. Garrison? I have a message for Lily Garrison from her brother."

Her heart sped up. They had been expecting Jacob and the *Sea Hawk* any week now.

"Yes. I'm Mrs. Garrison."

"Your brother has been wounded, ma'am. He asked for you and was barely out of surgery when I left. His man said—"

Andrew flung open the front door. "Who is this? Why are you disturbing my wife?"

Lily rose from the chair. She was again awkward with carrying a baby, but this one was a little easier than the other had been. "Andrew, he's come from Jacob. The *Sea Hawk* is in, but Jacob is hurt. He's asking for me." She leaned on her husband's arm.

"Is the cargo safe?"

"Yes, sir. But Mr. Hart is in bad shape. He took a piece of shrapnel in the leg and they don't know if he will live. He was unconscious and with fever when I left."

"I have to go to him," Lily said.

"Nonsense. You are eight months along and you will go nowhere."

"I could take a carriage to the station. The rails—"

"I said, no. We will take no chances with this baby. I will go. You will stay if I have to lock you in your room. If not yourself, think of the baby. Understood?"

She looked at him through bleary eyes, but she would not let the tears fall. Of course, she must think of the baby. His baby.

Garrison stopped by the hospital first thing after he arrived. He had to see for himself what sort of shape Hart was in. An orderly gave him directions to the far end of one of the wards, and he nearly turned around and left before finding him. Row upon row of sheeted beds full of wounded, moaning men lined both sides of the long room. No amount of washing in bromine could keep down the smell of blood, urine, excrement, and vomit. Garrison kept his eyes on the center aisle before him; he didn't want to look closely at any of the beds or what lay in them. Just as well his son hadn't lived and grown up to become part of this, though he would have paid anything to keep him out of the war.

Hart wasn't alone. His manservant sat on a chair next to his bed.

What was his name? A horse or something. Colt. That was it. The fellow looked like a half-breed. The man looked like he'd just as soon slit your throat as speak. The boy didn't look good—gray where he wasn't flushed with fever, and dark under his eyes. Blood had seeped through the sheet where one leg lay. Looked like it was still there. Maybe it shouldn't be. A glance at the half-breed told him he would get nothing from that one.

He hurried back down the row of beds as quickly as possible. If Hart died, possibly the whole cargo would be his, not merely twenty percent. Best to find out now, get to the factor and discover what was what.

He had been to the office with Hart and met Factor Armstrong P. Gallaway before.

"I've been expecting you," Gallaway said. He sat behind a big wooden desk covered with files and papers and didn't bother to get up. Garrison didn't mind. He was ready to get down to business.

"You know what condition Jacob Hart is in, I expect. You've been to see him?" Garrison said, taking one of the chairs in front of the desk.

"I'm afraid I have. He does look somewhat ragged, but we're not giving up hope. Dr. Campbell says he's young and strong. With the right care he may pull through yet."

"That may be, but I've got cargo that needs unloading, and the rest can't hang about on that ship either."

"Your cargo has been separated. You can see the master any time and unload it."

"What about the remainder? If Hart doesn't pull through, I'm the only other partner."

Gallaway sat back in his chair. "Actually, that's not true. Jacob assigned a Power of Attorney in case something like this happened. I sent for the man two days ago. He should be here tomorrow or the next day."

Garrison felt as though someone had struck him. *That young son of a. . . .* "Do I know him?"

"I doubt it. His name's Paien Villere, from up in Washington County."

Villere, Villere, I know that name. Damn, don't I, though. A mistake I didn't follow up on that family earlier. I won't make that mistake twice.

Chapter Thirty-Eight
Such a Fuss

Bernadette

As soon as Papa walked in the door, I knew he was bringing terrible news. He looked tired and years older, as though the ride from town had taken everything out of him. I went into his arms. *Who is it, who? Please, God, not Adrien. Not Lucien, but not Adrien.*

"Lucien," he said. "Lucien's been killed."

I heard the floor creak behind me and turned, saw Joanna in the parlor doorway, her face turn pale. Saw her collapse to the floor.

Papa gave Joanna a draught to help her sleep but, of course, took nothing himself but a little brandy he shared with me from a bottle put by years ago.

"This doesn't seem real," Papa said, staring into the empty hearth. "He's been gone, and now he won't be coming back." He lowered his head. "I'm sorry. I shouldn't—"

I raised from the sofa and lowered to Papa's feet, lay my head on his knees, and took his hand. "We will grieve together Papa."

He squeezed my hand and I squeezed back.

The following day a rider came saying Papa was needed in Galveston. Jacob Hart was sorely wounded and might not survive. I helped Papa pack, and he left early the next morning.

Watching him ride off, I wanted to drop to the porch, drop my head to my hands and give in to grief. Instead, I stared at the last trails of dust fading away down the road. *I cannot. I dare not, for I might not come back from it.* I took a deep breath and turned to the next task.

Action was the thing. Keep going, as there was plenty to do. Always plenty to do.

The light changed as September neared. A month later and we would be bringing in the fall crops. If only Lucien were here to see it. In the kitchen garden the children helped pulling weeds and picking insects off plants. Joanna had not told the children of Lucien's death. She couldn't. Not yet. Jacob's seven-year-old Michael loved making the younger ones scream by stomping tomato worms, *splat*. They had no time for moping around—not for more than a few days, at most, a week. No more than I had grieving for Will. Sometimes at night in bed, I still cried for him. I missed him most then, when everything was quiet and I was alone, when I could think and remember.

A week later Joanna and I were in the cellar under the hill next to Owl Creek adding Mason jars of tomatoes, green beans, corn, and fresh-pickled cucumbers to the shelves. The cellar, six feet wide by eleven feet deep, was always cool, though a mite dark, even on the hottest days. Ice stored in a hole at the back helped to keep the place cool. The only light was from what came in the open door and the two candle lanterns she had lit upon entering.

How satisfying to fill the shelves with summer's efforts. This was my second year growing and putting up food. Actually, last year I had been mostly learning from Betta. This year I could see the difference—the shelves were already nearly full.

Joanna put the last jar on the shelf and, rather than pick up her basket to leave, folded her hands at her waist and took a deep breath. "I'm going home."

"Home?" *What does she mean?* "This is your home."

"I mean to my parents' home, and I'm taking the children. I might be back. I'm not sure. I just, I want to be with my mother. Without Lucien, I need some time."

Oh dear, my energy collapsed. "You know we love you. There's a place for you and the children here. Any time you want."

"I know. I've sent for my brother. The one who's still at home." Joanna fumbled with the buttons at the bodice of her dress.

"Abraham will be good to me and mine and has little ones of his own."

I dare say nothing of Jacob's children, how well they have all gotten along. I can see she is determined. She has been lost since Lucien left.

A week later Joanna and her children were gone.

Jacob's two remained at Hartwood more than Blue Hills. Without so many children, the house and grounds were too quiet. Papa usually left for Hartwood Monday mornings and often did not return until Friday afternoon. I was grateful for Amos and Gideon. Gideon brought me wildflowers that wilted before the day was over, or an apple he had polished to a fare-thee-well from one of the trees out back. He often appeared at the back door with rabbits, pheasants, or a partridge or two, his ears turning pink beneath his hair when I thanked him.

In the middle of the night, or maybe it was early morning, something woke me. My room was dark, but there was noise, yelling, outside. "Fire!"

I saw nothing from my room window but a reflected glow to the east—the yelling came from behind the house—the cow barn! I threw on a shawl and, out of learned habit, grabbed the rifle from under the bed and ran down the stairs, stopping only to shove my bare feet into a pair of boots by the back door. I saw our people lined up and passing buckets from the well in the yard past the kitchen garden to dark outlines in front of the barn. I could make out Marcus's tall frame at the front of the line nearest the fire yelling encouragement and passing buckets. Then I heard a shot from behind me in front of the house.

I spun and saw a horse across the east house yard and the road—two horses galloping from the stables. A third horse had a rider, as did a fourth with more horses pouring onto and down the road. Two forms stood to my left on the road facing away and firing. The first rider fell, the second went down, and when I ran to see around the house, there were three more on the ground to the side of the barn firing back, and one of the two men, my men, went down, and I raised my rifle, took careful aim, and shot one of those men next to the barn. I took a bead and shot the other. I heard a shot and saw the third spin away and go down. I tracked with the rifle then lowered it a couple inches looking for someone else to shoot but there was no one else. The horses were running off, but they'd come back once they settled down. They'd come home where there was food and comfort. The rifle was heavy now so I lowered it all the way, put the safety back on and didn't recall taking it off. I started shaking. I'd shot two men. I thought they were men, though it was impossible to be sure in the dark. Were they dead? One of my own was down and I had to see to him. I moved forward, one foot before the other, and found I could still breathe.

That fire had been nothing but a ruse so those men could get at the horses. Thank the Lord for Amos and Gid, I now saw were the two men who'd been shooting at the thieves.

Amos was on one knee holding Gid. Gid peered up at me and smiled. *Not this boy with the flowers.*

"You are one mighty fine shot there ma'am," Amos said.

"How bad hurt are you?" I said and felt slightly nauseous.

"It's nothin'," Gid said.

Amos reached around under his arm to lift him up. "Hard to tell in the dark, but I 'spect it went right on through 'neath his ribs."

"Bring him into the kitchen. Betta will know what to do, and I'll send for Dr. Mills."

"I don't need no doctor, really I don't."

"Shut up, Gid. The Mrs. will do as she pleases."

What I pleased was to have a big gulp or two of that brandy Papa had the other night.

❧

I didn't find the brandy, but when I searched in Papa's study, I did find a couple bottles of something else. One was bourbon whiskey, which I took to the kitchen in triumph.

Gid was sitting on the kitchen table without his shirt looking a little green around the eyes. Betta had begun pushing him down onto a pile of clean rags she had placed on the table, and he didn't want to be pushed. I saw him from the back which was pretty rank with blood. *Not this boy. Please, God, not this boy.*

"I gots to clean that out and you gots to lie back for me to do it," Betta said.

"Have some of this." I came round to the front and held out the bottle.

"That looks too fine for the likes a him," said Amos. "But I'll have some."

"No you won't," Gid said, and chugged down a few good swallows. *He's pretty lively. Surely, he'll be fine.*

With that he commenced weaving and I easily lifted the bottle out of his loose hand.

"He ain't never had strong drink afore," Amos said, catching Gid and lowering him to the table.

"Whoa, hoss," Gid said.

"Why don't you go git dressed Miss Bernadette, while I clean this boy up. This ain't no place for a lady to be."

Goodness. I was still in my nightgown and these big boots. "I'll be right back, Amos, once I change."

"Yes ma'am."

I wasn't sure why I had to tell him that. I just did.

Once upstairs, I put the rifle on the bed. I was still carrying the whiskey in my other hand. I put it on the dresser, sat down and realized I had never checked on those men we had shot. I still didn't know if they were dead. What if they had only been wounded and were out there suffering? Damn them. They deserved to suffer. They shot that sweet boy and Lucien was dead and Will was dead and Adrien might be, and I hiccoughed and sobbed and sobbed into my hands and my lap and made a mess of my nightgown. I wiped my face with the hem. Ridiculous, making such a fuss. I was all in a muddle. Papa's people, my people, had surely taken care of them, their bodies, by now. I picked up the bottle and took a swig. *My lord that burned.* But it warmed me up going down. Another swig. That was better. Stuff tasted awful but it felt good.

I would get dressed and go downstairs and make sure everything was as it should be.

Chapter Thirty-Nine
Georgia
Not to Hide

Ethan watched the stallion reach around to nip Adrien on the backside as he threw a blanket and saddle onto the devious critter, and Adrien absently swatted his nose as though they were playing some game. Maybe the horse thought so, the way he shook his head and closed his eyes. Ethan had to admit he was one fine, hard-muscled animal—big shoulders and loins, high hooves and long, arched neck. A week ago, they had ridden all night chasing after Yankee raiders, and the stallion had barely broken a sweat. Ethan walked to the animal's opposite side and lifted a hand to the horse's shoulder while keeping one eye on the lowered head. He might appear harmlessly dozing, but Ethan was no fool.

"You taking the gray, too?"

"Thought I'd leave him as an extra mount. He'll be needed sooner or later."

"Expect so."

"Don't need more than one first lieutenant to head this thing."

Ethan shifted his feet. "Least I won't have to see you do something stupid."

Adrien pulled the cinch tight. One side of his mouth twitched. "I reckon it was that stupid thing I did that got me picked for this." He lay both forearms on the saddle, looking across at Ethan. "I won't need another horse, if that's what you're worried about."

"Hell, who says I'm worried."

"All right then." Adrien took his bedroll from the ground and tied it on behind the saddle. "This will be a nice ride around the country-side, while the rest of you fellows go charging Yankee infantry. I'll be less likely to face artillery."

Ethan settled his hand on Adrien's. They seldom charged any longer when facing infantry and artillery. It was dismount, creep forward or down on your stomach or aim from behind the nearest tree until some officer higher up said to go forward or regroup. Or you ran out of ammunition. "I count on you to come on back. Hear?"

"You. . . ." Adrien blinked at him, eyes filled with unspoken thought. He stepped back, slid his hand away, mounted, and was off.

Captain Shannon had picked Adrien, Riley Dillard, and Will Moore from Company K, two or three from each of the other ten companies, and one first lieutenant. They were to scout all over the country gathering information on the bluecoats for General Hood. Dillard would ride with Adrien most of the time.

The scouting part was sound, that's mostly what cavalry were for. Ethan didn't like the part about Adrien going off without him. Holy blazes. He was not Adrien's daddy, or big brother. Adrien was a grown man and could take care of himself—as much as any of them could, better than most.

There was nothing he could do about Adrien, but he had to take some sort of action before he went into a conniption fit. He'd write to Katherine. Letters took a coon's age to come and go, and these days many never reached their destination. It was best to write often.

He wouldn't consider how it might be if Adrien didn't return.

Chapter Forty
Watch and Turn Away

Adrien

I spooned with Riley Dillard on the frosty nights for the few hours we slept when we didn't return to camp. I liked Dillard except for the food remains that decorated the older man's gnarly beard. In his youth he had been a seaman out of Galveston, and it was always "aye, Slick." Dillard could always be counted upon for a rousing sea adventure around camp in evenings, and no one minded if his stories were a mite fanciful, as long as they were exciting.

Dear Papa,

    I am now one of Shannon's Scouts, and we report to General Hood in Atlanta, which is under constant bombardment. Our duty is to cut off Sherman's communications and supplies. Paper is under short supply so this will be brief. You may have heard General Hood left Atlanta, and Sherman has taken over the city. Perhaps you have heard about his orders to forage and destroy everything in sight. If you find it hard to believe, believe it, for Captain Shannon found Special Order 120 on one of our prisoners. I never imagined a war fought upon civilians. We ride up on burning homes, women, children, and grandparents standing and sitting around outside in falling ashes. No food, all their possessions destroyed or gone with Sherman's men. I thank God those people are not in Texas, and we keep fighting in hopes they never will be.

    Your son, Adrien

On the afternoon my fellow scouts whipped four Negroes for singing and dancing after the Yankees plundered their owner's home, I had the sensation I was disappearing. Or wished I would. I could do nothing because I had ridden with these men for years. Only they were no longer the same men who had joined up in Houston or fought at Chickamauga. We had seen too many ravaged women, children, babies, and old people left with no pride, no food, no future.

I made myself watch and turned my horse away when it was done.

It might have been me there on my knees, my back in red streaks.

By late October, it appeared Lincoln would be reelected, and Sherman was heading for Savannah and her sea ports. Dillard and I rode into camp, filthy, hungry, exhausted.

"My horse needs shod, and I need food and a bath." I dropped out of the saddle where Ethan was saddling up his mount.

"You certainly do." Ethan grimaced, wrinkling his nose. "I'm in similar condition, only not so desperate as you. We can get our horses shod in town. I heard there's a decent hotel that has hot baths and home-cooked meals, and they're right nice to us cavalry heroes."

"God, Ethan, I reckon a hot bath and something besides dry biscuit is all that can get me back on that horse right now."

"We'll likely have to return after dark and sneak past Yankee skirmishers."

"Why, I do that all the time. You're not scared, are you?"

"Get your skinny ass back on that beast."

Chapter Forty-One
Two Copper Tubs

Ethan

Such a portly proprietor was a positive sign, Ethan thought. Mr. Bedford T. Plummer must have found a way to hoard food to remain that way. What he had heard about the man's friendliness also proved true.

A darkie boy stood ready to fill not one, but two gleaming copper tubs. Mr. Plummer assured them that afterward there would be roast pork, potatoes, beans, and peach pie his wife had baked. Take as long as you like, boys, stick around. Plummer hoped they would, all of them, the whole cavalry. Ethan knew they wouldn't.

How wonderful to close his eyes and lay his head against the high curved back of the tub as the boy poured in more hot water. Couldn't imagine where the man got such fine, copper tubs as these two, obviously made for fancy women rather than a couple filthy rangers. Not outside either, but in a sunny little room with a fireplace and throw rugs on the floor. He wouldn't complain, not even if he had to smell rosewater, which, thank God, he didn't.

Adrien had been particularly morose since they'd met up again. He'd been riding hard with the scouts, but hard riding hadn't kept him this silent and solemn before, not since they'd come to their . . . understanding. Speaking of silent, Adrien was unusually quiet over there. Perhaps he had drowned. "Are you asleep?"

"I might have been." Adrien answered with barely a murmur.

"I wondered. There was a strange noise a moment ago."

"That was my stomach gnawing on my insides."

"I find it difficult to get out of this tub." Ethan hadn't felt this relaxed and warm for—he couldn't recall.

"Stay if you wish. Only do not expect any roast to hang around for you, or any pie, for that matter."

Ethan heard the roil of water, turned his head and raised his eyelids halfway. Adrien's shoulder blades rolled as he picked up a towel, skin glossy and steaming with hot water in the cool room, all aglow on one side from the burning fireplace on his right. He was thin, but fit, with the firm thighs and tight buttocks of a rider, though not as bowlegged as many of them were. Ethan followed a trace of water over the ridges of his spine and down the slope of his lower back. Adrien rubbed at his long hair, and Ethan watched as he moved across the room to where their clothes hung on the wall. He buffed at his privates, and Ethan wished he'd turn around—would chuckle at himself if his heart weren't beating so fast and hard. *Turn around, look at me, Adrien.* Instead, Adrien grabbed what was left of his ragged drawers and slid into them. Then grasped his trousers, the blue ones with a gold stripe, taken from some dead Yankee. That was when Adrien turned, trousers in hand. "I warned you," he said, softening the "you" at the end when he saw Ethan's gaze. He lowered his hand, the one with the trousers.

"I'm going to be hungry a while longer, aren't I?" Adrien said, the left edge of his mouth turning up ever so slightly.

Ethan grabbed the edges of the tub and flung himself up. "For food you are." Been too long since they'd had privacy. He padded to the door and latched it. That boy would have to wipe the suds off the floor. Couldn't be helped.

Chapter Forty-Two
The Whole Truth

Adrien

Mr. Plummer had such a grand fire going that it made me sweat. I was no longer used to being so warm or to this much food, so I ate slowly and noticed Ethan doing the same. The pork was roasted to a fare-thee-well, with plenty gravy to help it go down.

We'd fetch our newly shod horses and ride back to camp tonight, likely be there shortly after midnight, if we were fortunate. *I'm fortunate to be alive and chewing my way through peach pie.*

"Will you tell Mrs. Plummer that she makes a very fine pie?" I wiped my mouth with a cloth napkin after finishing a second piece.

"She will appreciate that, sir. She was afraid that lard for the shortening wouldn't do as well as butter, but Georgia peaches are still the best, if they be canned properly."

"I am afraid all we have is Confederate script for payment," Ethan said.

"Never you mind. Mrs. Plummer has packed some victuals to take back to your mates when you go."

"That's right kind of you, sir. We'll be sure to tell them where it came from," Ethan said.

"I'd rather you boys have it than them Yankees. Weather's turned a mite nasty. Sure you wouldn't like to spend the night? I got a real nice corner room with two windows and a goose feather mattress. Be a lot safer than riding back now, what with Yankee patrols about."

"What do you think Adrien? Could you manage to sleep under a roof on a real bed for a change?"

"We'll have to make sure we can leave our horses with the farrier and get our gear." *A bed with pillows . . . and Ethan.*

"Burke has plenty of room in that old barn of his. Yours are likely the only horses he's got these days." Mr. Plummer was busily removing the dishes, one in each hand—obvious he hadn't done so often. I glanced at Ethan, who caught my eyes. Except for that boy, the rest of the Plummers' slaves had likely run off like so many others hereabouts.

The room was at the far end of the hall whose floorboards creaked with nearly every step. The common room downstairs had an eight-foot ceiling. This room had a seven-foot ceiling with barely enough room inside for the bed and a side table with a kerosene lamp, turned low. The walls moved in on me, and I had difficulty breathing in the close room. I tried to recall the last time I had been inside anything so tight as this. Even the room in Corinth had been bigger. Ethan dropped his gear and opened the left wall window. I walked around the bed and opened the window on the back wall. Swirling wet snow blew in on cold air. The room was cooler than the downstairs hall. What a relief.

"Lord," said Ethan, "after that hot bath and that hot room, this is a blessing."

"I thought I would pass out until we got out the door. I reckon we are no longer fit to live in buildings."

Ethan sat on the bed and began removing his boots. "Nothing will keep me from trying out this excellent mattress. For once, I might not wake up with aching bones."

I was doing the same on the other side. "Shall we check it for company first?"

"In such an establishment as this?" He drew back the blankets. "My Lord, real pillows. I spy no little hoppers."

"God be praised." I got to my feet and removed my shirt. Ethan did the same, the same we had done countless times in the tent, only then it was much colder, and generally done a lot faster. I got down to my drawers, sat to pull off my socks, the ones Berni had knitted, that matched Ethan's pair. Ethan came around the end of the bed and sat down next to me, close enough our wool-covered thighs touched. Ethan lay a battered left hand on mine. Our hands, lying on our knees, were equally red, knuckles scraped, nails ragged.

"You are randy tonight," I said.

"I want to talk . . . about what's got you so dogged out and wrathy since you came back from that last scout."

"You mean besides this war?"

"You know it's more. We're not to hide what's bothering us from one another. You recall that?"

I slid my hand from beneath Ethan's, stood and stepped to the window and closed it against the snow. I folded my arms and stared out at the dark. "I believed we were in the right when we started. Now it's all turned wrong." I stood there, eyeing my reflection in the window glass, ghostly in the light of the kerosene lamp, and shivered. Maybe Ethan would understand.

"We often come upon burned houses and fields, the animals run off or killed, families standing around in shock—Yankee bummers loading up everything they can carry and burning the rest. We ride down on the bummers and shoot them, even if they drop their arms and lift their hands in surrender."

"What if you run into more than you can handle?"

"Signalmen are positioned so we can call on one another when needed. Shannon has it all planned out. He's a good commander, though a might harsh. I can't blame him or the others when their anger gets the best of them. I often feel it, myself." I stopped speaking, waiting to see if Ethan would comment, but he didn't. The silence made me continue.

"A few days ago, we rode up on a burning plantation. Four slaves, one no older than fourteen, were dancing and singing out front, celebrating the downfall of their master or their freedom or both. The men—the men I have been riding with—beat those defenseless people with their quirts, struck them harder than ever they would their horses, over and over again. They beat those four to their knees. I watched and did nothing."

"Would it have served them if you had?"

At least Ethan didn't say I was stupid for being concerned about mere slaves. Ethan had never indicated he thought slaves were less than human. I wiped my hands across my face, my mouth. "I don't know. I suppose not."

"Some sort of self-righteous vanity, maybe."

I snorted, slowly shook my head. "Hardly. You don't know the whole truth, Ethan, or you wouldn't say such a thing."

"Tell me then."

God. My heart was in my throat. I turned my head from the window to look at Ethan. I had to see how my closest friend would take what I was about to say. "Those people, those slaves, are *my* people."

Ethan stared at me, unmoving. His brows lowered; his mouth opened the tiniest bit.

I swallowed. Had Ethan understood? "My grandmother was a mulatto." I kept my voice soft but enunciated clearly so Ethan couldn't mistake what I said. "I'm one-eighth, Ethan. One-eighth Negro." My friend remained silent. I turned back to the window, again saw the kerosene-lit reflection of myself against the black, a white ghost. I was holding my breath and breathed into the silence, fogging the pane and my own image.

"That day in New Orleans at that house," Ethan said. "You went back, didn't you."

I turned to face him. "Yes." I went to the chair and snatched my trousers. Turned back, holding them in shaking hands. "I never meant to deceive you. Will you give me a head start?" Surely if Ethan meant anything he said in the past. Unless he felt too betrayed.

"A head start?" Ethan appeared confused, then angry. "You fool. You really think. . .? You think I'm going to tell everyone I've discovered a Negro posing as a white man and we'd better string him up? Is that it?" Ethan was up off the bed and coming at me.

I stood there unable to move like some . . . fool, as Ethan said.

"Look at me!" Ethan grabbed my arm and jerked me so hard I dropped the trousers. "I thought you knew me better than that. I thought we knew one another better than anyone and you come up with this shit. Who in hell do you think Louie was? I'll tell you. He was octaroon, son of a white man's mistress and I was fifteen and loved him beyond all reason. I love *you*, damn me. Damn you."

Dear Lord, Ethan was kissing me hard now, right on my mouth. *Thank God, thank God, it's all right, I'm all right.* We were all pinned muscle, flesh and bone, shoving free of wool and somehow managing to sidle, shuffle and stumble to that wonderful bed.

And Ethan loves me.

Ethan closed the window against the cold and we leaned back against the iron headboard, pillows stuffed behind our shoulders. Ethan had pulled a flask of whiskey from his saddlebags and who knew where he got it? Likely won in a card game if I knew Ethan. *My* Ethan.

We had gotten halfway through the flask when Ethan looked past our feet and said, "I'm going to tell you something I've never told anyone. I was fifteen when I saw my father killed on a Mississippi riverboat. The man was drunk, accused my father of laying bottom stock and shot him. My father was a square player. He never cheated, never had to. The man was arrested and taken off the boat at the next stop, but escaped.

"I tracked him to hell and gone for five weeks, caught him in a Mississippi bayou and told him I was going to kill him. He didn't believe I would. I was only a boy and he laughed and walked away from me. So I shot him in the back. It took a while for him to die. He cussed me with blood spurting from his mouth. Then he grabbed my hand, real tight, and wouldn't let go. I had to pry his fingers away. I hauled his body two hundred yards to a levee and pushed him in. I think the gars got him. Must have because I never heard anything afterward. No one came for me."

Ethan's hand was lying on the covers between us and I covered it with my own, curled my fingers around Ethan's palm. "I love you, too," I said.

The following morning, we rode through a low mist spread along the muddy ground, birds warbling in the trees like wet flutes. My heart was full of music, I felt buoyant, lightheaded, yet calm. The air was cold but soft, everything was soft: the trees, the grasses, the fence line to our right. A miracle I could feel this way in the midst of this . . . thing. I looked at Ethan riding alongside at my left. *Strange how I know Ethan will go to Katherine, and I don't mind. I truly am happy for him.*

Chapter Forty-Three
Texas

Bernadette

Dr. Mills praised the poultice Betta put on Gid's wound. Fortunately, the bullet had passed by the edge of his spleen and had not hit bone or any other important organs. The boy gratefully smiled at me for any little thing I did, from giving him tea and honey cookies, to wiping his forehead with a cool cloth. However, his smile did not reach his eyes as previously, eyes I now noticed were quite a lovely green, and were lately too often the dark of redbud leaves in the shade.

Early summer sun through the curtains of the south window lay a checkered pattern across the bed where he lay propped up on pillows, the counterpane pulled up to his waist, fresh bandages beneath a loose, open cambric shirt. He no longer appeared so embarrassed in my presence as he once had, which was some improvement, but he had not gained much weight, despite my and Betta's addition of wholesome food and rest.

I placed a tray of mint tea and cookies on the side table, pulled a chair up next to the bed and sat, tucking my skirts aside. As I learned with my brother, often it was best to face these things head-on. A bribe helped, as well. "I can see you are somewhat disheartened. For the price of a biscuit, do you care to tell me why?"

He glanced at me out of the corners of his eyes, then looked down at his lap, or the counterpane there, his fingers anxiously pulling at its fabric. He took a deep breath, as though gathering his thoughts.

"I've shot plenty critters, miss. For food. I never took pleasure in it, though, like some." He turned his chin, his face somewhat askance to glance again at me, then away, back at his hands that were now folded, grasping one another. "I never killed a man afore . . . before, I mean. It took some thinking on. I just did it—shot before he could ride off with your horses. But it took thinking on afterward. I'm getting over it, I guess. But as Grandpa said, you don't ever get over it entirely, or want to." He looked right at me then. "Mind you. I don't regret it. He deserved what he got. And you. You were amazing."

His lips curled into a bud of smile then, one that reached his eyes. I reached my hand out without thinking and he took it, I believe in the same way, and his was dry and warm and his smile grew warmer, too. I felt an empty place in my heart fill just a little. Perhaps I had found one more source of comfort in this war. With people of like mind one could count on—there was help in that—that was everything.

Both Jacob and Papa returned to their respective homes in early October. Jacob had been over two weeks in hospital and *Sea Hawk* had been nearly a month in dry dock for repairs. Jacob had not been up to a sea voyage afterward, but had taken the rail home to Hartwood to recuperate and remained there.

I visited the "invalid" once a week, taking baskets of apples, muffins, or whatever I could put together. I included a little honey put by last summer with my deliveries. Those bees have become my pride and joy. Amos and Gid have become hive guardians ever since I gave them a few cookies from a batch I made. Those two were as bad as Jacob's children when it came to sweets.

If only Amos had been more circumspect about the shooting when Papa came home. "Shoulda seen that daughter of your'n. She is one fine shot. Took two a them down like nobody's business."

Of course, Papa felt guilty he had not been there. Marcus, Amos, Gid, and I had to work on him ever so much to make him leave for Hartwood later that week.

Jacob, on the other hand, was horrid. "Thank you, Bernadette, but I can get it. I'm not a cripple, you know, at least not yet. Really, that's not necessary." It was the tone of his voice—who needs you? One little push and I could have knocked him flat. Nearly did, once or twice.

I forgave him when the children pounced on him, especially little Louisa. He did go down then, and didn't mind a bit the way she crawled all over him hugging, kissing, giggling. Michael, who had just turned eight, was more reserved, but Jacob got him in his arms too, eventually, made him laugh with his growling and tickling. I backed out of the room, found myself embarrassed and didn't know why. I passed their Negro nanny standing there with a smile on her face as though she'd seen this behavior before.

I felt as though I had spied on something I shouldn't have. This was not a Jacob I knew, not even when Adrien and I were children—and Lily and . . . Will. Of course, Jacob had been much younger, himself, then. In his teens? Goodness. He had always seemed so much older at the time.

Thanksgiving Day arrived warm and sunny, and the midmorning carriage ride to Hartwood was especially nice. Papa handed me down, taking the basket from me and turning as Jacob pushed open the front door and strode out onto the veranda, leaving his butler, Henry, standing in the doorway. Jacob's cane was gone and he limped only a little. Papa shook his hand.

"It appears you are well on the mend."

"Yes. Good morning, Bernadette."

"Good morning, Jacob."

"Lily and her husband and children arrived yesterday. Everyone's in the parlor."

"I can't wait to see her." I could hardly believe our good fortune. What a gala day—nearly the entire family for a real Thanksgiving. Jacob had invited Joanna and her family, who had sent regrets. Who would feed the animals, see to the work on their farm now that most of the men were in the army?

Adrien was somewhere in the Carolinas. We had received two

letters at once, one from Atlanta, Georgia, and one from South Carolina. He was with a group of riders called Shannon's Scouts. Everyone had read about horrible Sherman and his army, tearing around the countryside burning homes and entire towns.

Maybe next year we would all be together for Thanksgiving. I prayed every night it would be so, that Adrien would return.

Lily looked wonderful, much happier than I expected. "We are going abroad," Lily said. "Andrew promised me a trip to Paris and London as soon as Martha is old enough to be left with her nanny."

"Goodness." I glanced at Mr. Garrison, who sat in a comfortable chair next to the hearth with, by the smell, a cup of coffee in his hand, and wondered where real coffee had come from.

Garrison glanced at Berni, then the others in the room. "I thought it would be a good idea to get away from this war, give Lily a chance to rest and recuperate."

"Why, how considerate," I said. He was removing her from her family, getting her away as far as possible.

"Yes." Lily looked down at her cup of tea. She wore a beautiful blue silk taffeta brocade the color of her eyes—surely the height of fashion.

Just then Joshua bumped against Lily's skirted knee and nearly spilled her tea. He was attempting to walk from one safe place to another. "Mae, will you take Joshua for a lie-down with the baby?"

"Please," I said, "let me take him up to the nursery where he can play with Jacob's two." I leaned over and lifted him up—poked him in the belly, making him laugh and wave his little arms and legs. "You're much too jolly for a lie-down just yet, aren't you?"

If Lily and Garrison were going to Europe, I would talk to Lily about leaving Joshua and Martha with family, not with some nanny.

If only I had been able to.

Chapter Forty-Four
Stand and Bear

The meal had been more sumptuous than Paien had eaten in some time. He, Garrison, and Jacob had retired to what had once been Randolph's study, and was now often used for after-dinner drinks and smokes. Garrison lit a cigar. Paien would have liked a pipe and . . . surprise, Jacob turned from a cupboard with a small supply of the sweetest-smelling tobacco.

"I hope you brought a pipe," he said.

"A habit of which I've never been free." Paien pulled a pipe from his inner coat pocket. Jacob held a lucifer match to the bowl. *Dear Lord, how fine those first inhales . . . aah, familiar, too.* His own homegrown tobacco, by God. He smiled and Jacob gave him a knowing smile back. Paien was beginning to like Jacob, and trust him. The young man had been coming into his own since his father died. Maybe getting out from under Randolph's influence was the best thing for him. He had made solid decisions for Hartwood and his people since then and, according to Bernadette, cared for his children. Only time would tell whether he would remain on the right track.

"You two think you're quite the pair, don't you?" Garrison's right hand lay on the fireplace mantle, the cigar between his fingers. "Inviting me and my family up here after that little investigation you pulled."

"Paien knows nothing about that," Jacob said, and limped over to the desk to sit on its edge, easing his sore leg.

"Well, Mr. Villere, you ought to. You're involved now, whether you like it or no, with your Power of Attorney and that son of yours."

Paien had been calm until now. "I'll thank you not to speak of my son in that tone."

"I believe I have more right than most, don't you think? You should know once we all start investigating one another it never stops. I've done a little investigating of my own—into that Maryanne DeLeon woman you've been seeing so much of these past months."

Paien took in air, stiffened, crushed the bowl of his pipe in his fist. "Stop," he said. Jacob rose from the desk.

Garrison lifted his chin and continued. "You and I have something in common. It seems we have both been handed secondary goods from your son. He was her paramour for nearly a year before he rutted with my wife. He does get around, doesn't he?"

I'll kill—Jacob grabbed him around the shoulders, hung on. "Don't, Paien. He wants you to. He'll have you arrested!" Paien had promised himself never to lose his temper again. Not after the last time led to tragedy. He took a deep breath, let Jacob hold him. Forced himself to relax.

"Ask her if you don't believe me," Garrison said, and stalked from the room.

Paien again breathed deep, settled back onto his heels. He lowered his head, looked down at their shoes on the carpet, facing one another, felt Jacob's presence, thought about his son, about Maryanne, about Lily. He looked Jacob in the eyes. "You know how this feels, don't you?"

"I know," Jacob said.

"He's, he's a good son. He didn't mean. . . ."

"I know that, too. He can also be rash and foolish. But so can I."

Paien raised his hand between them, and Jacob took it. A strong grip, Paien meant to assure Jacob of his intentions.

"Do you mind telling me what you've got on that vile weasel?"

"Not at all. I found documents proving he was skimming funds from the railroad, which is one way he's been living high off the hog when the rest of us have been barely getting along."

"Jesus, Mary, and Joseph. If his partners discover. . . ."

He saw he had surprised Jacob with his exclamation. "Pardon me. Seldom does my childhood Catholic upbringing show itself in such a manner, particularly in the guise of an Irish chum I had once long ago."

The fact he had been negligent enough to say such a thing worried him. He must not let emotion affect his frame of mind. That, as he well knew, led to misjudgment.

"He and I are in a precarious balance at the moment, neither revealing what we know. But when this war is over? If the Yankees win and the railroad goes under?"

"I believe you mean, when, Jacob."

Jacob shifted uncomfortably under his gaze, moved to sit again on the edge of the desk where he could relieve his bad leg. "I didn't want to say that, but it's what you believe, don't you."

"I'm afraid I've been skeptical of our ability to win this thing from the beginning. Not from the South's resolve, mind you, but from her lack of modern equipment and organization."

"If that happens, Garrison will be the least of our problems."

"We need to be working both sides of that coin now, Jacob. However we can."

That night Paien gazed out the bedroom window in his dressing gown, thinking: of Garrison a few doors down, of his son somewhere in the Carolinas, of Maryanne. She had told him of her past. He had suspected as much from the ease with which she took him in. They found comfort in one another. He wasn't sure how he felt about her having been with Adrien. The idea was ludicrous. He was only a boy. A boy who had fathered two children. A boy who had likely killed more than one man and had been wounded and nearly killed. His son was a man, not a boy. That was what he could not wrap his mind around. *When Adrien returns from this war, I must see him as the man he is, not as the boy I knew.*

Would he be able to look at Maryanne and not see Adrien? Could they speak of this? Must they speak of it to continue? Did he want to continue?

More important, what were they all to do to prepare for what was to come?

❧

Thank the Lord the current three-day rain had held off until after they arrived home. No thunder and lightning, it was one of those steady downpours that appeared to be never-ending and would leave the Brazos in flood and with downed trees in its wake if any wind came up. Marcus had knocked at the back door right after supper asking if he could borrow the tub from the back porch to catch a leak in the roof of their cabin. Everyone had been too busy to check the cabin roofs before the rainy season, and this was the result.

"Of course," he said. "And you and Betta come on into the house and spend the night with us. You can use the guest room."

Marcus looked taken aback at that but, after a moment he nodded and went back out into the wet night.

Don't know why I did that, except I felt like it. Maybe I'm feeling a mite lonely in this house lately, with practically everyone gone. I built it for more folks than are here now, and maybe I'm tired of playing at something I'm not. Besides, no one's going to be out in this weather, and Amos and Gid are in town visiting Amos's nephew and his family.

Which was why he, Bernadette, Marcus, Betta, and even Simon were all sitting around the dining room table drinking tea together when they heard knocking at the front door. The rain had covered the sound of hoofbeats which, of course, there must have been. Any of their people would have come to the back door.

Without comment Betta quickly removed three saucers and cups, Marcus the pot, and headed for the Hive. Simon hurried to answer the door. Paien followed a moment later. With Simon in the light of the single kerosene light in the foyer stood a big fellow wearing a wet slicker. Paien stepped forward to shake the man's cold, wet hand. "Stan, what brings you out in this weather? Come on in."

Husky, sheriff Stanley Ford was as tall as Paien, and proud of his thick mustache. He appeared anything but proud at the moment. He removed his hat and dripped in the hall. "Sorry to disturb you like this."

Bernadette came into the hall next to Paien. "Sheriff Ford. Remove your coat and come in. We were just having tea. Or would you rather have coffee?"

"Tea, please." Few wanted coffee these days since it was most often chicory rather than real coffee. "But you won't want me to stay long for the news I bring."

Paien had taken the sheriff's hat and coat and hung them on a peg. "We don't shoot the messenger, here, Stan. Come in by the fire." Though his chest had clutched at the sheriff's words. *What terrible news had brought him out on such a night? News from the war? Please, please, not my son.*

His spurs jingled as he headed into the parlor. He stopped, "My boots . . ." he was already tracking mud.

"Don't worry about it," Bernadette said. "We learned how to clean a little mud a long time ago. Blood, too." She smiled at him.

He sat on the edge of a chair and ran a hand through his graying brown hair. Betta came in with a tray containing the steaming pot and a cup. Bernadette poured. The sheriff lifted his cup in both hands, blew on it and sipped, then gulped. "Nice and hot," he said, and put the cup carefully down on the coffee table.

"No way to make this easy," he said, brushing his hands on his knees. "I came here as soon as I heard 'cause I didn't want you finding out from the paper or someone else. Raiders attacked the Wheatley place a couple days ago. They believed the Wheatleys were Union sympathizers and set the house afire. Shot the old man and his son and the rest never got out of the house. I'm awful sorry."

Paien felt numb. He looked at Bernadette. She had lost all color. He reached around the corner of the table and took her hand.

"The children, too?" she said.

"I'm afraid so. A couple raiders were caught. One was no more than eighteen. He said they didn't know there were children inside. Hung himself from the beam in his cell after he found out." A moment of silence. "Lord." He lowered his head to his hand. "This whole thing, this war, I can't. . . ." He sighed. Took a gulp of tea, another gulp and finished it off. "Well." He stood.

Paien and Bernadette stood. "Thank you for coming, Stan, especially in this weather," Paien said.

"Least I could do."

"You are a good man." Bernadette took his hand in both of hers.

He gave her a short nod, a little embarrassed, Paien thought.

After showing the sheriff to the door, Paien returned to the parlor and took a distraught Bernadette into his arms.

"I don't believe I can stand any more of this, Papa. I can't bear thinking of Renee, Gabriel, and the baby. I can't bear it."

"You will stand and bear it as we have borne everything else. As others have. As Adrien is bearing his part in the war. We must hold Blue Hills together for when Adrien comes home."

"For Adrien," she said into his chest.

"Yes, for Adrien."

We have no choice but to stand and bear what we are given by God. All my grandchildren are gone but two. One is being raised by a man I despise; the other by a free Negro in New Orleans, back where I began. There may never be any others. Does God punish for such duplicity as mine? Must I relieve myself of this burden to those I love before I may be forgiven?

Chapter Forty-Five
Georgia
You Never Know

Adrien

We rode through the state capital of Milledgeville, where the north and south wings of Sherman's army had previously closed around the town like the jaws of a Carolina alligator around a rabbit. The town was empty and silent, its air acrid with smoke, its trees burned black sentinels, papers rolling, lifting, hugging the sides of buildings and broken windows. A few people stood in the doorways watching the army pass, silent women clutching their shawls close. What good was our army, nipping at Sherman's heels?

By the time we approached Sandersville, twenty miles east, I could look in any direction and see smoke trails from burning buildings on the horizon and nearer.

Shannon knew Sherman was collecting his army, including foragers, so that evening he brought all us men in. Of the ten men who had begun with our squad four years ago, besides me and Ethan only three remained: Crane Forbes, whose fiftieth birthday we had celebrated last month; red-haired Arch Lovell, the youngest, from Washington County like me; and blond Bob Fields. We rangers no longer received conscripts, for there weren't any decent horses to be found.

"You do any more good than us when you're scouting?" Young Lovell said as we stood around the fire that night. We were all, likely the entire army, frustrated by following in Sherman's wake. We couldn't stop him. We did so little for those he and his army had plundered.

"We came upon what had been a fine plantation home burned to the ground," I said. Nothing was left but two brick chimneys. "Everyone had run off except for one old lady on crutches and three small children. Yankees had taken everything, and she didn't know where they were going to go."

"You didn't just leave them there, did you?" Lovell's tangled red hair fell below his shoulders, and Forbes had been threatening to cut it with his knife.

"We found a neighbor moving into town who made room on their wagon for them."

"Not much left of that town," Fields said, scratching his head. His once-beautiful blond locks were dirty and greasy, as no one had time to bathe any longer, or any place to do so if there had been time. We all smelled of horse, sweat, ash, and woodsmoke.

The following morning, we rangers rode through Sandersville. Sherman's army had torn up yard and garden fences for fires. Dead cows, horses, and other stock the Yankees left lay in barns and fields. We dismounted and wandered through destroyed homes looking for anyone left behind. Meals had been left half-eaten. Yankee soldiers had taken hams, turkeys, sugar, flour, lard, salt, wheat, grain, potatoes, and even baked pies off tables. They had thrown books from library shelves and broken china, stomped upstairs and filched hair brushes, destroyed mirrors and sliced into pillows, blizzarding feathers everywhere.

I wished I had ridden straight through town without dismounting. Even so, the smell of burned animals and death would have told me what my eyes hadn't.

Sherman and his bummers moved north. Wheeler's cavalry and we rangers followed hard on their heels.

Our complement of rangers raced down a causeway that led to a rain-swollen creek and the escaping federal army. The constant rains and unusually warm November Indian summer had made the creek into a raging river. The federals had pulled up their last pontoon bridge, and abandoned on this side of the deep, furious water hundreds of newly freed slaves that had been following Sherman's army since Atlanta.

I was tearing along the causeway with everyone else, letting my grand stallion stretch his legs, urging him on and, by God, I was passing one rider after the other. I was among the first to see the slaves rushing into the swirling, muddy water: men, women, children, screaming at one another, at the Yankees, at Wheeler's riders crashing down onto them, knocking them this way and that, tumbling in the red mud of their horses.

Riders charged into the water after the leaders, swinging at them, striking this way and that, beating them down and back.

I hauled to a stop, the chestnut circled and pulled on the bit, all het up like other horses and riders. Small children struggled and splashed in the raging water, as well as women whose skirts dragged them down. One old fellow with white hair floated off with the current and went under, all silent and easy.

Those are people, I thought as my mount spun beneath my indecision. *My people.*

I aimed Horse—closest to a name as I would get—and heeled him on. We had never been in such roiling water as this, but me and Horse were of like mind, and I clutched a boy by the hair, then his collar, got him up on front, and my stallion lunged back to shore. I dropped the boy and splashed back for another—glimpsed Ethan, then a few other rangers, following my lead. One woman beat at my arms, screamed, "no suh, no suh!" When she scratched my cheek I nearly let her go, nearly let her drown. I dropped her next to a small, crying girl. "This child needs you," I yelled, and reined away into the water before she could respond.

Late that night, Ethan and I took a walk away from the fire and the others, as we could not make a habit of sleeping by ourselves. Yet it was common for someone to go off alone to write a letter or speak with a friend.

"Did Doc Matthews say what Wheeler is going to do with those people?" I was pretty sure I knew.

"They'll be sent back to their owners, or sold."

"It's only a matter of time before the Yankees set them free again."

"Be glad, then," Ethan said.

"If today's any indication, those northerners treat them worse than we do."

"We're at war. Everyone's treated poorly."

Ethan was right. War excused everything. I found a log to sit on, and Ethan joined me.

"As a boy, I thought what I had to say, and I said a lot then, was important, I was so in love with my family, myself, and the world. Then Jacob's harsh words, my father's secrets, and this war—something I thought so beautiful turned ugly. I was betrayed, time and again. It was all about me, you see. Now, I'm trying to find a way to live with myself, knowing what I know and unable to do anything to help those people, my people."

"You mean like John Brown?"

"I don't mean anything like that."

"Don't play martyr. You've shown common sense, so far, and you did what you could this afternoon. That's all any man can do. Unless you hope to have a place in the history books, or want your statue displayed in some town square."

I grabbed the edge of Ethan's hat and jerked it down over his eyes.

I picked up a leaf from the ground. "Look at this dead leaf, how many shades of red and orange, how they bleed into one another and the bit of green that remains in the center." I twisted it round by the stem. "Such a beautiful death. Those people today. Some wanted their freedom bad enough to die rather than lose it."

Ethan took the leaf, leaned on his knees, regarded the thing.

"Lord, I miss my family." I had just realized how true this was, how I ached to have a long talk with Berni, how much I would like to be sitting in the parlor with everyone and smell the scent of Papa's pipe. I hoped Lucien was all right. And Isaac. Lord, how I missed Isaac.

"I miss my sister. Our discussions. She had an opinion on everything. And was generally right."

"Katherine is the same, in her quiet way."

"Speak of her to me, if you like."

He turned his head to look at me, as if to confirm the truth of this, then away. He dropped the leaf, sat up, stretched, hands on knees. "It's difficult to explain."

"What do you admire about her?"

"Her forthrightness, to begin. She doesn't mince about in actions or words. She's different from other women I've known. She looks right at me, as though she can see deep into my soul. She won't let me get away with any nonsense. She can make me laugh at my own absurdities. She's strong—I can depend on her. I have never wanted any woman so much. When she enters a room, she smiles and takes in everyone at a glance. I love the scent that follows her, the sound of her voice." He was gazing off into the shadows, as if he saw her among the trees.

I felt a tightness in my throat, my chest, and almost regretted asking. Then Lily came to mind, and I realized that, though she was still there in my thoughts, my heart, so was Ethan, and one did not negate the other. "I'm glad you have found such love, Ethan."

Ethan blinked at me, as though coming out of a daze. "You are." He raised a hand to my cheek, stroked with his thumb, bent forward, placed a kiss on my lips that drew us into one another, grasping tight.

No more, not here where anyone might come along.

After Sandersville, Indian summer fled and the land dropped to a flat rain-swamped mire, good for nothing but frogs and rice. I had begun noticing things besides signs of bluecoat soldiers. First up before dawn, in frigid air I uncovered and blew hot coals from the night's fire to life, enjoying the warm glow, the minute crackling of the first tiny pieces of wood in the silent morning. The fire heated my face and hands by the time I stood and watched the soft sky change colors, rubbed my upper arms, and heard the horses shuffle in their knowing of fodder soon to come. It was the best part of the day and would get me through the rest because, at that moment, all was peace and beauty. Until the next man threw his blanket aside and sat up.

All day the sky drizzled a soft, cold rain. Near sunset we were strung out on one of the small rises that separated the rice fields. The sun only now broke through a few, thin clouds to the west, and I halted the chestnut. The land here was so flat, a person could see nearly to the next county. Low-lying water appeared to be one infinite lake, as the horizon line disappeared among glowing pastel colors of earth and sky. The three men behind me stopped. Dillard moved up alongside, stood in the stirrups and stretched to relieve his back.

"I thought this was the ugliest country we been in, but that is right purty."

"You never know, do you?"

"Guess not."

We sat in silence as the colors spread and changed, and I marveled at the world opening itself to me as it had when I was a boy. I had only to recall how to open myself.

Chapter Forty-Six
S. Carolina
Time for Herself

"Goodbye, goodbye."

The new year had come and gone, her family was leaving, and little Marjorie scowled behind her wave. Her and aunt and uncle insisted her sister would be safer with them, and Katherine agreed. She watched the carriage move off down the drive, dropping mud from its wheels. The wagon, loaded with portmanteaus, household goods, and two servants—as many valuables they could get into one wagon—followed more slowly.

She would have gone with them, but the trip would have been too rough for Father, for the stroke that had laid him low and the broken leg that may have indirectly caused the stroke. With the Yankee army nearing Columbia, her aunt and uncle could remain no longer. Everyone had heard stories about what Yankees did to towns and homes. They may have already waited too long in hopes Father would more fully recover, and she hoped they would make it safely to Raleigh, especially for Marjorie's sake.

How she would deal with the servants left behind, she didn't know.

Katherine turned and entered the house, which was not near so grand a plantation home as some around here, but was sizable, none-theless, and well-furnished. Father's bed had been brought down to the east sitting room where it was easier to tend to his needs. She went there now to spend the morning reading to him, though she was not sure how much he understood. Since Mother's death he had not seemed to care for life. The fall from his horse was the most obvious carelessness. He had always been such a strong, robust presence in her life. Day after day he now lay staring at the wall or sleeping.

She must have let something show for, when Cass brought a tray at lunch, she said, "Why don't you take the air, miss, and let me do this? I took care of my own daddy and I know how these gentlemans be."

Katherine waited long enough to see that Cass knew what she was about. Cass was her aunt's Negro, and Katherine wished she had paid more attention earlier. She hadn't known their lives would come to this. Hindsight, some homily about hindsight, but she couldn't recall it.

"Open up here suh, this be right tasty soup Cass done fix for you, and you must git your strength back." She was patient, yet firm, so Katherine left the room and passed through the kitchen to the back porch, where she grabbed a wool jacket and sat on a bench to pull rubber boots over her shoes, tied her skirts into a large knot on each side and headed off toward the barn and woods beyond. Father and Mother would be mortified, but she no longer had patience for all those crinolines every morning. Who would see her? The slaves didn't care. This situation gave her freedom she'd never had before.

She should be checking to see that Sam and the others were at their work, but she would ignore guilt for a while and take a little time for herself. These woods had beckoned ever since her family arrived, and she planned to take a nice walk beneath the pines—to clear her mind, away from everything that bore down upon her.

It was not so muddy here on the cushy layers of needles and leaf. Her palm on the rough trunk of a pine, she leaned close, smelled the sweetness of damp bark. Last spring there had been pink rhododendrons everywhere. Her uncle said folks got lost in these old, dark woods if they did not know their way. He had instructed her to hide the stock in these woods, as they so abounded with massive, gnarled trees, vines, ravines, and animal trails that lead nowhere that marauding Yankees would never find them. A large lake lay to the Northeast, and less than a mile south of her uncle's land a boundary of swampland above the Congaree River began—a fine place for childhood fancies. Uncle Furman said runaway Negroes hid in that swamp and were never found, not to this day.

There were so many trees, her uncle and all the other owners had to clear the land to grow cotton. No one had done any clearing since the war began. Like her father, she would rather have the trees.

Once the war was over, and she prayed that would be soon, Ethan would come home. She had written that she was here outside Columbia, but she hadn't received a letter from him for weeks—longer than usual.

He was still alive. She would know if he wasn't. Somehow, she would know.

She had wanted to ask his friend to take care of him, but she hadn't known him well enough. Besides, Ethan could take care of himself. He exuded quiet confidence—one of the things she admired about him. He didn't need to take up so much space in order to do it either. She had never cared for those men who walked into a room as if they owned it and spoke as if everyone ought to listen to what they had to say, especially each and every woman who happened to be present. Generally, the loudest were the least to be depended upon.

It had taken only a few hours in Ethan's company to know he could be depended upon.

She could not decide what to make of his friend. She could not abide a man who was too handsome. To have so much of that one quality must mean a lack of something else, of something she deemed more important in a man than his appearance. It had worried her the way her sister had carried on about him, but then Marjorie was a child and easily taken in by a man like Adrien Villere. Yet Ethan deemed him a friend, a very good friend, so she would withhold judgment.

Chapter Forty-Seven
Plague of Locusts

Ethan

The cavalry had been five months without supply wagons or decent food besides crackers and a little meat wrapped around sticks and cooked over their fires. No one had been paid in over a year, and their only clothes were what they scrounged along the way—mostly from Yankee soldiers.

Ethan felt the sneer on his face now the shooting had ended, that sneer he got when he was killing. They'd made these Yankees pay, right here on the main street of Aiken, South Carolina. They mounted pretty quick and got out of there, knowing there would soon be more bluecoats than they could handle.

The next night a group of Shannon's scouts rode in and spread the news about what happened at one of the farmhouses. How a woman and her teenage daughter were left alone and Yankee bummers found them, raped the girl and left her dead. Some of Shannon's scouts caught the rapists, slit their throats and left their bodies on the road where the federals could easily find them.

Ethan hoped Adrien hadn't been involved. Adrien wouldn't cut a defenseless man's throat. But he might have seen the thing being done. He might have seen the woman they said was out of her mind with grief.

He was relieved that Katherine was surrounded by her family, including an aunt and uncle. Except he didn't like how the Yankee army kept moving north toward Columbia like a plague of locusts.

Katherine was with her aunt and uncle a few miles southeast of Columbia. Maybe the foragers or the army wouldn't find them. Surely, she was safe.

On February 16th, the mayor of Columbia surrendered the city. Two days later, Federal General Hugh Kilpatrick, chief of Federal Cavalry, the instigator of many of the atrocities and much of the thievery, discovered seventeen of his men slaughtered and a note attached: DEATH TO ALL FORAGERS. He wrote a letter to General Wade Hampton in protest, threatening to execute a Confederate prisoner for every one of his men "murdered." Hampton wrote back with the same threat.

Adrien and Riley Dillard returned with other rangers from their group, and Adrien's chestnut was limping.

"A couple days rest will set him to rights," Adrien said. He joined their squad at their little fire and Ethan held out his meat-decorated stick. Adrien took it with, "Thanks," held it with one hand and with his other carefully picked at the piece of pork sizzling on the end. Men moved about making the usual sounds, muffled conversation, clank of a tin cup against a rock. The fire spat and crackled.

"You have a hand in dealing with them foragers?" Lovell sat on a stump picking at a foot blister.

"Why, Red," said Dillard, who had joined them, "we just brung in six prisoners today, and one of 'em was old Sherman hisself. Ain't you heard?"

Arch halted his foot inspection and opened his eyes and mouth wide. The chuckles and snickers clued him in. "You knucklehead, I meant those rapists, the ones that got what they deserved."

"I figger the good Lord give us all what we deserve in his own good time; it ain't up to me," Dillard said.

Adrien pulled his biscuit apart, gave Dillard half, and the way they chewed and looked at the fire caused the rest to look in there, too. As tolerable a place as any to find answers, Ethan thought. Or maybe just look and think of nothing at all.

Later, as Adrien and Ethan wandered away from the fire, they passed Crane Forbes returning from his own nightly routine. "You boys be careful. This place is full a them bogs where you least expect it."

A few steps farther on Adrien said to Ethan, "He knows."

"Suspects, maybe."

Adrien kept walking through the trees and Ethan followed. Adrien stopped, leaned both arms against a trunk and lowered his head, murmured something Ethan couldn't hear. Ethan stepped closer. "Don't speak to the ground if you want me to hear you."

"I'm swearing. I'm not meant to be here. I was born in the wrong time and place. I hate this war."

Ethan placed his palm against Adrien's neck. "All of it?"

Adrien turned and pulled Ethan against his chest. They gripped one another. Ethan leaned, pushing Adrien back against the tree, and Adrien wrapped a leg around Ethan's leg, chins on one another's shoulders, slouched hats mashed where they met. It was enough, must be, until time intruded a warning and they parted, eyes glancing down, then at one another, palming thigh, forehead, stepping back, away.

Ethan made a place under some shrubs for them, where he hoped to keep off the worst of the icy dew. He thought, again, how nice it would be to have a tent, but none of them had such luxury any longer. They moved every day. They had burned the wagons that slowed them down. He stripped to undershirt and drawers, what was left of them. There were patches on patches, and both of them had sacrificed wool leggings to repair the rest. He pulled Adrien in close, spooning, and they bundled their clothing and canteens of heated water under the blankets with them.

Ethan murmured in Adrien's ear, "There was this girl when I was eighteen. We were all watching fireworks in the park, and she and I had this blanket over our laps. I gave her what she wanted right there, Adrien, and no one could tell. She just grabbed onto my knees, so I knew, but no one else did."

Ethan trailed his hand down Adrien's stomach, reached under the top of his drawers which were pretty darn loose these days, like his were, all of them were. It was nice and warm under there.

"You're crazy, Ethan. We're too close." The last word turned into breath, and Adrien clamped a hand on Ethan's wrist.

"You wanted to forget." His hand was stroking, and Adrien let his wrist slide between his fingers.

"I . . . cannot do it, be so silent."

"You had better."

When the time came, face in Ethan's left biceps, Adrien bit down hard on the bundle that was his own trousers.

"Ethan, you're like a dog with a bur in his tail."

It was early morning; he was staring at pale lemon rays between the thin trees and . . . *Have Yankee bummers found her? Is she safe?* They were separating again, Ethan and Company K with the rangers to slow down the federal approach to the town wherever they could, and Shannon's scouts to spread across the country to search for bummers. Adrien grabbed him above the elbow.

"Tell me where Katherine is, and I'll see what may be done."

Ethan reached into his shirt pocket and smoothed a wrinkled, smudged paper across his thigh. He hesitated, looked at Adrien. "You sure? I don't—"

"Of course, I'm sure." He bent over the paper.

"She sent me this little map, just in case," Ethan said, and traced the penciled line of a road with one dirty finger. "The house is white, and the barn is red. Cotton storage sheds line the road before you get there. Of course, the fields will be empty now. There's a picket fence in front and a porch facing south. The garden's in back and farther behind are woods that curve around to the east." He stared at the map, unmoving. Adrien lay a hand on his shoulder.

"Don't worry. If she is there, I'll take care of her, Ethan. You have my word."

Ethan straightened, folded, and replaced the letter.

"Don't risk your neck."

"You mean no more than usual." Adrien grinned.

"Yeah, fool. That's what I mean." Ethan palmed his neck and gave him a sideways shove. Wanted to pull him in, but that wouldn't muster, not here and now.

He shouldn't be asking this of him, but he had volunteered. Then why this guilt, this feeling of having swallowed a stone as he watched him ride off?

Chapter Forty-Eight
Yankees Is Comin'

Georgia summer twilight had been Katherine's favorite time, for it tempered the day's heat and hinted of mystery with its softened outlines, deep blue shadows, and magic of fireflies. Here in South Carolina, twilight in March was cold, and she was alone. Dusk heralded the unknown, when anything might creep forth from the approaching darkness. Dusk was being a child again after Mother left the bedroom and her imagination saw gremlins in the black corners.

She had been too long here among these graves under the laurel oak, and turned away to follow the overgrown path that led up the rise to the back of the house. Mother lay in the freshest grave. Her father, a man who had always been so strong, the bulwark of their family, had been laid low by the death of his wife. How ironic, that her aunt, the sister who had been ill, should live, and Mother should die.

The moon was rising and the kitchen window was alight; Cass would wonder where she was.

Katherine stepped onto the back porch where the brindle coonhound, Bob, greeted her with swinging tail and sad, anxious eyes. Poor thing. Everything had changed for him, as well, and his understanding was less. Few animals were left now: a couple sows, three cows, chickens, two horses, a couple mules and old Bob. Aunt Millicent took the cat when they left.

The smell of chicken stew from the kitchen was wonderful. Sam stood in the doorway from the hall, his large, boney hands folded below his rope-tied trousers.

"Sam? Where is Cass?"

"She done left, miss."

"Left? Where has she gone?"

"With the others, all of them, jus' a bit ago. The Yankees is comin', miss. They's in Winnsboro. It be Hiram got the niggers all het up; they took the mules."

Oh. Fewer mouths to feed. But, Cass? "What about you, Sam?"

"I grew up here an' spec I will die here. Sides, it not right to leave you an Marse Wheatley alone."

She clutched her skirts and refused to release the tears from her burning eyes. Such consideration coming from this old dark person. "Thank you, Sam. I hope you will have some of this chicken stew Cass has seen fit to leave."

"Thank you, miss."

She lay awake in her bed that night. If the federal army was in Winnsboro, they might come here in the next day or two. Uncle James had taken what he could, sold and buried much of the rest of their valuables. They left the least valuable of the silver and old plate, furnishings, a small amount of gold and currency for her and her father's use. And the animals. She heard the federals took the animals, or slaughtered them. Tomorrow she would send them into the woods. How to hide the food they would need? She also heard of houses burned, of people killed. Were she and Father safe?

If only Ethan were here. Just thinking of him made her feel safer.

The following morning it was not Ethan who rode into the front yard.

Chapter Forty-Nine
Ragged Highwaymen

Adrien

Our group of five had ridden down a muddy, rut-filled track and seen no foragers. I hoped to keep ahead of bummers. I had convinced one small family to leave their home and move in with another, hoping for safety in numbers. Stubborn old men were the worst, risking their families for their pride. One had cussed me and my men for being cowards and not holding the Yankees off. Old piss-and-vinegar had stood at the top of the steps on the gallery, waistcoated stomach hanging over his trousers, disclaiming the loss of his cotton crop. For the first time, I considered maybe Sherman had the right idea, after all. A flash of white movement in an upstairs window caught my eye, likely the man's wife, maybe his grandchildren in the room beyond. I sat my horse and let the man ramble on, then turned my stallion and we rode off.

I saw the cotton sheds lining both sides of the road first, then the red barn and the woods. Once I reached the next rise, there stood the white house on a smaller rise with the same woods behind it spread to the horizon.

For the first time in months, I worried about my appearance. We must look like ragged highwaymen. I was not sure what made me hesitate, except Katherine and I loved the same man, and it seemed unfair she was not aware of it. Though she would get Ethan in the end.

Chapter Fifty
Where Our Duty Lies

Katherine had buried a few keepsakes, including her mother's pins, her own pearls, earrings and daguerreotypes, and a little gold near the graves, praying the Yankees would believe the freshly dug ground was a new grave. Food, as well, she buried here and there in the woods. They would likely find some of it, maybe not all—please not all. She and Sam set the pigs, chickens, a horse and cows loose in the woods. A few chickens and one horse remained in the barn. She left the silver in the cupboard, easily found, hoping it would be enough to satisfy the Yankees.

She was reading to Father when she heard horses galloping up the road. She carefully lay the book on the nightstand, smoothed her skirts and turned to the hall door. *God, please give me strength.* Her heart thumped against her chest; her hands shook; she buried them in her skirt, clutching fabric as she walked on coals to the front door.

Boots crossed the porch and someone knocked, didn't pound. How dared they be so polite. Her hand trembled as she reached for the door. She took a deep breath, gratifyingly saw her hand steady before she pulled the door open.

She had expected a blue Yankee uniform, not this ragged—person—holding his hat in his hand. Certainly not such deference in the way he held his body and the appeal in those deep-set eyes.

"Miss Wheatley? Katherine?"

He knows my name. Impossible.

"It is me, Lt. Villere, Adrien Villere. Ethan's friend?"

Blood rushed. Breath went out, she was falling into sparkling blackness.

Air against her face, that other face looking down at her, and he was waving something at her. His hat? She was on the floor, how embarrassing. His arm was around her, helping her sit up.

"Easy now, not too fast," he said. "I am sorry. I know I look pretty awful, but I did not think to make you faint."

She sat, skirts all tangled, and he crouched next to her. "The smell," she said.

"Well," he said, "that ought to wake you right up if anything can."

She nearly smiled. She did smile, a little, and had the first intimation of liking him, of why he was Ethan's friend. Ethan. She looked into the man's eyes, asking, before the question reached her lips.

"Ethan is fine. He's with the 8th Texas and Wheeler. I have more freedom than he does, so I came in his place."

He came. This should be Ethan. Not him. Her eyes burned. Damnation, she would not cry.

She gathered herself to rise. He held her by the elbow until she was up and he slid his hand away. He rubbed his hands on his trousers.

"I am sorry I'm in this condition. We have not had time or any place to wash, no soap either or. . . ." his voice trailed off as he lowered his head, stepped back.

"You can wash here," she said. "We have plenty soap and water, enough for. . . . How many are you?"

"Five, only I fear little time remains. Where are the others?"

"Gone." She clutched her skirts, again. Glanced away, then back to his face. "My aunt and uncle took Marjorie to Raleigh weeks ago. My mother died a month before that." She had said it out loud for the first time. "My father is ill—from a stroke and a broken leg. The doctor said he should not be moved. That was two weeks ago, the last time he was here. He never came back. No one has come. Even the servants have left, all but Sam. Sam should be here somewhere. Oh God, she is talking, talking, talking. She must stop. "Sam?" She turned halfway, "Sam?"

"I is here, miss." He was there in the back doorway. "I was in de kitchen, miss."

Adrien looked at Sam. Sam lowered his eyes, as he should.

"It was decent of you to remain, Sam," Adrien said.

"I had nowhere to go, suh."

"Nevertheless. I thank you for remaining with your mistress."

Sam lowered his head and shuffled. "Yes, suh."

Of course, Ethan would have such a friend, she thought.

Adrien turned to her. "You will have to move your father now. It is not safe here, alone. There have been incidents. Do you have a wagon, anything, we can carry him in?"

"A surrey and mare are in the barn."

"Sam, will you hitch her up and bring her out front? If Dillard questions you—he'll be closest to the porch— tell him I told you to."

"Yes, suh. I will."

Adrien turned back to her. "Take what you need of clothing and food. We can spare maybe thirty minutes. I have fellows out watching, and we will help move Mr. Wheatley when he's ready."

"Where are we going?"

"There is a plantation southeast of here, the Forresters? They have plenty of room and have already taken in another family. They are closer to town and medical help. They also have a sizable house in Winnsboro if the Yankees burn down the plantation home."

She wanted to reach out to him, but could only say, "Thank you. Wash up in the kitchen if you wish, and there is fresh-baked bread, a roast chicken, and potatoes. Take whatever you find for you and your men."

"Thank you, Miss Wheatley. We all surely appreciate it." He gave her the merest smile.

She was relieved to go upstairs, to get away by herself and throw a few things into a portmanteau she pulled from under the bed: an extra blanket, underthings, warm stockings. She would like to get the buried photographs, but there was not enough time. *Perhaps I will see Ethan soon. Why did Adrien come to my door and not Ethan?* She flung a pair of stockings at the bed, caught her reflection in the dresser mirror, her face red and screwed up, ugly, tears in her eyes.

These thoughts were unworthy and unfair, but she could not help it. The army and the war ruined everyone's lives. *Enough, you must do what is needed.* Those men, if they were all like Adrien, they needed whatever she might find. She wiped the back of her hand across her face, gathered as much as she could of her father's clean shirts, trousers, socks, and carried the bundle with her bag down the stairs.

She left her bag by the front door and found Adrien in her father's room seated on his bed. Father was sitting up and leaning toward him, one arm stretched out across the covers. Adrien turned to her.

"I told him where we are going and why. I believe he understands. I hope you don't mind my coming in." He turned back to her father. "We got along pretty well before, talking of plants and insects."

She was tongue-tied, hadn't seen Father look so, alive, since, since the stroke.

Adrien's hand settled on her father's. For a moment, it seemed war and all it entailed moved back and everything was as it should be—civilized. Father in his white cotton nightshirt, pale, his silver beard neatly trimmed, and this dark vagabond, unshaven, clothes in rags, his dark paw over her father's frail white one. He must have washed in the kitchen, for his hand was tanned but not dirty, and his hair was damp, the torn shirt clung where his skin was yet moist. Father's eyes reached hers, his mouth opened, and his tongue moved a sound that ought to be a word or several words, and the veins at his temples stood out.

"Yes," she said. "We will help them. I have brought clothing. Here," she held out a cream wool flannel shirt toward Adrien. "It's a little large, of course, and I noticed the rope you had to hold your trousers . . ." she lowered her head and actually blushed, had thought she would never blush again, and held out a pair of faded red galluses. "You can tighten them to fit."

"Thank you, Miss Wheatley."

"Call me Katherine, please."

"These," she pumped the bundle awkwardly, "are extra clothes and blankets to cushion Father, then your men could have them when we reach our destination."

"Excellently done," he said.

Sam held the horse steady when Adrien and another man, introduced as Riley Dillard, lifted her father into the surrey. Adrien had picked him up off the bed and carried him outside as though he were a small boy. Father used to be so large, larger than Adrien. All of these men, she suspected, were in the same shape—exceedingly thin but stronger than they appeared.

When she had pulled the covers from her father to dress him for the journey, Adrien had turned his back to her to remove his old shirt. She looked out of the corners of her eyes because she had never yet seen Ethan without his shirt. Adrien was all skin and bone and sinewy muscle. His pants looked likely to slide right off his hips. Ethan would look like this. She wanted to get every bit of food they had and load it into the surrey and round up the pigs.

Her father's shirt ballooned out of the top of Adrien's trousers, and she thought the galluses looked quite fine. She brought a dove gray shirt and blue galluses for Ethan.

Someone galloped down the road and into the yard. Adrien strode out to meet him, and everyone else held their horses steady. "Yankee bummers coming up the road," the rider said, loud enough for everyone to hear.

"How many?" Adrien said.

"I counted ten, nine on horseback, one with a wagon."

"Hell," one of the fellows said, "easy pickin's." He turned toward her. "Excuse me, ma'am, I'm not used to the presence of ladies."

Adrien moved toward his own horse, a large chestnut. "You know where our duty lies. Dillard? Head off across country with the surrey. Avoid any fighting if you can." He mounted; the chestnut nervously circled. "The rest of us will see if we can lead them off. A little charge and run ought to do it. Remember, nowadays these groups are not always alone, but are often followed by bluecoat cavalry."

Katherine was in the surrey and, with all the active horses about her and long time in the barn, the little brown mare pranced and arched her neck.

Adrien brought the chestnut up close to where Sam held the reins. "It's up to you and these boys now. Take care of Miss Katherine."

"I surely will, suh. You can count on me."

"I'm sure of it." He fingered his hat and nodded to her.

She wanted to say something but didn't know what, felt sorry she hadn't told him how grateful she was, how much she hoped to see him again alongside Ethan.

Chapter Fifty-One
For Love

Adrien

The bummers were spread across the road on both sides of the wagon when we galloped over the rise. They had either seen my lookout or heard us coming, likely both. Not a Yankee had dismounted—they were ready to run in case they were outnumbered—which gave us a chance since a mounted man could not shoot accurately at this distance. I nabbed my shotgun from the scabbard and turned the chestnut north across a field before we rode too close for a lucky shot to shorten our own number. A glance to the rear told me the Yankees followed, all but the wagon. We headed for a cotton shed on the other side of the field where we could dismount and find cover.

We were two hundred yards out when bluecoats swarmed from behind the shed. By the sound some of them had Spencers that were accurate at two hundred yards and could fire more than once without reloading.

My breath hitched. I threw my weight hard right, almost pulling the stallion over but the fine animal caught himself and broke into a run as though the devil were on his tail. Thank God my men were spread out and tore in all directions. *Bummers are a poor lot or they would have held their fire until we were closer.* No sooner thought than a thwack like a pellet popping into meat, Horse stumbled.

I followed hard upon Bob Myers past the red barn and toward the woods. Myers slid off his horse and rolled rag doll loose through the dead cotton stems; he wouldn't be getting up. Damn, he must've been hit in the first volley. His mount slowed to a canter, moved off to the right out of sight as Horse ran on by, his gait off, an uneven lurch. Something hot punched me from behind and low on the left, nearly knocking me from the chestnut.

If we could make the woods, I might lose them. Fire crawled up my back, chewed up my strength, and made it difficult to sit in the saddle. Even shot up, the chestnut was leaving the damn bummers behind. I was crying, damn it, such a fine animal.

We went crashing into the woods. I let Horse decide the best course. He was a smart horse. Twigs and wet, springy, needled branches stung my face. I bent low against the chestnut's neck, blurry-visioned, my face pressed into the wet mane, warm horse smell, heard sopping and splashing—a creek or puddles. The distant sound of voices and hoofbeats replaced by the constant drip of water, the stallion's heavy huffing, hooves thudding, saddle creaking . . . a jay called. I rocked in the saddle, a forward jerk, another and another and accompanying harsh jab as we lumbered down a ravine, crossed another creek, up the other side. On and on, deeper and deeper into the pines. Gray woods, and I lost my shotgun, clutched Horse's wet mane in one hand, hugged myself with the other until exquisite weakness faded me into obscurity.

Maman is leaning over peering down at me. Not Maman—some other woman. Her face is black and her eyes are spinning gold and I know her but cannot recall her name. Must remember, must wake up.

The thick smell of horse and blood and wet leather and pungent earth. Horse no longer moved forward, but trembled—he's going down. *Get your leg up or you'll be caught beneath!* I fell onto soaked leaves. Nearly passed out. The chestnut gave a moan. Blinked at the hump of him and the blood-soaked saddle washed by a drizzle of rain. Crawled off through brown and green grass, leaves, moss, ferns, bark, twigs, all soft and drooling rivulets. Got to my knees. A cartridge or whatever had made a ragged furrow on the outside of my calf that burned like hell. Whatever was in my back would stay there and kill me if I didn't bleed to death first. But Horse showed me how to do

this—dying thing properly. Tried to get to my feet, fell against a tree
or tripped. They might track Horse, but maybe not me, not with the
rain, if I was lucky, if they didn't try too hard.

Isaac. Had Isaac felt like this? Please God keep him safe.

Didn't know if I believed in God any longer, but the habit of praying . . . never gotten over.

Puked all I'd eaten into a stream, no, a bog, water sloshed above
my feet. Water under me, over, constant sound of gurgling, splashing,
slipping, kept on, how far, hoped it was far enough. Would have to be,
could go no farther. Musty dank smell of leaves and earth here on the
ground. Lost my hat, somewhere. Rain plopping, trickling, dribbling
my hair, into my eyes.

Must have passed out. Water dripping and must be dusk, hard to
tell in these dark woods. Reached back, lifted the shirt that stuck to
my flesh where blood yet seeped. Felt something hard tucked inside.
God-awful burn. Pressed moss and leaves back there while I chewed
at moss on the tree. Stupid to worry about bleeding to death out here?
Sweating despite clammy cold.

⁂

I am sitting on the cracked dry mud banks of the Brazos and sixteen-
year-old Jacob sits cross-legged there and we make marks in the dirt
with sticks, marks for where the armies go. Pebbles are the armies and
for some reason I do not have a hat, and the sun burns my head and
the back of my neck. Maman will be upset. Where is my hat? Jacob has
it behind his back.

Come get it, Jacob says and smiles.

I grab, only Jacob keeps it just out of reach and backs off laughing.

Give me something for it, Jacob says. You know what I want.

I walk down a dark street between ornate buildings and the sky
is full of stars. A city. New Orleans? An empty city. Where have they
gone? Have to find them—someone. Someone important.

Lily. Lily.

Mine, she says and smiles, exposing that wonderful gap in her tooth. This changes everything.

You see now, Ethan says. Ethan, who is close behind me, close enough to lean against. I am tired, and leaning on Ethan is easy and comforting. Ethan holds me. Where I am now, nothing matters.

My eyes gritty; a quarter moon glowed beyond the leaves and ghostly clouds drifted across it. It gave pale outline to the trees and branches. Recalled the fawn beneath the moon beams that night. *Here I am, curled up under a bush in much the same way. Will some animal find me or will my bones remain undisturbed throughout summer like that fawn? Curious. Led them away from Katherine. Hope someone finds Myers. Not likely anyone will find me in these swampy woods. Fine. Better to die trying to help Ethan than in some stupid charge.*

Not so cold now. Nice here, really. I always liked the moon. Fairies and such. Berni.

Chapter Fifty-Two
Epilogue

Dillard explained what happened, and led Ethan to Katherine. She understood when Wheeler gave him and men from Company K permission to search for the others, for Adrien. The two missing men from Adrien's squad rode in an hour later on exhausted horses. That afternoon they found Myers's body, and it was dusk when they found the stallion in the woods, and only because Crane Forbes was an excellent tracker.

Something had been at the horse. "Panther, looks like," said Forbes, crouching, fingering the bloody leaves. "No sign of Slick—Villere." The boys stood silent while Forbes walked in ever-widening circles. "Here," he said, bending low, then moving into the brush. Ethan saw the trail, and the blood. It got black real fast in those woods, but they kept looking, using a couple of kerosene lanterns, before giving up. Forbes had to speak harshly. "You don't want to risk the rest of these boys out here for a rescue that's not going to happen, Captain. You saw the trail. He won't make it through another night, and you'd better accept it."

The following morning, holding his hands, Katherine said, "You loved him."

"I did."

"I got to know him a little, Ethan. I would have come to care for him, too, I think."

He loved her more for that.

248

✤

It was July before Papa brought the news home. We had learned the war was over and had been waiting as so many others had been waiting.

I knew the news was bad the way Papa walked in the door, how he had aged ten years in one day. In a trembling hand he held out two letters—one official and one personal.

The official one said: "Missing and presumed dead attempting to save the lives of Georgian civilians from marauding Yankees. Adrien Denys Villere was a true hero in every sense of the word."

The signature on the personal letter was "Ethan Childs," and I knew. The 8th Texas never found a body.

"He's not dead," I said.

"Bernadette," Papa said.

"Adrien is alive. I would know if he were not. Believe me, Papa. I would know."

No matter how many months passed, I refused to believe Adrien was dead, that he would not come home.

Paien told Jacob.

"I am more sorry than you will ever know," Jacob said. "I never thought when this war started that it would end like this."

"What do you mean?"

"With Adrien's death. I sent him off, Paien."

"You sent him?"

Jacob turned away, momentarily unable to face Adrien's father, and planted fisted knuckles on the top of his desk. "I threatened to expose him and Lily." He turned back; would face whatever accusation Paien cared to make. Perhaps the man would kill him. "Adrien joined up to save my sister's reputation."

Jacob watched Paien breathe. His chest rising, in, out. A muscle in his jaw tightened. Jacob sensed, rather than saw, the rest of the man's body tense, then, relax. He spun, walked toward the door, stopped, turned back. "I have made mistakes I will forever regret," he said. "I think you have become a different, better, man than you were. A man who will carry his regrets with him as I have carried mine. I can wish you no further ill will than that."

He walked out the door.

❦

"Here's a letter from your brother," Garrison said, handing Lily the open envelope. "I'm going for a walk, may stop at that cafe across the street for coffee, do you want to come?"

Of course, he would ask her now, just when she had received a letter, when he knew she would want to read it privately. He had already obviously read it, as he read all her correspondence.

"Perhaps I'll meet you there a little later, say, thirty minutes?"

"Yes. If I'm still there. You can't stay there alone, you know. The French are more indulgent, but a lady must not be seen alone in a public place." He grabbed his hat and was out the door before she could respond.

She knew the rules. Why must he always treat her this way? As if she were some common . . . person.

He had been smiling and practically bouncing on his chubby toes. She had discovered his feet were surprisingly small for such a big man.

The letter was short.

I'm sorry. So sorry. Adrien . . .

Her heart skipped a beat.

. . . is missing and presumed dead.

She froze. She must have, because everything stopped. Then she became aware of birds chirping outside the window. Horses clip-clopping by on the street. She breathed. Oh, God. Never again. She would never see him again. Or feel him. She had thought she would. In the future. After. No, never. She swallowed. Breathed again. Swallowed. She felt tears run down her face. She would let them now, but never again.

Adrien had been right. Those books, all those romances, were absurd fairy tales.

Thank God, she had his son.

Acknowledgments

Though this is a work of fiction, except for the main protagonists, officers and exploits of the 8th Texas Cavalry are historical fact. I am indebted to the journals and diaries of rangers that were available on the internet as well as two books in particular: *None but Texians, A History of Terry's Texas Rangers* by Jeffrey D. Murrah and *Terry Texas Ranger Trilogy*, a compilation of the journals of three rangers.

We may argue who was on the "right" side in the Civil War, but I doubt anyone can deny the courage of the men who fought it, on either side—they displayed courage without regard to sexual orientation.

For history of the nineteenth century regarding sex between men before it was labeled "homosexuality," I recommend *Love Stories* by Jonathan Ned Katz.

I also wish to acknowledge my Critique Circle buddies whose attention and suggestions helped improve the many edits of this manuscript, especially Toni Morgan, Ben Zehabe, and Casey Robb.

I thank my publisher, Brooke Warner and She Writes Press for their assistance in bringing this story to life.

About the Author

Karen began reading before entering first grade and began her career drawing imaginative adventures in the margins of schoolwork which, unfortunately, few teachers appreciated.

After completing her formal education at Kent State University and San Diego State, her love of nature sent Karen to wandering the U.S. west and parts of Mexico and Central America hiking and backpacking before settling in Tucson, Arizona, with her cat buddy Dickens. Although she enjoyed minor success as a watercolor painter, she discovered her true passion when she began writing fiction at the age of sixty. Her interest and experience in psychology and therapy inform her writing about individuals who persevere through difficulty and crisis in order to become stronger and accept themselves for who they truly are. Karen is a child abuse survivor, and humbly hopes her stories give readers pleasure and confidence to face their own difficulties, knowing they are not alone.

Karen believes in taking risks, for this is how we grow. With over fifty years of overcoming her own fears and challenges she hopes to help others find their own true selves, to not only survive, but to thrive.

The following is a preview of
Book 3 of The Texian Trilogy

1861

Isaac

That first night on the Nueces Strip he had caught himself grinding his teeth, whether from fear or anger, he wasn't sure. Maybe both. Angry that he had to do this, leave everything he cared for and loved behind. Resentful and fleeing like a scared rabbit.

When the sky began to lighten, he found his "rabbit hole"—a deep arroyo amid a thicket of creosote and stunted mesquite—deep enough for both him and the horse. Roman was a goer all right. He slid out of the saddle, hauled it off, and laid the blanket over the upturned skirt in a small patch of shade. Roman nuzzled him and poked his jacket pocket looking for a treat. Adrien had given him treats. He felt a surge of longing for all he had lost. *Don't. This is no time for reflection; keep your mind on what you're doing.* Isaac gave the bay a few oats, hopefully he had packed enough oats to keep them going into Mexico. Along with scarce patches of grass that grew among the vicious cactus and acacia that was so thick he had to abandon even a halfway straight line in order to find a way through. Every plant had thorns, and he rubbed Mama's salve on Roman's cuts. Having planned to ride southeast, he was being forced farther and farther south, and he didn't want to end up on the Rio Grande at Brownsville on the coast. Bound to be soldiers at the fort there.

But he couldn't keep making his way through this thorny brush in the dark, despite being familiar with the map he'd memorized. He'd kept that secret even from Adrien. Maybe he should've tried farther north where the wild horses and cattle roamed. Still, if he had such a difficult time getting through this sea of thorns, so would anyone else. Too late now, anyway. Thank God for numerous deer trails—plenty of deer, jackrabbits, and javelina. When a roadrunner took off practically under Roman's nose, the horse startled—threw up his head, snorted, and watched the bird dash through the brush yipping like a coyote. Obvious why Adrien put so much store in the horse.

He slept for a few hours before the hot sun on his legs woke him, and the smokey smell of creosote ticked his nose. Maneuvering while leading Roman through the thorny scrub was his only course. Lunch of jerky helped pass the time until drifting off for another couple hours in the sweltering heat when even the birds he'd heard at dawn went silent. Except for an insect buzzing by every now and then, he'd never imagined such silence. Even Roman was as still as a statue, but for his flicking tail.

Once the sun got low enough to kick up a breeze that swayed the long, thin branches of mesquite above him. Another short drink out of his upturned hat for Roman before saddling up again. They stayed in the arroyo as long as it went in the right direction, not long enough. Early evening brought out birds flitting and chirping among the scrub, and when they heaved up out of the arroyo a flock of quail went scrambling and clucking into the brambles.

The following morning was the same flat, thorny brush country, a rest in the silent, baking afternoon, and ride till too dark to see.

His greatest concern had been bandits, of which he'd heard plenty. But maybe they were farther north. He hoped. But there were plenty other dangers, like the six foot rattler he'd nearly forced Roman onto— the one time the horse refused.

Another day and night—the land changed and the air became thicker. Brush opened up into grassland dotted with mesquite, yellow-blooming huarache, and a live oak here and there. Eventually the grass turned long and green, and the mesquite became a forest. He didn't stand out against the horizon so much here, but neither would anybody else. No time to relax his vigilance. Though it was grand to rest in plenty of shade for a change. Except this particular change told him he had come too far south.

He didn't sleep well. For one thing, a packrat kept running across his legs half the night. The critter had no fear of this human stretched across its territory. He didn't have the heart to learn it any better.

The following day told him he'd come too far south—riders—in uniform. He slipped off Roman, held and caressed his nose. Didn't want the him signaling those other horses they were here. He needn't have worried, Roman seemed to understand they must keep hidden.

Early evening and Roman lifted his head, ears pointed forward. Shortly after a soft breeze brought the scent of water. Water with a slightly sulfurous odor.

He had come upon the Red River.

Halting in the trees, he dismounted and scanned the open area where the land dropped off, and there the muddy red-brown river sluggishly flowed, at least a hundred feet across. Best to remain here and watch for possible activity. The moon had been waxing prior nights and ought to be full or nearly full tonight. Perhaps the best time.

Best to make one fast drive across to avoid being seen.

When the time came, he stored pistol, powder, and the clothes he wore into a gutapercha bag and tied it securely to the top of the saddle.

The river was low this time of year which maybe accounted for the two-foot drop-off. Roman didn't hesitate and, once again, Isaac was thankful for Adrien's gift of the animal. Once he knew what was required, the big bay slid on his haunches down the bank and right into the water. Giving Roman his head, Isaac hung onto his tail, being careful to avoid lashing hooves. The far side wasn't as steep, and he and the horse stood on sand, dripping under a full moon.

He was in Mexico. And from the sound of voices and smell of woodsmoke so was someone else.

Looking for your next great read?

We can help!

Visit www.shewritespress.com/next-read
or scan the QR code below for a list
of our recommended titles.

She Writes Press is an award-winning
independent publishing company founded to
serve women writers everywhere.